It's Oh So Quiet

It's Oh So Quiet

Ted Darling Crime Series

'a killer lurks behind the calm'

LIVRES
LEMAS

L M Krier

Published by LEMAS LIVRES
www.tottielimejuice.com

Cover design DMR Creative
Cover photo Neil Smith

IT'S OH SO QUIET

ISBN 978-2-901773-52-8

Contents

About the Author

L M Krier is the pen-name of former journalist (court reporter) and freelance copywriter, Lesley Tither, who also writes travel memoirs under the name Tottie Limejuice. Lesley also worked as a case tracker for the Crown Prosecution Service. Now retired, she lives in Central France and enjoys walking her dogs and going camping.

Contact Details

If you would like to get in touch, please do so at:

https://www.teddarlingcrimeseries.uk/

tottielimejuice@gmail.com

facebook.com/LMKrier

facebook.com/groups/1450797141836111/

twitter.com/tottielimejuice

For a lighter look at Ted and Trev, why not join the fun in the We Love Ted Darling group? on Facebook. FREE 'Ted Darling is billirant' badge for each member.

Discover the DI Ted Darling series

If you've enjoyed meeting Ted Darling you may like to discover the other books in the series. All books are available as ebooks and in paperback format. The First Time Ever is also now available as an audiobook. Watch out for audiobook versions of other books in the series, coming soon, as well as further books in the series:

The First Time Ever
Baby's Got Blue Eyes
Two Little Boys
When I'm Old and Grey
Shut Up and Drive
Only the Lonely
Wild Thing
Walk On By
Preacher Man
Cry for the Bad Man
Every Game You Play
Where the Girls Are
Down Down Down
The Cuckoo is a Pretty Bird
Dirty Old Town
The End of the Line
It's Oh So Quiet

The First Time Ever is also available translated into French by Jean Sauvanet, under the title of 'Darling.'

Acknowledgements

I would just like to thank the people who have helped me bring Ted Darling to life.

Alpha and Beta readers: Jill Pennington, Kate Pill, Karen Corcoran, Jo Baines, Jill Evans, Alan Wood, Paul Kemp, Eileen Payne, Valérie Goutte.

Police consultants – The Three Karens.

Medical advisor – Jo Baines

Military consultant - Chris Flounders

Emma Faulkner - UK Head of Publishing, Livres LEMAS.

Special thanks to Sgt Simpson and PC Newton for taking the time to talk to me about Rural Crime.

Finally a very special thanks to all Ted's loyal friends in the We Love Ted Darling Facebook group. Always so supportive and full of great ideas to be incorporated into the next Ted book. FREE 'Ted Darling is billirant' badge for all members.

To Young Chris

Many thanks for all your valuable help

Author's Note

Thank you for reading the Ted Darling Crime Series. The books are set in Stockport, and Greater Manchester in general, and the characters use local dialect and sayings.

Seemingly incorrect grammar within quotes reflects common speech patterns. For example, 'I'll do it if I get chance', without an article or determiner, is common parlance.

Ted and Trev also have an in joke between them - 'billirant' - which is a deliberate 'typo'.

If you have any queries about words or phrases used, do please feel free to get in touch, using the contact details in the book. I always try to reply promptly to any emails or Facebook messages.

Thank you.

L M Krier

Chapter One

Detective Inspector Jo Rodriguez looked around him as he got out of his service vehicle. This had to be one of the most remote parts of his new patch that he'd yet visited since his transfer from Stockport to Ashton.

A solitary Police Community Support Officer was waiting near a gate next to her area car. She was visibly shivering in her waterproof coat from the steady drizzle borne on what locals might call a lazy wind - one which preferred to go through you rather than around you.

They knew each other by sight. PCSO Fiona Murray reached into the car to pick up a clipboard on which she was logging any visitors to the incident site.

'Morning, sir,' she greeted him as she noted his name then asked, 'Is it an S at the end or a Z? I never remember.'

'It's a Z, and there's no need for the sir when only the sheep can hear us. Jo is fine,' Jo told her with a smile. 'So, where am I going from here?'

'Through that gateway there, then diagonally to your right at about two o'clock on a clock face. Across the first field then through a gap in the stone wall into the next one. You should be able to see Sergeant Thomas there, near to a waterfall. He's waiting with the body. He's informed the coroner, who's delayed but is coming later. He's also requested the attendance of a pathologist because he thinks the death is suspicious, but he hasn't bothered asking for the police surgeon to certify death. You'll see why when you get there.'

Her parting shot was delivered with a cheerful smile which filled Jo with trepidation. He usually had a strong stomach for such things, but all he knew was that he'd been called out to a suspicious death, and not a recent one, at that.

Jo trudged off across a field in what he hoped was the right direction. The fine rain, being driven straight into the side of his face, made visibility difficult. He was soon aware that his town shoes and short raincoat were more a fashion statement than any adequate protection against such weather. His boss, Detective Chief Inspector Darling, would have been far better equipped because of his fondness for hill walking. Jo's idea of the great outdoors was attending a football match with his sons or going for a walk in a park with his family.

He found the gap in the drystone wall easily enough. He had the rain, driven by even stronger wind, full in his face now but he could spot the fluorescent jacket of PS Cai Thomas easily enough, right over the far side of the field near a rocky outcrop down which water was tumbling and splashing, being blown back upwards by the gusts.

'Hello, Jo, they've sent the big guns in already, have they?' Thomas asked as Jo reached him. 'I might be completely wrong in thinking this isn't an accident, of course, though I've got my reasons for thinking that. But let's see what an experienced detective makes of it all.'

'Hello, Cai. So what have we got?' Jo was looking round for a body but not yet seeing one. He was getting a whiff of something he didn't much like the smell off at all, though.

Thomas saw his expression and chuckled.

'That's why I waited up here. I thought it was only fair to warn you in advance. It's a body, but not a very fresh one. In fact it's been here long enough for the crows to have had the eyes and it looks like foxes have made a start on the fingers.'

For one anxious moment, Jo felt bile rising up in his throat and desperately hoped he wouldn't suffer the indignity of throwing up in front of a sergeant who clearly had more years of service under his belt than he did.

'Are CSI on their way?' he asked, more to have something to say than anything else.

If it did turn out to be nothing but a natural death or a tragic accident, it would be a costly waste of resources to bring in a full Crime Scene Investigation team when there was no crime.

'Not yet. I wanted a second opinion before pressing the red button on it. Shall we go and take a look, then?' Thomas asked him. 'It's down below, in the dip. Only watch your footing. It gets a bit slippery where the water splashes onto the bank, and your shoes don't look ideal.'

The body was that of a man, lying on its back on rocks at the bottom of the waterfall. The head was twisted to the side at an unnatural angle. As the sergeant had told him, the eyes were nothing but empty sockets. Close to, the smell was worse, the body bloated. Sergeant Thomas seemed unaffected by either the sight or the stench.

'Dead about a week or so, would you think?' he asked.

'What makes you think it's not just an accident?'

Jo was looking up at the rocks as he asked the question. They weren't high, but a fall from up there could possibly quite easily result in a broken neck, if the person was unlucky enough to land the wrong way, he thought.

Thomas smiled at him through the rain.

'You're the detective, Jo. Are you not seeing what I'm seeing?'

Jo steeled himself to look in closer detail at the corpse. Then he said, 'His footwear is even worse than mine, to go scrambling about on wet rocks. So what was he doing out here? Running away from someone, or something? And who found him, come to that? The farmer who owns the fields?'

'To answer your second two-part question first, it was a woman out taking photographs who found him. She tramps about all over the place, apparently, and puts her snaps up in some Facebook group or another. She apparently wanted to get shots of the little waterfall here. I had her taken to the station because she was very shaken up, understandably. We'll need her witness statement whether it was accidental or something else.

'As for what he was doing here, I have a slight advantage over you there. Hard to tell for sure from the state of him now, but I think I might know who it is. Luckily the foxes didn't run off with his ring finger as I'm pretty sure I've seen that ring before. If it is who I think it is, it's a bloke who called himself Spike and I don't know his real name, not for definite. Hippy type, but more than that. He's one of this new breed of militant vegans, you might call them. You know them - "Meat is Murder" and all that stuff.

'Fair enough, their opinion, they're entitled to it. But they don't always stop there. Look around you, Jo. It all looks so quiet and peaceful enough in the pastoral landscape, doesn't it? Sheep may safely graze, and all that. But it's turning into a seething cauldron of lawlessness, as any of us who work Rural Crime can tell you.

'The sort of stuff Spike and his mates get up to doesn't seem to have an official name here yet, although some countries call it agri-bashing, I've heard. They let livestock out of fields, for one thing. Even out of barns and outbuildings, under the notion of setting them free. Of course the poor beasts usually finish up on the road getting killed. Not to mention causing serious accidents. If they do survive, it can often lead to the farmer getting fined for straying livestock.'

'So you're saying, what, that Spike here was up to something like that and some farmer chased him off with a shotgun, so he fell over the waterfall?'

'Because I've worked in a rural area for years, I've seen a good few deaths in my time from various causes. But I've never seen a neck broken like that from a fall as short as this one. Not without any other visible injuries, for sure.

'I think someone may have broken his neck, perhaps even

with their bare hands. Someone who knew what they were doing. That's why I called in the cavalry. I think there's a good chance that this was murder.'

* * *

Even above the noise of the waterfall, they both clearly heard the booming voice from up above them calling out, 'Did anyone here call for a pathologist?'

Then the sturdy, short figure of Professor Elizabeth 'Bizzie' Nelson appeared at the top of the slope above them. She was suitably dressed for both the location and the weather, with tweed trousers, green Wellingtons, an old but well-waxed jacket, and a battered deerstalker pulled down hard to keep her head dry.

She began her sure-footed descent of the slope, totally undeterred by the tricky going, carrying her medical bag in one hand.

Sergeant Thomas had not met her before so called out a concerned, 'Careful, ma'am, it's quite slippery. Do you need a hand? Shall I carry your bag, at least?'

Jo hid a smile as the professor stopped in her tracks to reply.

'For goodness sake, please don't call me ma'am, sergeant. I'm neither a serving police officer nor the Queen, so Professor is perfectly adequate. And I'm completely at home traipsing round the countryside, thank you, so no assistance is required.

'So, where's my body? I do hope you two gentlemen haven't been fiddling about with it before I've had chance to examine it. You should certainly know better, Inspector Rodriguez.'

Looking suitably abashed, Jo and PS Thomas stepped aside to allow the Professor her first look at the body. She shooed them away with one hand as she approached.

They withdrew to a good few yards away and Jo reached in his pocket for his packet of cigarillos, offering one to the sergeant, who shook his head.

'I don't smoke, you understand,' Jo told him as he lit up. 'Gave up years ago. At least that's what I tell the mother of my children. Just in case our paths should ever happen to cross when we're in the company of our better halves.'

He tipped his head back to blow smoke up into the mizzle then said, 'So what other kind of rural crime do you deal with? Cattle rustling? Is that a thing? And is this cattle country? I'm a real townie. I have no idea what goes on out here in the sticks.'

As he spoke, he kept one hand cupped underneath the other to stop any bit of ash from landing on a crime scene. He'd put a carefully folded clean handkerchief into the palm, and between each flick, he closed his fist to smother any hot ash. He wouldn't normally light up close to the scene but he felt the need of something to ward off the smell.

'Livestock theft happens, for sure. Sheep especially, and this is mostly sheep country. They're easy enough to round up into a trailer, especially if the thieves bring a trained dog with them. A few farms run some beef cattle but there's very little dairy just here. Some dog thefts, too. Mostly puppies, especially of good working dogs, which can fetch a fortune, even without papers.

'And you'd be surprised what else goes on. Night hawking is quite prevalent. That's using metal detectors illegally to steal archaeological artefacts. Then there's the wildlife crimes - badger baiting, lamping, coursing of hares, organised fox shoots. All illegal, but it's getting to be a thing now that people will pay money to come out to places like this just to kill things. It's often organised crime gangs behind it, too. Another lucrative string to their bow.

'Then, not long ago we got a call about a farmer who'd found a couple in a field getting frisky with his bull. Well, she was, while he was trying to film them. The bull didn't seem to mind but the farmer was furious.'

They both laughed, then Jo said, 'We must be pretty near to

the border here, aren't we? This is definitely on our patch, is it? Not one for Derbyshire?'

'The boundary's about a mile as the crow flies from the waterfall. So it's definitely ours, if it turns out to be criminal at all. Although we might need to liaise with them, perhaps, if our victim has come in from their side of the line.'

Although she couldn't have heard them above the sound of the waterfall, the Professor chose that exact moment to look up and beckon them closer.

'I can't, of course, be certain without a full post-mortem examination, but my initial observations would suggest, sergeant, that you were correct in your suspicions. The only apparent injury is the broken neck, which appears not to be consistent with a fall from any height. From higher up, I would expect more injuries than I can find. From lower down, I would not expect to see a broken neck at all. Certainly not one broken with the force which appears to have been applied in this case.

'Once again, but with the caveat that none of this is certain until after the PM, I am leaning towards the theory that this man had his neck cleanly broken by a person using their bare hands. And that takes a degree of skill not known to the average person. So I would suggest ...'

Jo jumped in before she could continue, already seeing where she was going.

'Someone with special skills training, perhaps those taught to certain military personnel.'

'Exactly so. A strong possibility. And also I can offer you no shred of evidence for the assumption, but I would suggest it's likely that the victim was killed elsewhere and left here in the hopes that whoever found him would jump to the conclusion that he had simply fallen from the top of the waterfall. And that would have been a seemingly logical conclusion. So thank you, sergeant, for not accepting it at face value.'

'Thank you, Professor,' Jo told her. 'Right, Cai, can you chase up CSI and let's get this started as a murder enquiry. I need to make a phone call of my own.'

'We'll both need to go back up the slope in that case. Radio and phone signals are patchy at best sometimes, out here in the sticks. Down in this dip, there's virtually nothing at all.

Jo's call was answered on the first ring. Detective Chief Inspector Ted Darling responded with, 'Hello, Jo, to what do I owe the honour? Are you missing us already?'

'We've got a suspicious death on our patch, boss. Something a bit out of the ordinary. I needed to find someone who might know ways to break a man's neck with their bare hands. So of course, I thought of you.'

Chapter Two

'So what's he like to work with, then, this DCI Darling?' PS Thomas asked Jo Rodriguez, as the two of them stood waiting.

Jo tried hitching the collar of his raincoat up a bit higher, in the vain hope of stopping at least some of the trickle which was finding its way down the back of his neck, inside his shirt and all the way down his spine. It felt as if he'd been standing out in the wet and cold for hours.

'I've heard a lot about him, of course,' the sergeant continued. 'He seems to be a bit of a legend in the force. But I've never met him in person.'

'First off, don't go by appearances,' Jo told him, shifting his weight from side to side to try to restore some circulation to his frozen and sodden feet. His town shoes seemed to have even fewer waterproof properties than his coat.

'He's smaller than you might expect from his reputation. Slight. Very quiet and polite. But a bit of a ninja on the sly. Excellent detective and the best boss I've worked with, by far. He's a bit formal and old-fashioned, though, so you're best off calling him sir, at least to start with.'

His tone turned wistful as he said, 'Once he's had a look here and we've got Uniform and CSI on site starting a search, we'll probably adjourn to Ashton nick to set up an incident room.'

He was thinking of the drive back, the heater on full blast for his feet, which now felt like blocks of ice. Of hot, strong, black coffee back in the warmth of his office, or the briefing room.

Cai Thomas was looking at him appraisingly, reading his thoughts with a smile.

'Don't forget I warned you it will take time to get the various teams out here. Then there's the headache of how and where we're going to park them all, to get as close as they can. Especially those bringing in equipment. I'll need to speak not just to the person who rents these fields but to the owner of them. They're going to want some reassurance that we're not going to rip up their grazing land. Not even for a murder case, if that's what it turns out to be.'

He was now looking across the field to the opening in the drystone wall through which the short, slight figure of DCI Ted Darling had just walked.

Thomas's gaze was appraising. He was noting the high quality jacket. Not new, not bought for the occasion to impress. He couldn't make out the footwear in the grass but if the hiking gaiters were anything to go by, they'd be the business. This was clearly someone used to being out and about in all kinds of terrain and any type of weather. Unlike Jo Rodriguez.

Jo perked up visibly at the sight of his boss. It wasn't that he didn't think he could manage a murder case without him. It was simply that the boss's arrival on the scene meant he might be able to go back to the nick first on the pretext of sorting out an incident room.

He made the introductions, hoping his genuinely chattering teeth might earn him the right to go.

'Boss, this is PS Cai Thomas, from the local Rural Crime Team. He spotted some things which made him suspect this was a suspicious death rather than an accident. The Professor's already been and gone, and she agreed with him.'

'What things in particular, sergeant? Can you run me through your initial thoughts, please?'

The 'please' came as a surprise to Thomas. He hadn't come across much of that from other senior officers he'd encountered. Especially ones dragged out of their cosy warm offices to trudge across fields in unrelenting rain.

'Well, sir, as I told the DI here, it's hard to tell from the state of the body, but there's a ring on his hand which I recognise, so I think I know who it might be. We have some of what you might call militant vegan hippies living in the area. I think this might be one of them. A bloke I only know as Spike.'

'Living or squatting?' Ted asked him.

'Oh, they own the land they live on, although they live in a bit of an eclectic collection of accommodation rather than conventional housing. Gypsy wagons, converted buses, that sort of thing. The council gets lots of complaints about them, but they're sharp. They know the planning laws inside out, so they always stay one jump ahead.'

'Hippies? New Age Travellers? That sort of thing?' Jo queried.

'Probably not quite what you mean by that, Jo. They're not your average benefit-seeking drop-outs, if that's what you had in mind. You'd be surprised at the background of some of them. I go up there quite often. Trying to keep the peace, like, between them and the farming community. They have their own lawyer on tap there, for one thing, and a sharp one. Most of them are well-qualified in something. They just prefer an alternative lifestyle.

'Spike reckoned to be a singer-songwriter. He says he wrote that theme tune. You know the one, for that big smash-hit TV drama.'

He started to sing a bit of a tune, in a good baritone; a haunting, melancholy piece which Ted and Jo recognised immediately.

'So we could find his real name from that,' Jo suggested.

'Well, if it was really him who wrote it. He did spin a good yarn. But I imagine it would be easy enough to verify. I've never found reason to check out his story.'

Ted had been looking around on his walk across the field

and was still scanning the lie of the land.

'I haven't seen any livestock in this field, or the last one, but I presume it's sheep grazing, normally? Was he here looking to see what animals he could liberate, or whatever it is they do?'

'Possibly, sir, I suppose. But I still can't fathom what would have had him scrambling up or down a waterfall. Certainly not in old trainers with very little grip.'

'Boss, Professor Nelson's initial thought was that someone broke the victim's neck, probably in another location, then dumped the body here to make it look like an accident,' Jo told him.

'If it hadn't been for a woman out with her camera, the body could have been there for a lot longer, which would have made the cause of death harder to determine,' Thomas put in. 'Certainly from the position of the head in relation to the neck, it seemed to me likely that that's what caused his death, sir. The DI said you might have some ideas on who would know how to do that manually, if that's what happened.'

'It's a very specialised skill. Some Special Forces might be taught it, but not many I don't think. Certainly fewer than you might imagine, although I'd have to check on that. Those types of operatives prefer to keep much further away from their enemies than that would require, as I understand things.

'You must know the people on your patch very well, I imagine, sergeant. Have you any ideas if any of them would fit that profile?'

Thomas's gaze was steady as he locked eyes with Ted and replied, 'It's not really the sort of topic which comes up over a cup of tea when I call in to see how lambing's going, sir.'

Ted smiled at him as he replied, 'Fair point. But I would imagine you spend a good bit of time talking to the people around here. It's surprising how much you can pick up just chatting to someone. So you'd know if any of them have served in the Forces, for instance.'

'Most of them are farmers back a few generations. Sometimes a son or daughter will rebel and go off and join up or do something else, but they generally get pulled back, especially as parents get older and can't manage so well. There are a couple I can think of like that.'

'So who have we got coming out, to get us started?' Ted looked at Jo as he asked the question.

'I came on my own, boss. My team are tied up with a biggish assault. Two rival groups - gangs, if you prefer - decided to start knocking lumps out of one another. One of the injured lads is in a bad way so we're bracing for possible murder charges. DS Ramsay and DC Burgess will come over as soon as they're free. DC Sharp and our Civilian Investigator can take over with the paperwork for now. If it does turn into a murder, we'll need more bodies for that, though.

'The coroner's not been here yet. He was delayed by something else, but he's on his way.'

'I've asked for as many officers from Uniform as can be spared to come and start a site search, and Cai's got those members of his team who can drop what they're doing to come over and help with house-to-house. But as Cai warned me, the problem is the length of time taken to get here. Not long now though, hopefully.'

'Right, well I'd like to view the body in situ before it's taken off to the morgue, if you show me where, sergeant. Jo, you'd best get back to Ashton before your vehicle gets blocked in, and sort out an incident room. I'll come and find you there once I've seen what I need to see here.'

Jo had to resist an urge to smother the boss in a man hug of relief at the prospect of getting to somewhere warm and dry. He'd had enough of the great outdoors to last him for some time. He was whistling jauntily to himself as he trudged back across the fields to the sanctuary of his car.

And not a moment too soon. He was nearing the end of the access road when the first of the police and CSI vehicles started to arrive, forcing him so far up onto the verge that branches of the hedge shrieked against the sides of his service vehicle. He'd need to report that, especially if the damage was as bad as it sounded.

Now that PS Thomas had seen the DCI's boots at close quarters he didn't even bother to warn him about the slippery slope down to the base of the waterfall. Those bad boys were clearly designed for terrain much more challenging than that. Again, they had certainly seen some use.

He did, however, give a timely warning about the smell, although no doubt the DCI had experienced the same, if not worse, a few times in his career.

Again he got a smile which was more like a grin in response, as Ted's hand went into his jacket pocket.

'I never visit crime scenes without my secret weapon,' he told him, pulling out a packet of Fisherman's Friend lozenges and offering the sergeant one.

They both sucked in silence while Ted stood, some distance from the body, experienced eyes taking in details.

Then he said, 'Well, if for some reason he was trying to climb up or down there in those shoes, it's easy to see why he would have fallen. The big question is why on earth would he be climbing there in the first place? Either up or down.'

'First thing that went through my mind, sir. There are far easier and quicker ways to get round the waterfall and they're easy to spot. Unless he was here in the dark. But then I have no idea why he would be.'

'This is a question for elimination purposes, not a judgement. I try not to do those. But, drugs?'

'Spike used a bit of weed, for sure. Most of them do, up there where they live. But something strong enough to make him think he could fly off a waterfall? I doubt it very much.

'The Professor said he could have been killed elsewhere and dumped here to make it look like an accident. That sounds plausible to me.'

'You know the people on your patch a lot better than anyone, I imagine. And you clearly know what's going on. If one of the farmers wanted to kill a militant vegan, I can think of less complicated ways of doing it. A shotgun blast to the chest, for a start. A cover story of disturbing someone breaking in to get at their livestock. A farmer being afraid there were more of them and their own life might have been in danger. A case like that, it would have been very hard to prove pre-meditation. They might have got away with it. But breaking his neck then dumping him here? That's something else entirely.'

Even above the sound of the water falling onto the rocks, both men could clearly now hear the sounds of vehicles approaching, coming down from the road.

'Sounds like the cavalry's arrived, sir. Shall we get this show on the road?'

As they climbed back up the slope, Ted told him, 'Your team are the best placed to talk to the locals, but I'd like someone from CID in on each visit, please. The best combination of skills that way, so we're less likely to miss anything.'

Again with the please, Thomas noted. The politeness made a pleasant change.

They started walking towards where the vehicles should soon be arriving. Ted said conversationally, 'Gwynedd, somewhere, but I can't be sure exactly where.'

Thomas looked at him in surprise, rewarded with another of those grins which made the DCI look even younger than he did anyway.

'Your accent,' Ted told him. 'I told you it was possible to pick things up from talking to people. That's what I picked up from listening to you. Am I right?'

Thomas was looking impressed.

'Not bad at all. My family farmed very near Yr Wyddfa, as it happens.'

The slip into Welsh for the name Snowdon may have been natural, or, Ted thought, it could be the sergeant seeing what he really knew.

'I've been up it a few times,' Ted told him.

Cai Thomas had heard so many people say that when what they actually meant was riding the train to the summit then taking the easiest walking trail back down. Watching the way Ted moved and how he was dressed, Thomas suspected he meant he'd done the toughest ascent of all, Crib Goch.

'You didn't fancy the farming life yourself, then?' Ted asked him.

'I don't know if you know it, but the figures for depression and suicide in farming are way above the national average. My dad went out to the livestock sheds one night to check for early lambs. When he didn't come back, my mam sent me to look for him. I found him hanging. I was thirteen.

'Mam and I kept the farm going, somehow, until it could be sold. Then we moved to a nice little house on the coast and I decided pretty much anything but farming was the future for me.'

'Sorry to hear that.'

They were in sight of the arriving vehicles now. The PCSO was directing some of them through the gateway. Ted could see that the coroner had arrived, and the mortuary van was further up the lane, waiting to get through to remove the body. He nodded to the coroner and gave him a polite 'Sir', but knew he'd be keen to make his inspection then let everyone else get on with their work.

'Clearly we need a site search as soon as possible. We're already looking at a long delay before the body was found so some indicators may have been lost. But let's see if Uniform can find anything at all to help, both above and below the waterfall. Then we need to get on with asking anyone in the area if they saw anything, as soon as possible. We'll need your local knowledge for that, to know who would be the best officers to send where.

'Are you happy to set the site searches in place, then come

over to Ashton to brief us on who lives where so we can plan that stage? I suspect we'll be better starting on that fresh in the morning. Another few hours shouldn't make much difference in the long run, if that's all right with you. Thank you.'

That was definitely a first. Not just please and thank you, but being consulted on what needed doing. PS Thomas stood for a moment to watch Ted walk off back to his service vehicle. He had a feeling he might enjoy working with DCI Darling on this case.

Chapter Three

Ted used the drive to the Ashton police station to make some phone calls. The first was to his long-suffering partner, Trevor, to warn him that he might well be home later than planned.

Trev had been pleased when Ted was made up to Head of Serious Crime, giving him a more administrative role and much more regular hours. He'd been less than happy when Ted had agreed to a sideways step to Deputy, with a changed role which saw him back doing the hands-on policing he loved best.

'I'm just calling to say I might be a bit later than usual this evening. We've got a suspicious death out on Jo's patch and it's a bit of an unusual one, on the face of it. I'm on my way to a briefing now, to see how it's going to go, but with luck, I should still be home for seven-thirty or thereabouts, so we can hopefully eat together.'

'Is Jo not running it? And I suppose, if you're getting involved, it means you're not going to make judo tomorrow or karate on Thursday?'

Trev didn't sound thrilled. He'd got used to having Ted around a lot more, eating together frequently, but he'd always suspected it wouldn't last. Ted preferred to be where the action was.

'I'll have to clear it with Sammy, of course, but Jo called me in to consult, so depending on how it pans out, I might stay as SIO. Whatever happens, I'll need to attend the first briefing to set things off in the right direction. I'll try to get back as soon as I can, though.'

He made himself a mental note to try to take a clearly disgruntled Trev out for a meal as soon as he could. A small gesture of gratitude for his support. Then he phoned his current boss, Detective Superintendent 'Sammy' Sampson to give her all the details, including the unusual probable cause of death. He'd like to head the case as Senior Investigating Officer, but she would have the final say. He hoped it would be nothing but a formality to get the nod from her.

'It sounds an intriguing one, Ted. But is this going to be another opportunity for you to start playing cowboys, and will I get another phone call from a disgruntled Firearms Commander who wants you kept firmly on a lead?'

He'd had a token rap over the knuckles from her over how he'd dealt with the last big case. No more than that, because his actions, although unorthodox, had brought down a gang the Drugs team from Manchester had been after for some time.

'No reason to think so,' he reassured her.

She made a sceptical noise. He'd told her the theory on the type of people who might be capable of inflicting the fatal injury, if it was what it appeared to be on first sight.

'I've not known you all that long but as soon as I hear the words Special Forces in the same sentence as a case you want to take on, I start to get nervous.

'Here's what you can do. Go and do your initial briefing now to get things started. Give them the benefit of your undisputed experience, but then pass the reins over to Jo Rodriguez tomorrow morning while you come and see me and convince me why I should make you SIO and not him.'

Ted smiled to himself as he ended the call. It was very much as he'd expected. So now he'd better find out some specialist information to show why his knowledge would be an asset leading the enquiry. Time to call in a promised favour.

The voice which answered the call was hoarse and indistinct. Ted could barely identify it, especially from the one word, 'Hello?'

'You sound rough. But I need your help, and you did say you owed me one.'

Mr Green. Ted's Special Skills instructor, but sounding nothing like he'd ever heard him before.

'I can't speak.'

The voice was so weak Ted had trouble hearing him. But if anyone would have the answers to the questions rattling round in Ted's mind, Green would.

'I wouldn't ask if I didn't need your help. If I tell you what it is I need to know, could you text me a brief reply, please?'

Green clearly rallied his forces for his reply as it was slightly stronger.

'Piss off, Gayboy.'

Then the line went dead.

Ted frowned. He could have done with the information which Green could have supplied him with in an instant. He didn't know anyone else likely to have the same knowledge at their fingertips. But he did know someone who had served in the armed forces. Given how cagey he always was about talking of those days, Ted had always suspected he might also have been with a specialist unit and might therefore have at least some of the knowledge he needed.

'Dave? Ted Darling. I don't know if you can help me. I need some info. About the armed forces. My usual source has laryngitis or something so I can't talk to him and he doesn't text. I wouldn't ask if it wasn't important.'

Dave, the landlord of The Grapes, the pub nearest to Ted's own station, was usually jovial, full of bonhomie. Ted could almost hear the shutters clang down at his question. Ted knew little of the man's military service, only that he had served and didn't talk about it, which made him think he might, at least, be a starting point for some of what he needed to know.

'Those days are long gone, Ted.'

'I know, and I don't want to let skeletons out of cupboards for you. But I really could do with some help.'

There was a long pause. Ted and his team were good customers. Ted always saw to it that everyone behaved, even when letting their hair down off duty.

Eventually, Dave gave a sigh of resignation and said, 'Can you come round tomorrow morning? Before opening time? I'll do my best to tell you whatever it is you need to know.'

* * *

Jo Rodriguez had made good use of his time back at the station, pulling in extra hands to sort out an incident room which looked the business. His sergeant, DS Ramsay, had told him their assault victim was now off the critical list, so at least that was looking like a serious assault rather than a murder charge.

He'd started a white board with the scant information they had to date and had got someone to print off a large-scale map of the site where the body had been found, and the surrounding properties.

As he'd thought from his visit there, the farms in the area were widely scattered, all of them some distance from where the body had been lying at the foot of the waterfall. It would be a question of getting officers round each of the isolated properties to talk to the locals to see if they had seen or heard anything which could be of use to them.

There'd be no CCTV to help them with this case, unless any of the farms had their own security cameras. From what Cai Thomas had been telling him about the value of farm machinery, he suspected quite a few of them might well have them. It had come as a surprise to Jo, who'd never had occasion to ponder on the cost of a tractor. Cai had told him that some farm machinery was worth more than a Ferrari driven by a Cheshire celebrity's wife, although the theft would not always be taken as seriously as that of a WAG's sports car.

Jo had now briefed DS Pete Ramsay on the details he had so far. Jo had been transferred to Ashton to sharpen up the team there. Ramsay had the rank but was too much under the thumb of the older DC Alan Burgess and not managing to assert himself sufficiently.

Jo was relaxed and informal, happy to be called by his first name by everyone. He could still run a tight ship when he needed to, and already crime statistics in the division were much improved.

Jo had also called up a couple of the team members from Stockport, in anticipation of the boss's instructions. DCs Jezza Vine and Maurice Brown were already there and starting to catch up with details, together with some officers from the Rural Crime Team who'd been told to go straight to the briefing.

Once Ted arrived, he told Jo to start things off with the information they had so far, but they would need to wait for Sergeant Thomas's arrival for the detailed local knowledge he would bring on those living around where the body was found. Professor Nelson's suggestion that the man had been murdered elsewhere and dumped at the waterfall to stage an accident meant that he could have been killed anywhere. But the most likely witnesses would be those living close by, or who had livestock on any of the nearby fields.

'We don't have a definite ID on the victim yet, only his nickname, Spike. But Sergeant Thomas thinks it may be a local hippy type who claimed to be a singer-songwriter who wrote that theme tune everyone was singing a few years back after it was on telly.'

Jo hummed the opening bars of the haunting refrain. Immediately a few voices joined in. It was one of those songs that everyone knew as soon as they heard it, even if they hadn't seen the series. At one time it had been impossible to turn on the radio without hearing it.

Jezza's head was down over her phone, her fingers flying. Then she looked up and said, 'If it is the same man, his name's Brendan Doyle, sixty-four, originally from the west of Ireland. He wrote that piece years ago and it stayed unknown until it was picked up for that series. That seems to be the only major commercial success that he ever had, although he had a few minor ones. But he must have been raking it in with royalties, the amount of airtime that one's had since. As long as he had a tight contract to keep control of the rights.'

'Good, Jezza, thanks for that. Let's explore that avenue first, see if we can establish if it really is the same person. We don't want that identity to get out until it's confirmed, in case Brendan Doyle simply moved quietly back to Ireland and is happily living there.

'Hopefully we'll get a positive ID from DNA samples taken at the post-mortem, if there's anything on record. Jo, will you take that yourself? We'll decide who else nearer the time.'

'Will do, boss. I'll be interested to find out more about the injury, for one thing.'

'I'm hoping to talk to someone tomorrow who might be able to give me a steer on which forces personnel might have the training to break someone's neck cleanly like that.'

'The killer's a bloke, then,' DC Alan Burgess put in emphatically. 'A bird wouldn't have the strength or the bottle to do that.'

Ted opened his mouth to respond but Jezza Vine beat him to it.

'I'd be more than happy to show you exactly why that pile of misogynist crap is totally inaccurate.'

Jezza Vine was a kick-boxer and a good one. Her sharp tongue was also capable of inflicting some serious injuries. There were a few muffled laughs, hands going to faces to hide smiles. Burgess's face darkened and the look he flashed at Jezza was positively murderous. But he'd learned the wisdom of not making any comeback with the DCI present.

'DC Vine,' Ted told her sternly, a clear warning in his tone. Privately he agreed with her but he wouldn't allow disrespect from any officer during one of his briefings.

Then he went on, 'But Jezza is correct in what she says, DC

Burgess. It's foolish and dangerous to rule out anyone purely on the basis of gender. There could be plenty of unscrupulous so-called self-defence instructors who teach the most extreme forms of protection. So let's not jump to any conclusions here without proof.'

Burgess's DS, Pete Ramsay, spoke next. Ted suspected it was as much an attempt to defuse the situation as anything else.

'But if the Professor has said the body might have been killed elsewhere then taken to the waterfall and placed there, rather than thrown over, that would also take someone with some strength, wouldn't it? I'm assuming you couldn't get a vehicle down to where it was found, from what you said, Jo. Not even a quad bike, with a slope as steep as you said. So that implies a degree of strength, doesn't it?'

Jezza wasn't finished yet, but she was more careful with her words and tone this time, with the boss's eyes on her.

'If you like, sarge, I'll give you a fireman's lift round the room to show you even a mere woman can do it. It's technique as much as strength. We do similar stuff in training sometimes.'

'Hopefully a site search might still show up tyre tracks from a vehicle from around the time the body was put there,' Ted told them. 'Although there's been a lot of rain since, so we might be out of luck there.'

'Bit of a risk though, lugging a body about on the back of a quad bike, surely?'

The question came from a Uniform constable sitting near the front of the room.

'I can probably answer that one, sir.'

Sergeant Cai Thomas had just entered the room at that point. Ted had expected he would be swift and efficient at organising things at the scene of the crime, which he clearly had been, to arrive in such good time.

Ted indicated to him to continue and Thomas walked to the front so he could address all those present.

'First off, for those not used to policing in sparsely populated rural areas like our patch, let me just say that it's possible to go for days around some of those farms without seeing a soul from the outside world. So the risk of being spotted would be very low indeed.

'Those of us who spend a fair bit of time there will often see farmers doing their rounds on a quad with all sorts of things on the rear carrier, from livestock feed to sheepdogs, even to an injured or dead sheep. Sadly, especially in spring with lively lambs about, we can get a lot of sheep fatalities because of irresponsible dog walkers who think their precious pooch would never hurt a sheep and "just wanted to play".

'Now, I've never tried it with a body, obviously. But I think for one of those you'd need to fold it up, lash it and cover it with something like silage bale wrapper, to make it look less suspicious.

'The simpler solution, of course, would be to move it in the back of a Land Rover, which most of the farmers round here own. We get no end of Defender thefts reported. A skilled thief can get into one of those with a tin opener.'

'Sarge, all this is assuming he was killed on or near one of the farms,' DC Maurice Brown began. 'How far away is the hippy camp? Because maybe it was one of his mates who killed him for some reason. Especially if he had money. That's always a powerful motive. Perhaps he was killed there then the killer moved him and hoyed him down by the waterfall, either to make it look like an accident, or to try to frame one of the farmers.'

Jezza Vine was sitting next to Maurice, her best friend, and she nodded in agreement.

'Maurice is right. If he was still getting royalties from the music, or even if he had a lucrative buy-out contract on it, he may have had money stashed away. Serious money, possibly. We'd need to look at next of kin, for a start.'

'That's a good point,' Cai Thomas told them. 'We definitely

need to find out first if Spike and Brendan Doyle the song-writer are the same person. The legend always was that he was the one who wrote that song. I never looked into it, to be honest, because I never had occasion to.'

The first thing PS Thomas had done on arrival had been to scan the white board for any updated information, so he'd seen the possibility of Spike having been called Brendan Doyle.

'The hippy camp is about two miles away across country. And as for means, they have various types of vehicles there so that's a possibility.'

'What we need from you now, please, Sergeant Thomas, is a run down on who lives in the surrounding properties,' Ted told him. 'This is not me being judgemental, nor misogynist, DC Vine, but would I be right in thinking some of the people in the farms we'll need to visit will be wary of outsiders? And might there be places where we'd be better off sending in older male officers to talk to the occupants rather than younger female ones?'

Thomas smiled at that.

'Spot on, sir. Some of the old buggers might get a bit bristly being expected to talk to "a slip of a lass", as we've found in the past with some cases.

'This one here,' he pointed to a particularly isolated property on the map, 'is a woman living and farming on her own. She seems to hate everyone on principle, so it won't matter who we send there. She's not likely to be very forthcoming to anyone, except to complain and criticise us. I'd suggest sending a male and a female officer, mature ones who won't be put off by her manner. Miss Burrows, she's called.'

He covered most of the properties on the map with a brief description of the occupants plus any knowledge which would help determine who should visit each one.

'This one's Tom Taylor. He's harmless enough but a bit fanciful. He'll tell you anything he thinks you might want to hear so he's not usually a lot of use, but there's always a first time. He'll tell you he's seen Lord Lucan out in the lane if it will get him some attention.

'Then this one, sir, this is the only ex-Forces person I know of on the patch and I know very little about his military background. Jamie Robinson, he's called. I told you suicide rates are high in farming. Jamie went off to be a soldier and all I know about it is he served in Afghanistan. The farm was too much for his parents without him and his father killed himself.

'His mother wasn't well either. Always a bit odd and it turned out to be early onset dementia. Jamie was their only family but he had PTSD. It did at least mean he could get out of the Army to get back and help his mother, but in the end she had to go into a home so he's on his own and not always doing very well.

'We've been called in a couple of times, with the RSPCA, because of animal welfare concerns when he's not been coping. He's had a bit of help and he's mostly back on an even keel for now. If it's all right with you, sir, I'd like to speak to him myself initially. I've got a bit of a rapport with him. He talks to me, at least. I should certainly be able to pick up whether he's all right at the moment, or not. The sight of strangers and talk of a killing might not be the best thing for him.'

Ted nodded at that.

'That makes sense.'

'So now, if it's helpful, I can play my body cam footage of the crime scene and the victim. That way everyone can see what you and I and Jo have seen at first hand, although without the pleasant accompanying fragrance.'

Chapter Four

Ted put an arm round the open kitchen doorway first, waggling a wine bottle, before he ventured in himself, unsure of his reception. He hoped it was a suitable peace offering. The man in the shop had assured him it was an excellent Burgundy. For the price, it ought to be drinkable, at least.

He paused to scoop up Adam, the youngest cat, who was already trying to climb up his trouser leg, before he walked into the room. He wasn't quite as late as he'd feared he might be. The cooker was in full use and something was giving off inviting smells, but the atmosphere was a bit on the chilly side.

'I brought you some wine,' Ted told his partner. 'I won't come any closer until I've had a shower because I've been to a murder scene and the body wasn't all that fresh. I don't think my suit smells, I had my jacket over the top, but just in case. Is that all right? Have I got time?'

Trev looked at the bottle as Ted put it on the table and smiled, at least.

'That looks nice, thank you. There's time, if you're quick. The meal is nearly ready. Hang your suit up in the bathroom while you shower. The steam should help with the smell but if it's bad, I can take it to the cleaners for you tomorrow.'

His words made Ted feel slightly worse, if anything. He said a heartfelt, 'Thank you. I really don't deserve you,' as he put Adam back on the floor and sprinted up the stairs to wash and change.

Trev was certainly in a better humour when Ted came back

downstairs, hair still damp, smelling of shower gel, and wearing something more comfortable than his suit. The open wine bottle and half-empty glass suggested one reason for the thaw. Ted risked moving in close to give him a hug. He was about to apologise when Trev beat him to it.

'Sorry, I was being a mardy spoilt brat. I've just got used to seeing a bit more of you and I'm finding it hard to adjust to you going back to how things were before.'

The colloquialism made Ted smile. Any dialect always sounded out of place pronounced in Trev's posh accent.

'Sit down. It's all ready. I can dish up now you're showered. How's the suit?'

'It doesn't seem too bad to me but then I've had the smell in my nostrils all afternoon so I might not notice. Have a sniff when you next go up and see what you think.'

Ted sat down at his usual place, reaching for a glossy brochure lying next to the place setting.

'What's this?' he asked, picking it up, although he could see perfectly well that it was a catalogue of the kind of expensive, hi-tech big bikes Trev worked with in the motorbike dealership in which he was now a co-owner, thanks to Ted taking out a bank loan for him to buy into the partnership.

'Oh, that,' Trev said airily, putting down full, steaming plates of food and whisking the brochure out of Ted's hands. 'Just some of the new bikes Geoff and I have been thinking of stocking.'

Ted studied his partner's face as Trev sat down at the table with exaggerated nonchalance, took another drink of his wine then made a start on his food.

'See this expression?' Ted asked him conversationally, not yet touching his own meal. 'This is my policeman face. I use it in interviews. To let a suspect know that I'm not believing a word they're saying to me.'

Trev tried not to react but failed. His face slowly creased into a smile, then he laughed as he said, 'It's a fair cop, guv. I was tentatively thinking of an upgrade. I could get an excellent trade deal, of course, and a good part-exchange rate on the Bonny. Best of all, Geoff has said I can put the running costs through the business accounts and we'll claim it as a demo' model.'

The Triumph Bonneville had always been Trev's baby. He'd had his heart set on it for a long time before Ted bought it for him. But he'd had it a while now and was clearly in the mood for change.

'Can we talk about this another day? Please?' Ted asked him. 'That's not a no. It more an "I need to look at the figures to make sure we're not over-stretching ourselves". There's still the mortgage, and the bank loan on the dealership. But if it's what you want and we can afford it, then that's fine.'

He was rewarded with a smile which would have devastated the ice caps, followed by a spontaneous hug.

They ate in companionable silence and a better atmosphere. When Trev stood up to get the pudding, Ted picked up the catalogue again, looking specifically at the page with the casually turned down top corner. He had to read it at arm's length as he'd left his reading glasses upstairs in his jacket pocket. He'd need to retrieve those before it went to the cleaners, although Trev would automatically check for such things.

'I like the look of the Tiger 900, but I still need to look at the figures,' he said, putting the brochure back down as Trev put a bowl in front of him. Sticky toffee pudding with clotted cream. Ted's absolute favourite. Trev had brought out the big guns, right from the start.

Ted was further rewarded by a bone-crushing hug and a lingering kiss.

'I do love you, Mr Policeman, and I really don't deserve you. Eat up your pudding then let me show you how much you're appreciated.'

* * *

Ted was heading down the corridor to see Detective Superintendent Sampson, now installed in what had been Superintendent Caldwell's old office on the ground floor. Superintendent Caldwell, the formidable Ice Queen, had moved up to the hallowed ground of the top floor, leaving the easily accessible ground-floor office to Sammy Sampson, who was recovering from surgery.

On his way there, Ted bumped into Inspector Kevin Turner, from Uniform, who had just come out of his office chuckling to himself.

'Morning, Kev. What's put you in such a good mood?'

'You know we're always complaining about how the baddies keep managing to stay one jump ahead? Well, we've just had a bit of a breakthrough on that spate of burglaries we've been getting nowhere with because whoever it is manages never to leave DNA traces at the scene. We only got lucky because they didn't recognise PCs Firethorn and Berberis, they got too close and left their DNA all over them.'

Ted frowned at the unfamiliar names.

'Hedging plants, Ted. Murderous ones, with savage thorns. Our burglar picked the wrong property. He must have thought an older single male occupant would be easy prey. But our man is a retired professional gardener, and he knows how to use his plants as lethal weapons. He planted up the entire perimeter of his property with those two, and others, which will cut any potential intruder to ribbons. And they did. Our hapless villain left his blood all over the thorns and spikes, because he clearly hadn't yet covered up like he does close to and inside the property.

'Once we had his DNA, a couple of my officers went round to knock on his door and even without going inside they could see the hall was stuffed full of the gear he's nicked, so they were able to arrest him and haul him in.'

Ted laughed at that.

'More people need to know about that. Forget dodgy burglar alarms that might let you down unless you pay a fortune for them. Plant spiky hedging for DNA traps. A whole new angle in crime prevention and detection.'

'I'm on my way up to see Her Majesty now, to get her to agree to us starting an initiative. Send out flyers round target areas suggesting it. Got to be worth a shot, eh? Anything which makes life harder for the criminals and easier for us has to be a good thing. It should put a bit of business the way of local garden centres and landscape gardeners too, I imagine.'

'I could do with that sort of a breakthrough on this latest case out on Jo's patch. Body's been out in all that rain for a week or more before it was found, so I'm not holding my breath for any such miraculous DNA breakthrough with it. No CCTV out in the wilds, either. I think it's more likely we'll have to rely on good old-fashioned policing methods of going door to door and asking the right questions.'

'Yes, I heard about that one via the jungle drums,' Kev told him. 'Can't say I envy you. Hard to say who's likely to be the least receptive to answering police questions, especially from strangers - the farmers or the hippies. Good luck with it.'

Ted found Sammy in her office, starting to sort out her priorities for the day. Like putting the kettle on. Looking at the accumulated paperwork on her desk, he felt not a single pang of regret at having stepped sideways to leave her to that side of the role.

'You only want this case so you don't have to deal with that lot, isn't that true, Ted?' she asked him, nodding towards her desk, as if reading his thoughts.

'I can't say I envy you dealing with that little lot,' he replied. 'I genuinely think, though, that I might be able to bring something to this latest case. I'll be going to see someone shortly who can give me some inside information about possible suspects. People who might have the necessary skills. Mike Hallam is fine here for now running the gold bar scam case and he can always call me if he needs my help.'

Sammy frowned at the mere mention of their latest case.

'I know a murder trumps a fraud on SIO bingo, but I really would like us to wrap up that nasty one as soon as humanly possible, if not sooner. The thought of pensioners, of all people, losing their entire life savings, and possibly the roofs over their heads as well, makes me start to have murderous thoughts myself.'

'We've had a similar one in the past, only that one was getting people to buy expensive watches, rather than convert all their cash to gold bars. And I wanted to ask you if there's any chance we can borrow back Sal Ahmed, from Fraud, for some expert help with this current one? He used to be with the team, he's a DS now and a case like this is right up his street. Ours is unlikely to be a case in isolation and he'd be the one to pull all the threads together.'

Sammy busily scribbled herself a note on her desk.

'Leave that to me. It sounds like a sensible pooling of resources. Now tell me more about this case over Ashton way and why it interests you so much.'

'I'd be surprised if Professor Nelson was wrong when she says someone snapped the victim's neck for him with their bare hands. She's usually spot on. The full PM may reveal something she didn't see on her initial examination, though. But to manually break someone's neck like that, with no other visible injuries, is highly unusual. Because of course, you need to be up close and personal with someone to do it. And even then there's a fair bit of skill involved to do it quick and clean, as seems to have been the case with our body.'

'I'm almost afraid to ask this question, Ted, but is it something you know how to do?'

Ted gave her his most disarming smile.

'Theoretically, yes. It's something I've never had to do, though.'

'Well, I'm bloody glad to hear that. I'm not sure I'm keen on the idea of being alone in my office with a DCI who's sizing up the best way to snap my neck.'

She'd stood up to make herself some coffee, which necessitated her turning her back on him. She threw a, 'Cuppa?' at him over her shoulder.

'No, thanks, I'm going out shortly to talk to someone who may help me on the possible armed forces connection and no doubt he'll have the kettle on when I get there.'

She made her coffee and sat back down. Then she asked him, 'So purely out of academic interest, how easy is it to do? Would it suggest a killer bigger and stronger than the victim? Was he a big person? Presumably he saw the perpetrator as being unthreatening if he let them get that close to him. Unless he was drunk or drugged at the time, perhaps?'

'That thought has been going through my mind as a possibility, but we won't know until after the PM results. The victim was about five ten, five eleven but very slim, by what I saw of the body. Skinny, almost. Not that build alone is indicative of strength.'

'Does it take a lot of strength to kill like that?'

'Technique, rather than strength. But you're right, it does require the killer to be up close, in the victim's personal space, for it to work. You can probably find a video online easily enough that tells you how to do it. But that's a world away from actually doing it. You're not likely to get a second chance if you try and it doesn't work, because then you've totally lost the element of surprise. But as I said, I'm going shortly to talk to someone who may know a bit more about such things. I just wanted to check that you're all right with me leading on the case for now.'

'It seems to make sense. Make sure that DS Hallam knows he can come to me at any time if there's anything I can do to help while you're out in the country. I do hope you have green Wellies to look the part? You could probably claim them on expenses.'

Ted went on his way smiling, both at the humour and her

agreement that he should run the murder case. It had sparked his interest. Not just a novel means of killing but an environment unlike any of the urban cases he usually worked.

DS Mike Hallam, the senior of the Stockport team's two sergeants, was in charge while Ted was out of the office. He had what remained of the team, with Jezza and Maurice now over at Ashton, working away on the latest scam case, involving supposed investment in gold bullion. Ted went over to Mike's desk for an update.

'How was your body, boss?' Mike asked him.

'Fragrant,' Ted told him drily. 'How are things going here? Oh, and I've asked the Super if there's any chance of getting Sal over to give some input on your case. She's looking into it.'

'Speaking of bringing in experts, boss, when is Steve back from the States? We could really do with a computer investigator on loan for a few days. Gina's on it for now but she's the first to admit it's not her speciality. She's still better than the rest of us, and we do need to get to the ins and outs of the suspect's exchanges with the various victims, amongst other things.'

Ted was already shaking his head before Mike had finished speaking. Former team member DC Steve Ellis was on extended sick leave. He had a long, hard road ahead of him if he wanted to rejoin them at some future point. DC Gina Shaw, formerly from Drugs, was filling his place on the team but had nothing like his computer skills.

'I think he's back from the States this weekend. I'll check with Bill. But he then has another week's leave, and there's no way he can come back here straight away. You know that, Mike.'

'Not on the team as such, boss. But we need someone more adept with the intricacies of a computer than any of us are.'

'I'll see what I can do, but almost certainly not Steve. There's just a chance I'm going to need to pinch another team member for Ashton, too. There's a lot of widely spread properties where the occupants will need to be questioned at length and it risks being slow work. I'm reliably informed they're not the most forthcoming folk at the best of times, especially with strange faces on their territory.'

He was looking round at his depleted team. Mike Hallam would need to stay to run things, Gina Shaw seemed to be doing well with what she was working on, which meant the choice was between the second DS, Rob O'Connell, and DC 'Virgil' Tibbs.

Sensing the boss's eyes on them, both men looked up expectantly. Whilst not eavesdropping, they had both nonetheless caught the gist of what Ted had been saying. Virgil's face slowly split into one of his beaming smiles.

'You're going to pick Rob, aren't you, boss? It's because I is black, isn't it? Seriously, though, if these good country folk don't even like the sight of any copper they've not seen before, I can imagine what their reaction would be to my black face appearing out of the blue. They might take a shotgun to me.'

He grinned across at Rob O'Connell as he said, 'I think it needs someone of higher rank than me. Over to you, sarge.'

Chapter Five

Ted went round to the back door of The Grapes and rang the bell there. Dave appeared swiftly to open up to him. He had a tea towel slung over his shoulder and a half-eaten bacon sandwich, dripping with brown sauce, in one hand.

'Morning, Ted, come on in. Sorry, you've caught me having a late breakfast. Come into the kitchen. Do you fancy a brew? And what about a butty?'

'Nothing to eat, thanks, Dave, but I seldom say no to a cuppa.'

Ted sat down at the table as indicated. He'd not been in the kitchen before, only ever the bar and other public rooms. It was bright, clean and airy, professionally set up for the meals the pub served.

Dave was putting the kettle on and taking mugs out of an overhead cupboard.

'NATO standard?'

'I'm a bit of a tea wuss, so a lot weaker than that, please. Make it like you wouldn't touch it with a bargepole and it will probably be fine.'

There were noises coming from a room off the kitchen. Ted assumed it was a food prep area, and that the sounds were from the mystery woman who did all the cooking. He'd never seen her. As far as he knew none of the customers had. Dave only ever referred to her as "the trouble and strife", but Ted didn't even know if they were married.

Dave made the mugs of tea and put them on the table then

sat down opposite Ted to finish his sandwich, saying as he did so, 'So tell me how you think I can help you. But as I warned you, my military days are long gone. I took the Queen's shilling, did my bit and now I try not to think about it, so my information could well be out of date.'

'Any help at all would be great, Dave. Like I said, my usual source appears to be dying somewhat self-indulgently of man flu or something. I know I can trust your discretion but I have to say, for the record, that this is all in confidence.'

'No worries there at all. Anything you say to a publican is bound by the same code as to a priest in the confessional. You'd be surprised at what I know about some of my customers.'

Ted gave him the basic outline of his case and the pathologist's reasoning behind thinking the broken neck was the result of a deliberate act rather than of a fall or a similar accident.

Dave listened in a silence broken only by occasional bites of his sandwich or slurps at his tea.

'Right, first off, I need to dispel a few myths,' he began. 'Your average line soldier is not trained to kill with his bare hands. He has sophisticated weaponry to do that from a safe distance.

'He will be taught arrest and restraint, using an Aikido-based method, as part of his basic training and ongoing development, but definitely no lethal holds or interventions. That's only in the films.

'That holds good, too, for the Special Forces. The theory is that if you need to resort to that sort of thing, you're too close to the enemy and should have taken them out from a distance.

'It's worth remembering that the initial mission of the SAS was Recce and Prevention. Causing a distraction but not necessarily a body count.'

He paused for more tea, checking that Ted was all right with his and not needing a top-up. Ted was fine talking to Dave but was becoming acutely aware of the seemingly increasing sound of pans being banged down on surfaces in the other room. It bothered him slightly that he really didn't know who it was who was listening in on their conversation.

Dave had clearly seen and correctly interpreted his expression as he asked, 'Are you all right if we move to the back room now, Ted? So she can get in here and get on with the cooking without us jabbering away and getting in the way? I'll be in the doghouse for a week at least if I delay her getting the lunchtime food ready on time.'

Once they'd relocated to the small, intimate dining area off the main bar room and sat down at a round table, Dave picked up where he'd left off.

'So let's start by taking a look at the Specials who might have such skills. SAS you probably know about. They're almost certainly the best known to the general public. But then there's Pathfinder Platoon and MAW Cadre, which most people have probably never heard of.'

Ted opened his mouth to ask for an explanation but Dave beat him to it.

'MAW Cadre are the Marines' training lot for Mountain and Arctic Warfare. Pathfinder are part of an Air Assault Brigade. Some of those might learn silent kills as part of their special skills.'

Ted was thinking of Jezza Vine's input as he asked, 'Might some female soldiers have those sort of skills? One of my DCs will doubtless accuse me of being sexist if I fail to check that point.'

Dave frowned and drank more tea as he pondered that one.

'Some of those who served in the now defunct Int and Sy units - that's Intelligence and Security - may have trained in lethal force skills, and a small number of them may well have been females. But seriously, Ted, these are very specialist skills and those trained in them probably number fewer than a hundred in total, in all probability. I've trained in some strange things but not that. I'd struggle to neck a chicken if the trouble and strife decided to bring a live one home from the market one day.

'I'd have said you'd be far better looking more closely into the martial arts lot, and that's your speciality, isn't it? It's probably something they're not supposed to teach anyone but might there be someone rogue on your patch who's doing just that? Maybe to make themselves look tough? And I'm honestly not trying to teach a copper of your experience how to suck eggs, but have you started with a Google search to see what info is out there for all to see?'

'I haven't yet, no, and I should have. But there's a long way between knowing the theory of something and actually carrying it out in cold blood. It's a hard thing to practise, of course, and we'd know if we were getting a spate of broken-necked bodies dumped on our patch or anywhere else.'

Ted drained his mug and stood up.

'Thanks for your help, Dave, I really appreciate it.'

'I hope I was some help. It didn't feel like it.'

'Oh, more than you might realise. I had a horrible feeling it might be a widespread skill in some units. Knowing that it's so specialised means I now know to spread the net much wider and not get fixated on a military connection, which I might otherwise have wasted time doing.'

* * *

Ted used the short walk back to the station to phone Jo for a catch-up.

'Any news yet about when the PM is, Jo? I might join you for that one, while it's clearly going to be an interesting one, and not something I've come across before.'

'Monday morning, boss. I've not long since had the phone call to let me know. I imagine Professor Nelson will want to share this one with her students. It's not likely to be one they'll come across often in their chosen careers. Assuming she's right, of course.'

'I'd be surprised if she wasn't. It would be a first. Any progress on anything else?'

'I'm over at the crime scene now to see if the site search has thrown up anything. Unfortunately the answer so far is a big fat zero. The weather's not been in our favour, of course, so there don't seem to be any traces of anything much left. At least nothing we've found so far.

'We've got teams out now starting to talk to people in the nearest properties. Cai Thomas has gone first to the hippy place to see if he can perhaps get a provisional ID on the victim. Something to show that Spike really was Brendan Doyle, and that's who the body is. Cai's got shots of the ring to show them. Of course he might just find Spike there alive and well and having had his ring nicked, or lost it, or sold it to someone, which would leave us back at ground zero.

'If it does seem to be Spike, there's a chance someone there might just know his real identity for sure, and perhaps even about next of kin. We're purely going on hearsay at the moment. I'll let you know if there's any update. Of course they might not tell him anything, or he might not find the right person to ask. Will you be over later?'

'That's the plan. I'm following up on leads about neck-breaking skills, because I think the Professor is more likely to be right than not. I'll see you later.'

Ted stopped at the front desk when he got back to the nick, to talk to Bill Baxter, retired sergeant and now the station's secret weapon against time-wasters. No one knew better than Bill which reported crimes needed urgent action and which could join the queue. He was also Steve Ellis's landlord.

'Morning, Bill.'

Ted's first ever encounter with the man had brought him a gentle rebuke for asking his question before giving a polite greeting and he had never forgotten that.

'Is it this weekend Steve is back from the States?'

'It is, but he told me he's going away for another week before he comes back. He didn't say where or why and I didn't press him. But he did sound on better form. Well, from his email, but you know what I mean. He's kept in touch and that's a good thing, I suppose.'

Back in his office, Ted started internet searches about techniques to break someone's neck. There were fewer results than he'd expected to find. He still couldn't see it being something anyone could learn to do from a two-minute video. A bit of lateral thinking gave him an idea which might just advance him, as well as getting him some good points from Trev.

He made a phone call.

'*Sensei*? It's Ted Darling.'

His karate teacher. He hadn't been for a few weeks, to his regret.

'Ted! I was beginning to think you'd forgotten about us. What can I do for you?'

'I'm hoping to get there tomorrow evening, work permitting, but I wondered if you could help me with something in the meantime. Have you heard of any martial arts or self-defence instructors teaching the theory of how to break someone's neck?'

'Seriously? If I had heard of anything like that, I'd have gone and had a word myself and probably told you about it. You of all people know that's not what martial arts are about, Ted. It would be well out of order.'

'Oh, absolutely. I'm simply trying to find where and how someone might learn that technique. Could you do me a huge favour? Can you ask around and see if anyone has heard anything? It may not be in this area at all. I'm a bit clutching at straws here, so any information, even rumour, could be helpful. I hope to see you tomorrow for a catch-up.'

* * *

Sergeant Cai Thomas had chosen DC Maurice Brown to go with him for the initial visit to the so-called hippy camp. Maurice was solid enough but there was also something calm and non-threatening about him. Thomas had never worked with him before and knew nothing of his Daddy Hen reputation. Maurice simply gave off the vibes of someone who'd be more likely to defuse a situation than cause it to kick off.

'I'm not optimistic, Maurice. Even on a good day they're not always forthcoming. But let's give it a go, eh?' Thomas told him as he parked his service vehicle, a 4x4, at the end of a rough track, then led the way through a wooden gate.

There was an old stone house, scaffolding up against the front elevation, with an impressive bank of solar panels on the roof. Several outbuildings in various stages of disrepair and renovation were scattered about. Further away across the field, a collection of vehicles, seemingly converted as dwellings, parked in a semi-circle.

A man in a brightly coloured jumper, a strange, battered, black Homburg hat with a feather in the band squashed onto his head, sat by a fire where a kettle was boiling away happily. He had a lit spliff in one hand which he made no attempt to conceal at the sight of police officers arriving.

'All right, John?' the sergeant greeted him.

'All right, Cai,' he got in return.

'This is Maurice. We're here about Spike. D'you know where he is?'

The man made a show of looking round him.

'Not here, Cai. As you can see.'

'When did you see him last?'

'I don't keep track. Spike's his own person.'

The sergeant took his phone out, scrolled to find the photo he wanted then handed it to the man.

'Do you recognise this ring?'

John took the phone, looked at the screen, then his eyes narrowed as he looked back up at the sergeant.

'The wearer of this ring doesn't look a healthy colour. Are you telling me you've found a body?'

'Do you recognise the ring?' the sergeant asked him again, without giving anything else away.

The man's reply was equally as guarded.

'I've seen Spike wearing a ring similar to this one.'

'So now can you please tell us when you last saw Spike?'

'I couldn't say for certain. A few days, for sure. We don't live in each others' pockets here.'

A young woman had just emerged from the cottage with a wicker basket full of laundry balanced on one hip. A little girl, about four years old, trotted in front of her, large brown eyes in a heart-shaped face immediately locking on to the two strangers standing by the fire. Her small feet started carrying her nearer to them, as if unconsciously.

'Would anyone else know?' PS Thomas persisted.

Maurice was impressed with how patient he was in his questioning. It was like drawing teeth. But then his own attention was distracted by the little girl. Maurice couldn't resist children.

'Ali, any idea when you saw Spike last?' the man named John called across to the woman.

'Who wants to know and why?' she asked in return.

The sergeant ignored her and carried on with the man.

'We have found a body, yes. Wearing this ring. We need someone to come and ID the deceased. Unless you can tell me you definitely know where Spike is and that he's alive and well. Could you do that, and can you tell me Spike's real name?'

'Spike,' the man replied. 'Spike is what he called himself, so to me Spike was his real name.'

The little girl had edged closer now, her eyes fixed on Maurice. He squatted down to her level and smiled at her. She was clutching a brightly-coloured picture, which she held out towards him.

'I drawed this. For Gracie.'

'That's lovely, pet. I'm Maurice. What's your name?'

'Ruby!' the mother called sharply. 'I've told you not to speak to strangers.'

The child turned and trotted obediently back to her mother. Maurice sighed and straightened up.

'As I told you, Spike has a ring like that. And no, I don't know where he is at the moment,' the man continued, in answer to the sergeant's question.

'So could you view the body for us and let us know if it could be Spike?'

'Shouldn't it be next of kin to do that?'

Thomas sighed.

'Come on, John, you're a solicitor, you know how it works. We need a positive ID. We can't begin to track next of kin with only a nickname to go on. Help me out here. Can you do it or not?'

'What happened to the body? How did he die?'

Maurice thought he'd better make some sort of input, as the token detective on the scene. He was already feeling like a spare part.

'All we can say at this stage is that it's being treated as a suspicious death.'

He saw the man's eyes narrow at that and chanced another question.

'Did this Spike have any enemies that you know of?'

'We get on wonderfully well with all our lovely neighbours. It gets embarrassing having to turn down so many invitations to Sunday lunch,' the man told him in a tone heavy with irony.

'Just a thought, John, but perhaps if you all stopped telling them their whole lives are built around murder, you might get on a bit better, eh?' the sergeant told him. 'So how about it? Can you come and look at the body for us, to see if you can ID him? I'll run you there myself, then fetch you back again afterwards.'

The man stood up, stubbed out his spliff on the side of the log he'd been sitting on, then put it into his pocket.

'How can I refuse such a delightful invitation? I'm all yours. Lead on, Macduff.'

Chapter Six

'Well, this is all very quaint and Escape to the Country idyllic,' Jezza Vine commented with customary irony as she paused in the passenger seat of the police car to pull on her Wellies before descending into the sea of mud which awaited her.

She was with one of the rural team constables, Colin Nield, who was also equipping himself with suitable footwear.

He smiled at her as he said, 'I should warn you that as well as having to wade across the Somme, Miss Burrows' normal form of greeting to anyone, including me who she's known for years, is the business end of a firearm. And if she doesn't shoot us on sight, whatever you do don't call her by her first name. She hates that.'

As if on cue, two skinny sheepdogs with matted coats raced out of the open barn doorway, closely followed by a thickset woman pointing a .22 rifle towards the two officers.

The two dogs circled the intruders, hackles up, teeth on show, but making no move to attack.

'Now then, Miss Burrows, that's not a very friendly greeting. Call the dogs off, please, and put the gun down. You know me well enough by now, and this is DC Vine. We just need a word.'

Her piercing whistle instantly brought both dogs cringing to her feet and the gun muzzle dipped by all of a couple of inches. The overall impression was still of extreme hostility.

'I didn't see anything,' she told him immediately, her voice surprisingly deep and powerful.

'I haven't told you what we've come about yet,' Nield explained patiently.

'Whatever it is, I didn't see anything. Like none of you dozy sods ever sees anything when I report them mad "Meat is Murder" bastards coming onto my land, interfering with my beasts. I'll just put a bullet into one of them next time and claim self-defence. Perhaps then you might start to take some notice.'

Jezza Vine thought she might as well have a try, since PC Nield seemed to be getting nowhere fast.

'Miss Burrows, as PC Nield said, I'm Detective Constable Vine. I'm with the Serious Crime Team in Stockport, which I hope will indicate how seriously we are taking things ...'

She got no further. With a snort of contempt, the woman spat into the mud at her feet and said, 'Save your breath, girl. Your bullshit doesn't impress me. You're here because you want something from me. Well, I'll give you precisely what the police have always given me whenever I've tried to report anything that's happened to me - bugger all. Now get off my property, before I set the dogs on you.'

PC Nield was patience personified as he tried again.

'You know how stretched we are most of the time. And you know I always try to call round as soon as I can. I'm here now, for instance. Have you had any of them around bothering you recently?'

Another scoffing sound, then she said, 'If it's got a beard and hairy armpits, it ends up here, telling me I'm a murderer. And that's just the women. I've had more than twenty at a time on the place and where were you and your cronies when I reported that, eh? I'm not doing anything illegal, just trying to make a living out of the farm. They're the ones breaking the law, yet you do bugger all about it.'

The muzzle of the gun crept ominously upwards again as she said, 'I might just as well shoot one of them. At least someone would bloody come round here if I did that.'

'But if you won't tell us anything now we're here, we're not going to make any progress,' Jezza told her, trying to keep her tone reasonable but starting to lose patience with the open hostility.

'And you can shut your gob, you posh townie twat,' the woman told her sharply, changing her position slightly so that her gun was pointing squarely at Jezza, which left her feeling more than a little vulnerable.

'Come on, Miss Burrows, put the gun aside and talk to us nicely. We really are here to listen, and to see what we can do to help. Don't make me arrest you for threatening a police officer with a firearm,' PC Nield warned her.

This time she laughed out loud with what sounded like genuine amusement.

'I'd like to see you try, Colin Nield. I'd shoot you dead before you got within six feet and claim self-defence. I called your lot the last time my sheep were let out onto the road and I lost five good in-lamb ewes. I reported it when the bastards stole my best tup, which cost me a fortune, and they were long gone before anyone did anything. And then it was just a phone call to tell me to go into the station to report it. So why the buggery should I help you now?'

'Is it worth hanging about?' Jezza asked Nield in a quiet aside. 'Is it likely to get any better?'

PC Nield chuckled as he told her, 'Oh, this is her being quite warm and welcoming. She's not set the dogs on us for real yet, nor even fired a warning shot. Let's give it another shot.'

'I really rather wish you hadn't said that,' Jezza told him darkly.

'So, which of them has been bothering you of late? Have you seen anyone about recently? Anyone at all? Someone coming on the farm, or hanging about here?'

'The one this week, I drowned him in the slurry tank. Last week's one I fed to the pigs,' she sneered, with heavy irony. 'There's always one or more. I don't bloody know who they are.

We're hardly on first name terms.'

'Can you describe anyone in particular? Perhaps one of them you might have seen on their own, possibly quite recently?'

Jezza was full of silent admiration for PC Nield's patience, and the way he was doing his best to get the information they'd come for.

'I told you. Beards. Hairy armpits. Hairy arses, for all I know. They all look the bloody same to me. And they're all just vermin who need treating like it. What they do is breaking the law, not that any of you lot seem to give a shit about that.'

'Well, if you do think of anything relevant - anything at all - you know where we are, so just give us a call. Anyone you've seen. Anything which stands out in your mind.'

'But do you remember where I am, half the time? I bloody wonder. You only manage to show up when you want something from me.'

With that, she called to her dogs to follow her as she stumped back into the barn.

'Well, that was truly delightful and edifying,' Jezza commented, as the two of them went back to the vehicle to change out of their boots, now covered in sticky mud with a strong fragrance of cow pats. 'How do you manage to keep it civil, if she's always like that?'

'Because I know what a tough life she's had. Still has. She's on her own, tackling jobs that would floor a couple of healthy young men, and she's likely to die trying rather than give up,' he told her as he shut the boot of the vehicle.

'Plenty of us have had lives harder than you might believe, but we don't go round pointing guns at everyone,' Jezza muttered, half under her breath, as she slid into the front passenger seat next to him.

* * *

Maurice had called ahead to the mortuary to let them know they were on their way there with someone who might possibly be able to identify the deceased. That would hopefully at least enable them to take the case forward a bit further.

He did his best to make conversation on the drive there, hoping he might pick up something of some use to take back to the end of day briefing. Not that he expected to get much out of this man, John, if he really was a solicitor.

'So did this Spike bloke really write that song, then, eh? That must have made him a bob or two, if it was him. It's still getting a lot of air time now and it must be years old.'

Maurice half turned towards their rear seat passenger as he asked his question. John's reply was more suited solicitor in his offices than bearded and colourfully-clad hippy.

'Spike was not only my friend but also my client. I helped him with his business affairs. So anything at all which passed between us is confidential and will remain that way.'

People often made the mistake of underestimating Maurice because of his affable and unthreatening manner. He didn't come across as the sharpest knife in the drawer sometimes. He was sharper than he looked, though. A plodder, certainly, but he got there in the end. And sometimes he was quicker on the uptake than he seemed.

'He had means, if he needed advice with business affairs, then? So was that only from his songwriting or something else?'

'I refer my learned colleague to my earlier answer,' John told him dryly. 'Unless and until Spike gives me his permission to discuss his affairs with you, it goes against my code of professional conduct to disclose anything to you. Unless you should happen to obtain a court order compelling me to do so.'

'You're still practising, are you? You're not struck off or anything?'

'Not struck off, no.' He seemed to find the question amusing, without taking offence. 'Still consulting, for hand-picked clients. I can dispense legal advice as easily sitting on a log in the fresh air as in an expensive office, wearing a suit and tie. And I don't need to practise any more, in either sense of the word. You might be surprised by my qualifications. Let me put it another way. I doubt a humble detective constable could afford my usual fees.'

As they arrived at the hospital and parked as near as they could to the mortuary entrance, Sergeant Thomas told their passenger, 'The body's not very fresh, John. It's only fair to warn you. You won't be in the same room as the deceased. You'll be able to see the body through a window, and it will be displayed so you can see the ring, which might help you with identification. Are you all right with that?'

'If it does turn out to be Spike, it's only right that I should be there for him. He didn't have many friends. He was a man who didn't trust easily.'

The sergeant and Maurice stood on either side of the solicitor as the curtain was pulled back to reveal the body, one hand on display with the distinctive ring.

The solicitor remained professional, his face not betraying much emotion as he said, 'It's not easy to be sure, of course, but going from the height and build, plus the ring and the general appearance, I would say there's a good chance that that is the body of the man I knew as Spike.

'If it helps, I can tell you that he had a significant abdominal scar from a few years ago. An emergency operation for an appendix on the point of bursting, so it was done in a hurry by open procedure rather than keyhole.

'And in the interests of cooperation, as I now believe that my friend and client is deceased, I can confirm for you that Spike was indeed the singer-songwriter Brendan Doyle, who wrote that famous theme music which brought him a great deal of money in royalties over the years.'

* * *

'So subject to the scar matching up, and the medical records, now we have his real name, it's fairly certain that our victim Spike is indeed this songwriter chap, Brendan Doyle. And from what John told us, sir, that throws up another possible motive, apart from the militant vegan one, which is money,' Cai Thomas summed up their visit to the hospital mortuary.

'He will have been building up a nice little nest-egg from the royalties. John, the solicitor, has promised to let us have a copy of the will as soon as identity is confirmed, because the inheritance issue will be very interesting. It's a good while since he sold that tune, and music royalties last for the lifetime of the artist plus seventy years, he told us. So if the beneficiary knows the terms of the will, and knows the sort of money involved, that could be quite a strong motive to murder someone. And then to have a go at dressing it up as part of a known ongoing feud between the local farmers and the vegans, of which Spike was one. It's probably only a matter of time before one of the protesters gets themselves seriously hurt going onto the farms.'

Ted nodded at that. He was back to attend the round-up of what the day had produced.

'That makes a certain amount of sense, sergeant. Thank you for that. Anyone else got any input?'

'Boss, Colin, PC Nield, and I went to meet the truly charming Miss Burrows today. Janice Burrows, but Colin warned me she might shoot me if I addressed her by her first name. She certainly gave us a warm, friendly greeting by pointing a .22 at us and sending in the dogs, although she did call them off before they did anything.

'She's the original hostile witness. Text book. We got the sum total of bugger all from her, except a lot of abuse and complaints that she never gets any attention when anything happens to her, like theft of livestock, so why should she be worried about whatever had brought Serious Crime round asking questions. But she did confirm that the protesters are often entering her property unlawfully, sometimes in numbers.'

'Sir, can I just say a few words here?' Sergeant Thomas put in. 'Not defending Miss Burrows, because a lot of her behaviour is indefensible. But just a bit of background to explain some of the reasons she's like she is.

'First off, she never planned to go into farming. She left the family farm as soon as she was old enough and got quite a decent office job. Accounts, I think it was. She was certainly doing well for herself there. But then her father disappeared without trace, maybe five or six years ago now, it must be.

'She had to go back to manage the farm more or less single-handedly- she's an only child - as her mother was always ill. Some sort of depressive illness, and then early dementia, I think, so not always very with it. She didn't live very long. She died in a fall.

'It was always assumed the father had gone off and committed suicide, because of the high rate of it amongst farmers, although his remains were never found. There'd always been various persistent stories about him being not at all a nice person, especially where women were concerned. He was pretty much universally hated by everyone who knew him.

'There had been suspicions of him beating and abusing his wife, which may have been a factor in her illness. Social services were called in once many years ago when concerns were raised at school that the daughter, Janice, might also have been being physically and sexually abused by him, but nothing was ever proved. In fact, to be honest, I don't think it was even properly investigated. Not as thoroughly as it should have been, for sure. So many cases slipped through the net back in the day, for one reason or another.'

There was a moment's silence while people digested the information. Then Jezza said, 'Well, yes, fair enough, something like that might knock the warm and sunny side out of someone's character, if it was ever there. But then if the parents are both gone, and she presumably inherited the farm, why does she stay there? Battling on against all the odds? Why not move away? Go back to an office job? Or retire, if she sold the farm? How old is she, anyway? Pensionable age? It was hard to tell.'

'You've met her, Jezza,' the sergeant told her. 'You must have picked up on how stubborn she is. Not one to admit defeat. Besides, I wouldn't mind betting there's nothing but negative equity left on the place by now. Plus, of course, with Fred missing but no presumption of death yet, she can't inherit the place, if he even left it to her.

'She's suffered a good few losses of livestock and I'm pretty sure if she ever had insurance on them, she wouldn't be able to get it after the first ones. Plus don't forget women have much longer to wait for a state pension these days. And she probably won't have a halfway decent work-based retirement pension like us coppers, with having to leave and go back to the farm.'

'Fair enough, sarge, it can't be easy for her. From the point of view of being a suspect, though, I'd find her unlikely, despite her aggression. She certainly seems as if she would have no qualms about shooting an intruder and as we've all said before, she might well get away with doing that as legitimate self-defence. She carried that gun as if it goes everywhere with her, so why would she need to do something like break his neck, and how would she get in close enough to do it, assuming she knew how?

'And if it was her, why bother to dress it up as an accident, away from the farm? She's made endless reports about intruders, apparently, so she's already established a need for direct action in self-defence. Or she could have staged a fall there and reported it so it wouldn't come back to bite her.'

'Jo, if time allows, and in case it's relevant, get someone to look into the abuse claims around the Burrows family, in case that leads us anywhere,' Ted put in. 'But I agree. She could have shot an intruder and possibly faced no action. Or if she was trying to stage an accident, as Jezza suggested, put him somewhere on the farm he could have fallen from. A hayloft, or somewhere like that. That probably wouldn't have raised any suspicions at all.'

A hesitant hand, creeping up, appeared from one of the officers sitting near the back.

'Sir, is it all right if I say something, please?' the young woman officer asked.

'Yes, of course, PC ...?'

'Newman, sir. Carol Newman. I'm a Wildlife Crime Officer and I just wanted to make an observation, really. I don't want to sound as if I'm telling anyone their job, though.'

'No one will take it that way, I'm sure. Please, go ahead.'

'Well, sir, I just wanted to stress how you really can't go off appearances. I've met Miss Burrows a time or two, and I wouldn't want to cross her. Yes, I agree, she'd be likely to fire off a shot, but you really can't tell what someone will actually do.

'We had a spate of really nasty incidents recently, with baby birds and animals being deliberately killed. Savagely, too. Beaten to death.

'People tend to get worried if they see baby birds on the ground, but often if you leave them alone the parents will feed them until they're strong enough to flutter to safety. Leverets, too. Baby hares. They're often left alone for long stretches, but the parents always come back to them.

'We found our culprit. It was a little lad, not even ten years old. I went and had a word with him. Too young to charge with anything, and he had a convincing enough tale. He said he thought he was helping them by putting them out of their misery because they'd been abandoned and were going to starve to death.

'Sir, he was bashing them to death with a cricket bat, and he must have spent his whole time out looking for his next victim, the number of them we found. And that's not counting any we don't know about.

'So I just wanted to say, sir, that you really can't go off appearances.'

Chapter Seven

There was no way Ted could get to the dojo in time for the children's self-defence club he ran with Trev, but he managed to get there, by the skin of his teeth, in time for his own judo session.

He needed the workout, but he also wanted to go for a drink with some of the other members afterwards to see if any of them had heard about anyone teaching extreme forms of self-defence in the area. If anyone would know, one of them might well.

There was a pub not far from where they trained. Ted got a round in for those he was sitting with and sat down to hear what, if anything, they might know when he explained what he was looking for.

'Bloody hell, Ted,' one of them, called Carl, said when he told them the information he was after. 'What mad bastard is teaching stuff like that? Imagine if kids start trying that out. It would keep you lot busy, for sure. Are you positive it's some-one round here?'

'I'm not sure about anything, to be honest,' Ted told him. 'I'm just exploring possibilities. I thought it might be a military thing but I'm reliably told it's not something that's routinely taught, not in the British armed forces, anyway.'

'How would you even teach it, though?' another asked. 'It's not the sort of thing you could practise. Simulation would never really prepare you for the real thing.'

Carl's sister, April, joined in.

'Some teachers use like a human dummy, for showing pressure points ...' then she broke off at the laughter the image provoked. 'Shut up, you mucky lot, get your minds out of the gutter. You know what I mean. A bit like Resusci Anne when you're learning CPR for first aid, only with all the limbs there, too.

'But then why would anyone be teaching that kind of lethal force? Plenty of other ways to stop an attacker in their tracks without killing them. Happy to show any of you, if you don't believe me,' she added defiantly as she looked round at them.

There was good natured laughter. They believed her. She was one of the club's black belts and as good as most of them there, if not better.

Ted took a pull at his Gunner then said, 'I know a few of you belong to other clubs as well as this, for various martial arts. So please, if anyone gets wind of anything like that being taught, or even being talked about, can you let me know? It's to do with a suspicious death case we've got on, but even without that connection, I'd like to see it stopped before it leads to any more unnecessary deaths.'

* * *

'So have we drawn the short straw, being sent to talk to this Tom Taylor bloke? Did I gather from this morning's briefing that he's the local time-waster, and operating at Olympic level?'

DS Rob O'Connell had now joined the team at Ashton. He was being driven by a woman from the local team, going to one of the farms not far from where the body had been found.

PC Heather Wright chuckled at his words.

'You could say that. But we always have to check with him. Most of what he says is pure fiction, but he is incredibly observant. So just occasionally, he does give us a solid lead that's worth following up on.

'What you have to watch out for, though, is he has an

amazing knack for reading body language. You have to keep as deadpan as you possibly can. Like, if he starts describing a supposed suspect and he says they were tall. He'll watch your face and if he sees the slightest hint there that that's not the right answer, or the one you were hoping for, he'll start with the, "Well, I say tall, but I was downhill from him, so I might have got the perspective wrong".'

'A total time-waster, then?'

'No, not entirely. Sometimes he's put us on the right track. You just need to learn to filter him. And not to give away anything for him to feed off.'

'And is he a possible suspect for our suspicious death?'

Heather had parked the car in a neat and tidy yard in front of a chocolate box small farmhouse, complete with flowers in window boxes on the ledges. A collection of different sized children's trikes and bicycles was lined up in an orderly fashion close to the front door.

'I'd be surprised if Tom was a killer. As you can see from all the bikes, he has a big family, lots of kids, and he seems like a big softy. Not that you can ever tell.'

They'd reached the front door now and PC Wright was just about to knock when Rob asked her, 'I don't know much about farming, so are we likely to find him at home at this time of day?'

Heather smiled as she replied, 'Oh yes, you could set your watch by our Tom. Barring natural catastrophe, this is second breakfast o'clock for him, every day.'

Her knock on the door was opened by a woman holding a small child in her arms whilst another toddler clung like a limpet to her leg.

'Hello, Maggie. This is Rob. We wanted a word with Tom, if that's all right?'

'He's in the kitchen, Heather, love. You know where to find him at this time of day. Go on through. I'll come and put the kettle on, if you fancy a brew.'

'Ta, Maggie, you know I never say no.'

She led the way along a hallway which looked narrower than it actually was because of the number of coats and small-sized Wellington boots piled haphazardly on the floor, and on a long low bench which ran the length of it.

Rob O'Connell had formed a certain mental image of the man they'd come to visit, whilst trying not to prejudge. It didn't at all match the person sitting at the table in the sunny kitchen wading through possibly the largest fry-up Rob had ever seen.

The man looked up, wiped bacon fat and egg yolk from round his mouth and gave them a beaming smile.

'Tom, this is DS Rob O'Connell, from Stockport. He's working with us on a case.'

'Mr Taylor, can I ask you if you've noticed anything unusual in the area recently? Have you seen any strangers about, anyone acting suspiciously, anything out of the ordinary at all?'

Rob was trying to keep both his tone and his expression as neutral as possible, bearing in mind Heather's warning about the man being a people-pleaser.

Taylor's smile was disarming enough as he said, 'Oh, please don't call me Mr Taylor. Only my bank manager does that, and it's never good news when he does. And no, I've not spotted anything out of the ordinary these past few days.'

Rob could have sworn he stayed as blank-faced as possible, but Taylor must have picked up on something as he added, 'Well, nothing for a good few days, to be honest.'

'How are things between the farmers and Hippy Valley now? Any more trouble from them?' Heather asked him.

'Oh, there's always trouble with them,' the man said immediately. He looked pleased to have been fed what he clearly took as a cue to what they wanted from him. 'Well, you know that, Heather. You know I always try to tip your lot off when it starts to kick off again. There's hardly a week goes by without them doing something to make our lives harder than they need to be. Letting stock out is a real favourite and it's dangerous.

Not just to the beasts, but to road users, too.'

'Any of them in particular that you've had problems with?' Rob asked him, watching for his reaction.

'Well, we're not really on first name terms, if you get my meaning. Some of the stuff they do we don't see who's done it. Sometimes a load of them come and do like sit-ins in the livestock sheds. That scares my kids, because they all have pet lambs and puppies and things in there, so I try to get them to leave. Peacefully enough, like.'

'Do you have a firearm, Tom? A registered one?' Rob asked him..

There was a flicker of something in the man's eyes now. A snippet of an idea of what it might be all about, so he could perhaps get some bonus points for being helpful.

'Is that what's happened, then? Someone's been shot? Was it one of the hippies?'

'Just routine questions, Tom, if you wouldn't mind answering, please,' Rob told him.

'Well, I think most of us have one, out here in the wilds. Licensed, like. Nothing illegal. We need them for lambing time, for the foxes and the crows. But I don't think anyone round here would shoot anyone. Except an intruder, in self-defence. Oh, but then I don't know about Janice Burrows. She's an odd one. I don't know about anyone else but she scares me. I wouldn't like to come across her on a dark night with that .22 of hers.'

It was clear that, despite his evident desire to help, Tom Taylor had nothing of much use to tell them, so Rob and Heather headed back to the car.

'I must say, with all the obvious signs of domestic bliss, I'm having difficulty seeing him as a neck-snapping killer,' Rob said as Heather turned the car round and headed out of the gateway onto the narrow road. 'How many children are there in total?'

She laughed.

'I've a bit lost count. Six or seven, I think, but there's at least one pair of twins. D'you have kids, sarge?'

'Not yet, but me and Sally are on the list to foster and we may be getting our first one in a couple of weeks. A little girl of seven. Faye, she's called. We can't wait. We've met her and she's gorgeous.'

'Aww, that's lovely, I hope it all goes well. But with Tom, well, we shouldn't forget what Carol said in the briefing yesterday. You really can't go off appearances when it comes to who might be a killer.'

* * *

As he'd said at the first briefing, Sergeant Cai Thomas decided to visit Jamie Robinson by himself. The man was unstable and unpredictable a lot of the time. He didn't see him as a personal threat, as such, but he didn't want to be the cause of one of his psychotic episodes by worrying him with the presence of strangers, unless it became necessary.

The signs weren't promising when he drove his vehicle into the yard and parked up. A small, tricolour sheepdog came out of the house to greet him, crouching low, frenetically-wagging tail so far underneath her body that it was barely visible.

Thomas squatted down and clicked his fingers to the dog who crept closer, lips curled in what he knew to be a smile of submission rather than a threat of an imminent bite. The dog was noticeably thinner than usual.

'Now then, Nell, good girl. Where's your dad, eh? Is he not managing again? Come on, let me see if I can find you something to eat, for starters, then I'll go and see if I can find him.'

He knew where things were around the place. It wouldn't be the first time he'd stepped in to take care of the animals when he'd arrived to find Robinson once again in a dark place, incapable of fending for himself, never mind the livestock. It wasn't that the man was uncaring. It was simply that when the bouts of depression hit, often without warning, he was incapable of doing anything at all, for himself or his animals.

In an ideal world the authorities would have helped him to sell up and go somewhere he could manage better. There simply weren't the resources, nor the time, to keep an eye on the Jamie Robinsons of the world.

Things in the livestock sheds weren't as bad as the sergeant feared. There weren't many animals in, just a few sheep in a pen. He gave them hay and fresh water, put down food and water for the dog, who fell on it as if starving, then went up to the house to find out what was what.

He didn't expect an answer to his knocks and there was none. The door was standing ajar, as it often was. Thomas always worried that one day, he'd be the one to walk in and find the man hanging, or having shot himself. At least today was not the day.

He found Robinson in the kitchen, sitting at the table. He was unshaven and clearly hadn't washed or changed in days, judging by the strong smell of sweat, and worse, coming from his clothes. There was one empty red wine bottle, lying on its side on the table, and another open one, down to the last dregs. Knowing Robinson, and judging by the state of him, they wouldn't be the only empties lying round. Dead soldiers, the ex-military man always called empty drinks bottles, with graveyard humour.

He looked dreadful. Thin, haggard, haunted. Distinct track marks of tears down his dirty cheeks. His eyes were bleary and unfocused as he tried to bring them into play on the face of his visitor.

'Now then, Jamie, what's to do?' the sergeant asked him. 'Have you not been taking your pills? You know you need them. Like you know you don't need the booze.'

'It helps to numb the memories. And the noises in my head.'

His voice was weak, hoarse, as if he'd been shouting. He might well have been. More than once Thomas had called in to check on him and found him raging at invisible enemies, sometimes clamping his hands to the sides of his head as if to block out sounds only he could hear.

'That's what the pills are for. The pills, and no booze.'

Thomas's voice was kind and caring, no trace of judgement. He had no way of imagining what the man had been through. Clearly he couldn't leave him in this state. He'd need to stay as long as it took to see that he was safe and not likely to harm himself.

He would usually simply get on with it. But with the DCI in charge on the latest case, Thomas thought he'd better cover his backside, if he needed to, and at least radio in a sitrep.

'I've fed Nell and seen to the sheep in the barn. Can you manage to get yourself in the shower to clean up, and put some fresh clothes on? Let me find your pills and put the kettle on. I'd better make you a bite to eat, too, to help them down. Can you do that all right?'

If it came to it, it wouldn't be the first time he'd had to physically undress and wash him, then get him into clean clothes and sometimes into bed where he usually felt safest.

'They were here again,' the weak voice told him. 'Surrounding the place.' Then his voice went up in volume, becoming clipped, staccato. 'Last man standing, Lance Corporal Robinson. It's up to you now.'

Quieter once more, his voice broken and desolate.

'But the noises. The guns. Got to stop them. Up to me.'

This was not good, Thomas said to himself. This was one of his bad episodes. He couldn't leave him alone like this. Not until he was sure he'd eaten and drunk something, had his medication and was safe enough to be left.

He helped him to the bathroom where he more or less had to undress him and stand him under the shower. Robinson was at least starting to show some instinctive reaction as the hot water needled down on him. His hand went automatically to the soap and he started to make some sort of an effort to clean himself up a bit, although his eyes were still vacant.

The sergeant carried the dirty clothes at arms' length through to the kitchen, put them in the machine and set a wash going. Then he went outside to the car to radio in his location and explain what was happening.

'Can you make sure DCI Darling knows where I am. Jamie's usually fine once I get him back on his medication. I always unload his shotgun and hide the cartridges, too, when he's like this. But more than anything this time, I need to try to figure out how long he's been like this, and what might have been the trigger which tipped him over the edge.'

Chapter Eight

Ted was at the Friday morning briefing at Ashton. He was half-perched on a desk from where he could see everyone, while Jo Rodriguez started things off with a summary of what they had so far.

'Post-mortem is first thing Monday morning, so with a bit of luck we might have something more to go on from that. For now I think we need to concentrate on motive, to see where that takes us. It may yet prove to be totally unrelated to the feud between the farmers and the hippies, although that does remain a strong possible motive.

'I've had a print-out done of all the calls for the last few months from local farmers reporting incidents likely to be linked to the militant vegan lot. There aren't quite as many as I thought there might be, but it's a start. There are a good few from Janice Burrows, though.'

'That's easy enough to explain,' Sergeant Cai Thomas responded. 'A lot of them won't call in to report a crime, even while it's happening. It's often not how they operate. They might well wait until one of us pays a call on them. Tom Taylor will phone us, of course. He can't resist making himself seem important and doing his good citizen thing. Miss Burrows will phone in because she avoids face-to-face chats with anyone.'

Jo looked down at the papers he was holding and said, 'You can say that again, about Tom Taylor. I wouldn't like his phone bill, the number of times he phones to report something or another.'

'There's often something to what he reports, too. But at the risk of sounding like I'm making excuses, most of you have now seen what our patch is like, so you can understand how long it can sometimes take to get a unit out there to investigate. We do what we can, but it's rare we arrive to find any sort of crime ongoing.

'Like I said, most of the other farmers are far more likely to wait to talk to one of us when we're next doing our rounds than to phone in. And of course by that time, there's not much trace of anything for us to work off. Janice Burrows always phones to complain long after the incident has happened, so we can never do anything useful for her. One of these days she really will shoot someone and claim it as self-defence, rather than call us for help while something is ongoing.'

'I'll vouch for that,' Jezza Vine chipped in, with feeling. 'With guns about on the farms, I really am struggling to see how or why a farmer would resort to hand-to-hand stuff. Miss Burrows looks as if she probably takes her rifle to bed with her, so I don't know when or how she'd be caught without a gun to turn on an intruder.'

'Boss, the vegan thing isn't the only likely motive though,' Maurice Brown put in. 'From what John the solicitor was telling us about the royalties, it looks like this Spike had a fair sum of money to leave to someone. That has to be a significant motive. And I didn't realise the royalties keep getting paid for seventy years after the artist dies. That's a nice little nest egg for someone, so surely it's a powerful motive, if the beneficiary knew about it.'

'Where are we up to with getting a copy of the will? Sergeant Thomas?' Ted asked him. 'Because I agree with Maurice. That could be a very strong motive.'

'Sir, John Alexander, the solicitor, is about as by the book as you can get, despite the hippy clothes and the odd sneaky spliff. He won't deliberately obstruct us, but he won't make our task easy, either. That's for sure. We might need a production order to get sight of Spike's will. I'll see what I can do.'

'Where are we up to with official confirmation of the deceased's ID as Brendan Doyle? Because if that is his real name, we should now be using that, please, rather than the nickname. What else do we know about him? Any known next of kin? And does he have any convictions that we know about, under any name he may have used?'

Cai Thomas made an apologetic face.

'Sir, sorry, but we don't really know all that much about him. Nor about many of them from that community. Unless we actually arrest any of them and run their prints and DNA through the system, a lot of them remain anonymous, apart from nicknames, until they come to our attention for any reason.

'John's one of the few of them we know something about and he's squeaky clean. No convictions, although he's been arrested a few times for various protests he's attended. He knows the law inside and out so it's hard ever to get anything to charge him with.

'His ID of the victim can't be definitive, because of the state of the body, but he gave us some other identifying factors, like the appendix scar, which have been passed on to the pathologist. But he's digging his heels in and refusing to give us a copy of the will until a positive ID has been made.'

'He has a point,' Ted said mildly. 'If he's still practising, it won't do his reputation any good if he gives out confidential client information. Especially if his client suddenly turns out not to be dead after all. It could still simply be someone of similar height and build who had the same ring. Although that would admittedly be quite a coincidence.

'Do you know anything at all about Mr Doyle's domestic circumstances? Was he living with anyone?'

'It can be a bit fluid there, relationship-wise, up in Hippy Valley,' Thomas told him. 'That's fine, I'm not judging, but it does mean there's not always a simple answer to a question like that.'

'How many people live there?' Ted asked him.

'That's fluid too, sir. Some have been there for years and are more or less permanent. Some come and go. I'd say that at any time there will be about twelve to twenty of them, and that's not counting the children, of which there are sometimes quite a few, but only one there currently, little Ruby, as far as I know.'

'Are any of the children Mr Doyle's, do you know, Cai?' Jo asked. 'I was thinking that possibly if he's fathered children, they might be in the will, which could be significant.'

'Again, it's not something I know for certain,' the sergeant replied.

'Ideally we still need to find witnesses to what happened, if there are any, to make much progress. Even someone who saw Mr Doyle at or near where his body was found, or someone who could place him at one of the farms at some point,' Ted reminded them.

'What about the woman who discovered the body? Did she have anything useful to say?'

'Nothing, boss,' Jo told him. 'First time she'd been out that way on her walks. She photographs landscapes. Not professionally, it's just a hobby, but her pictures are not bad. Atmospheric and evocative. I looked at some of them on Facebook. She'd heard the little hollow below the waterfall could look quite scenic in the right light, so she went for a look. If she hadn't, goodness knows how long the body could have been lying there.'

'And there's nothing at all about her which should raise any red flags? In connection to the victim, I mean?'

'Nothing that I can spot, boss. Admittedly she could have been playing the red herring card by reporting a body she'd killed, although why she'd leave it a week or more before doing so isn't clear. But part of the reason I checked her out on social media was to get a feel for her use of time. And she really does seem to spend most of her time taking photos and posting them in various groups.'

Seeing Ted was about to speak he went on hurriedly, 'But yes, I know, you can do all that from a mobile phone these days, wherever you are, although not from down in that dip. So we will be looking for any connections between her and Brendan Doyle, in any of his identities.'

'Sergeant Thomas, I presume you'll be paying a return visit to Jamie Robinson at some point today? If so I'd like to come with you. Also, I'd like you, please, to take me to Hippy Valley. I'd be interested in meeting this John Alexander and just generally getting a feel for the place and the people.'

Cai Thomas hesitated. He still hadn't quite got the measure of DCI Darling. He was clearly a lot more hands on than many SIOs, but whether that was going to prove to be a help or a hindrance on this case, he wasn't yet sure.

'Sir, Jamie can be quite unstable. Even if he's remembered to carry on with his pills today they won't really have had long enough to sort him out, and he's not good with strangers at the best of the time. He can get really paranoid. At least he knows me.'

Ted gave him one of his self-effacing smiles and said, 'People don't generally tend to see someone of my size as all that much of a threat, sergeant. I'll be quiet enough. I just feel it might help to see him for myself. And I agree with your message from yesterday. We probably need to find out as soon as possible what tipped him over the edge on this occasion, and when, in case it's relevant in some way.'

* * *

'I suppose most of the farms have dogs, do they? And what about the hippy place? Only I'm not very good with dogs,' Ted told the sergeant candidly as they drove out into the countryside, heading towards the farms they were interested in, and to what all the locals simply called Hippy Valley.

'None with the vegans. It goes against their principles about captive animals, so they tell me,' the sergeant told him. He risked dropping the 'sir' whilst it was just the two of them together in the car but that's as informal as he'd go until he felt he'd got to know the DCI better. So far, he'd characterise him as unusual, and he didn't want to risk crossing a line he was not yet sure of.

'The farmers all have dogs. Working dogs. Sheepdogs, mostly. Jamie Robinson's bitch Nell is a proper softy, although she's a very good working dog. She's what keeps him going a lot of the time. She'll squirm and squiggle and show you all her teeth but I swear she'd never bite anyone.'

'If you say so,' Ted still sounded uncertain. Then he went on, 'You mentioned cannabis use in Hippy Valley. Are they growing it there?'

'Not on any visibly large scale, no. I'd have had them shut down if they were. Rightly or wrongly we've tended not to kick off about small quantities for personal use. They mistrust us enough as it is, without coming down heavy when we might not need to. Especially with their own resident lawyer, and a very good one at that.'

Ted could hardly say anything to that as Trev was a recreational user and he'd even seen the forensic pathologist, Professor Bizzie Nelson, partake moderately at her own hand-fasting.

'We'd better go and check on Jamie first, if that's all right with you. I need to know he's back on the right track. But sir, is it all right if I say something? Ground rules, like?'

'Of course. This is your patch, so it's your call.'

'I really do know him pretty well. Better than anyone round here. He's never so much as threatened me. I've never felt concerned in his company. Not for my own safety, certainly, only for his. But he is unpredictable, and volatile. And I don't yet know how long since he stopped taking his medication. So if I ask you to leave, I need you to do it straight away, without question.'

The sergeant's eyes were fixed on the narrow lanes, with their tight turns and blind corners. He risked no more than a quick sideways glance at the DCI in the front passenger seat, but its message was clear. He was in charge on this visit.

'That's fair enough, sergeant. Don't forget, I know how much paperwork it would generate if I got one or other of us killed or injured in the line of duty.'

Exactly as the sergeant had predicted, the little collie ran to greet them, belly close to the ground, tail invisible, lips curled in a submissive rictus. She flopped onto her side on the wet ground when she reached them, underbelly exposed, and the sergeant bent to give it a rub as he spoke to the dog. Even Ted didn't feel particularly threatened by her.

'Where is he today, Nell? And more importantly, how is he?'

As if knowing he was being talked about, Jamie Robinson appeared in the doorway to the farmhouse. He was deathly pale, not entirely steady on his feet, but he was at least up and apparently functioning, to a degree.

'Now then, Jamie. How are you today? I just thought I'd bob round to see if you needed anything. This is DCI Darling. I'm showing him round the patch.'

He said it casually but both men were immediately aware of shutters clanging down, senses on full alert, as Robinson's eyes looked towards the stranger.

'Have you had your pills today? And what about something to eat? Do you need a hand with anything, while we're here?'

'I'm reet, Cai, thanks.'

His eyes were fixed on the unknown officer the whole time. There was nothing threatening about his gaze or his posture but his body language was closed, distant. It was clear they were going to get nothing from him, in that frame of mind. Not in front of Ted, at any rate.

'Well, don't forget to keep taking the pills, Jamie. And remember you can call me any time you need to, night or day. Nowt wrong with asking for help.'

'I'll remember that, thanks. And thanks for everything you did for me yesterday. Again. The memories, you know. They come back sometimes. Sneak up on me, like.'

'I did warn you we might get nowhere,' the sergeant told Ted when they got into the car and he turned it round to leave the farmyard.

'We tried, at least. I'd still like to get some sort of a clue as to what triggered him, in case there's a connection, but it's clearly going to be better if you try for that on your own. He obviously trusts you.'

'Let's see if we do any better with our bunch of happy hairies in the valley.'

The solicitor, John Alexander, was sitting in his usual place, wearing the same clothes as before and smoking another spliff when they found him. Once again the sergeant made the introductions.

'Mr Alexander, thank you for viewing the deceased and for your help so far. I'm sure you know that we can make better progress once we have a definite identification, so I wonder if you might give us permission to take something of Mr Doyle's for DNA testing?' Ted asked him, after introductions were made.

'Do you have a warrant?'

It was the question he'd been anticipating from the solicitor.

'I don't, no. I can get one, but it really would help to speed things up if we could take something like a comb or a toothbrush. Which is Mr Doyle's dwelling?'

'The Routemaster.' He nodded across the field to where a red and white double-decker bus was parked a little distance from the other vehicles. 'I can see that it would help with your enquiries, so I've no objection to you taking a toothbrush. Spike wasn't a hair-combing sort of person, so I doubt he had one. But I insist on being present the whole time you're in his personal space.'

'That's not a problem at all. Do you have a key for access?'

The question seemed to amuse him.

'Even Spike didn't have an access key. We don't lock anything here. We have mutual trust and respect so we don't need to.'

He led the way across the field to the bus, then stood aside to let the two officers go in first. Ted wasn't sure what he'd been expecting but he was stunned by the reality. The lower deck had been converted into high-end living accommodation. A fully fitted kitchen in light hardwood. A small dining alcove, and a comfortable seating area. It must have cost a small fortune.

Alexander saw his expression, and that of the sergeant, who had clearly never previously seen inside, and chuckled.

'As I said, I knew Spike long before he was famous. Luckily for him. I met him at a festival in Ireland decades ago and we've been friends ever since. It was me who negotiated the original contract for his intellectual property - that song everyone was fighting over - and made sure he got, and kept getting, every penny he deserved for it. And that was, and still is, a lot of money.

'So now I imagine you're going to press me for details of the will because clearly, we're not talking pennies here, and that kind of money is always going to be a strong motive for murder in your minds. Which is what I presume we're talking about here, since you used that police-speak phrase "a suspicious death"?'

Chapter Nine

'Brendan Doyle has a Wiki page, at least,' Jo Rodriguez told the assembled officers when they got together at the end of the day to report on further developments.

'And yes, I know they're not all that reliable, but it does give us something of a starting point. He's not lived in Ireland for years but he does still go back regularly for visits, apparently. Still sings in his local pub when he does, too. Never forgotten his roots, by all accounts.

'I've been speaking to the *Garda Síochána* in the nearest town to where he's from, which is a tiny village way out in the sticks. He's still highly regarded there. I've asked them not to say anything until we have a definite ID but the officer I spoke to sounded genuinely sad to hear he might have died.'

'Any family there? Possible next of kin?' Ted asked him.

'His parents are still alive but elderly now. Brendan, if it is him, was in his sixties. They live in a nice retirement bungalow which Doyle had built for them. They're well set up, no financial worries. There's also a much younger brother. A real "oh, whoops, where did that one come from?", as my contact put it. Conor, he's called. The black sheep of the family. Always getting into trouble, although nothing all that serious. Attention seeking, by the sound of it.

'He and Brendan never got on. The *garda* I spoke to said the logical thing would be to assume that Conor was jealous of Brendan for all the fame. Not to mention the money. Surprisingly, it was the other way round. Brendan was insanely jealous of the kid brother he never expected to have and who, he thought, took up too much of his parents' love and attention.'

'So on the face of it, it sounds unlikely that Brendan would leave anything at all to his brother in his will,' Jezza Vine speculated. 'That would also perhaps mean he wouldn't make his parents his beneficiaries either, if they're older, because he'd know the money would be likely to go to Conor when they died. Unless he could have a tight clause written in preventing that. And presumably Conor would know of Brendan's feelings towards him so he'd be unlikely to be expecting a windfall on his death. He'd know, or guess, it wouldn't be worth killing him for the money.'

'Let's not jump the gun, Jezza,' Ted cautioned. 'It's pointless to speculate until we get sight of the will, and a definitive ID. We do now at least have the means to run DNA tests on the toothbrush we took from where the man known as Spike was living. We might possibly get a quicker result that way than waiting for DNA from the PM. I'm assuming none of the photos of the singer-songwriter look anything like our deceased?'

'Not remotely, boss,' Jo told him cheerfully. 'But then his real moments of fame go back a long way. There's nothing recent online anywhere, not that I could find. The Wiki entry simply says that he dropped off the radar about fifteen years ago. There are hints about him joining a community of travellers, but nothing concrete. Certainly nothing to suggest he found his place in our very own Hippy Valley here. And nothing noteworthy on our system either.'

'And speaking of his place,' Ted went on, 'I think Sergeant Thomas was probably as surprised as I was at that. It's a converted double-decker bus, but the interior must have cost a small fortune. It's beautifully done. So if anyone saw that, they would assume there was money there somewhere, even if they didn't know who he was.'

'The officers I spoke to in Ireland are going to do some discreet checking on Conor Doyle's movements, to see if he's left the country recently,' Jo told him. 'But as Jezza says, it seems unlikely that he would even feature in the will, and even less likely that he would know about its contents.

'And until we get a positive ID we still don't know for sure if the man Spike really was Brendan Doyle. People often claim to be someone they're not, especially someone famous.'

'That's true,' Ted conceded, 'although whoever he was in reality, he had money, or had had at some time, judging by his living arrangements. But that could simply have been a lucky scratch-card, I suppose.'

'Boss.' Jezza Vine again. Clearly picking her words carefully. 'Trying to avoid racial or political stereotyping here, but if he grew up in Ireland during the sixties and seventies, might there be a hint of a motive there? Did he piss off the wrong people? Maybe even write a song with controversial lyrics about the Troubles?'

'But why bother to come over here to find him, Jezza? If he regularly went home and sang in the pub, wouldn't it be easier to attack him there, if that's what someone wanted to do?'

'If he was popular and well-respected there, he'd be surrounded by people who might well protect him when he was on home soil, though. But then if it was some sort of political punishment, it would probably be a gunshot, I imagine. A bullet to the back of the neck, or even just a simple kneecapping, perhaps, rather than a broken neck.'

'And with regards to that broken neck,' Ted put in, 'as some of you know I do some martial arts. I've been asking around my contacts to see if anyone has heard of such extreme forms of self-defence being taught anywhere in our area. Nothing so far, but I'll keep you all posted if I get word of anything. Even if it's not connected to this case, it's certainly not something we want happening on our patch so it needs clamping down on.'

'Sir, are we doing a public appeal on this one at some time?' Sergeant Thomas asked. 'I know, given the remote place where he was found, it's unlikely that anyone from outside the area would have seen anything, but it's surely worth a try. If we wait for an ID before we go public, are we risking a load of time wasters calling us? I know most people wouldn't know the name Brendan Doyle, nor recognise him, and we're not talking Elton John notoriety. But you'd have to have been living on another planet for years not to know that tune. And you know how people can't resist getting their five minutes of fame. Didn't someone once reckon they spotted Elvis Presley in a chip shop in Yorkshire, long after he was supposed to have died?'

'It's always worth trying, but in the certain knowledge that we're likely to increase our workload with a load of stuff which all needs checking but doesn't lead us anywhere. The press have already got wind of a body being found but so far they've only had basic details. I'll talk to the Super at Stockport and get something sorted. Anything else, anyone?'

An older Uniform constable from Ashton, sitting near the front, risked a comment.

'Am I the only one here who really hates that song? I always turn the radio or the TV off as soon as it comes on. I'd have happily strangled him myself if I thought it would stop it getting played.'

A ripple of amusement went round the room to end the day.

* * *

'If you smell of dead bodies again, kindly strip off before coming into the kitchen,' Trev called out as he heard Ted open the front door. Then he added, his tone mischievous, 'In fact, do that anyway. Supper isn't ready yet and I'm sure we'd think of something to pass the time.'

Ted chuckled as he walked into the kitchen, carrying young Adam.

'It would be just my luck if the day I did that the neighbour was leaning over her fence trying to attract our attention for some crisis or another.'

'The sight of you in your birthday suit would certainly attract her attention,' Trev laughed. 'Is this you finished for the weekend, or do you have to work?'

'I'll need to go in both days, just to stay on top of the paperwork, if nothing else. I also want to go and have a walk round this latest crime scene out beyond Ashton, probably tomorrow. I don't know that area out there much at all. You could come with me, if you like. It would be a bit of fresh air and a change of scene for both of us, at least. And a bit of time spent together.'

'Ah, the romance of living with a policeman. "Let's go out for a romantic walk and a picnic. I'll show you the spot where a body was found in a state so rank that you needed to get my suit dry cleaned for me". How could I resist such an offer? And I have done, by the way. Had the suit cleaned, that is, and it's back in your wardrobe.'

'Thank you.'

'And speaking of smart suits, let me give you fair warning now that if you even think of standing me up for the baptism of my gorgeous god-daughter, I should point out that a mere Tiger 900 would not be sufficient bribery to buy your way out of that. I know you. Just because it's in a posh traditional catholic church, and Cheshire's finest, to boot, you'll be desperate for an excuse so you can pull out at the last minute. But don't even think about it.'

'Noted,' Ted told him with a guilty grin. It wasn't something he was particularly looking forward to but he knew his partner was, so he fully intended to be there if he could.

'And the same goes in spades for our holiday in Corsica. Don't even try to pull the "all police leave cancelled" card on that one. We are going, and that's final.'

'Noted again. And I know my little suggestion for this weekend doesn't sound much like fun but we can avoid where the body was found. Or at least not get too close. I really want to explore all the various ways of getting to that spot, either on foot or in a vehicle of some sort. Are you up for it?'

'Well, if it means that I at least get to spend some time with my husband, of course I am. On the condition that we take a gourmet picnic and I can be Poirot this time, while you play Captain Hastings.

'Now, what can we think of to do to fill half an hour before the supper is ready?'

* * *

They stood at the top of the waterfall looking down into the dip where the body had been found. It was a grey, damp day but at least there was no persistent rain this time.

Trev peered over the edge as he said, 'So, Hastings, you say the body was down there but that the Professor says there's no evidence that it was thrown or fell from up here.'

'That's right, Poirot. So, now we've walked the various paths and tracks around here, if you were the one dumping the body, how would you get it out here, then put it down there, while attracting as little attention as possible?'

'Quad bike,' Trev said immediately, with a note of triumph. 'Fold the body up, then wrap it in plastic like a silage bale. You could get a quad quite close to that little hollow. Up to the edge for sure. And then if you didn't unwrap the body straight away, rolled it down as it was, it wouldn't leave any DNA traces until you unwrapped it at the bottom, presumably.'

'I'm impressed,' Ted told him. 'That's as sound a theory as we've come up with so far. Because no one would take any notice of someone riding round like that. As long as they weren't a complete stranger, of course. I have a feeling that everyone knows everybody round here and a stranger would stick out like a sore thumb.'

'Especially someone they didn't know playing at farmers,' Trev agreed. 'I know people like to feed horses they come across in fields, although they shouldn't, it's not always good for them. But I don't think anyone would buy a cover story of someone bringing silage out to livestock they didn't own out of some kind of sense of altruism.'

The comparative quiet of the rural scene was suddenly broken by strange sounds.

A sharp crack.

A loud pop.

A stuttering rattle.

Trev jumped visibly.

'What the hell? Are we coming under fire?'

Then he laughed out loud as he said, 'Oh, good grief, what kind of a townie have I turned into? You'd never think I grew up spending holidays on a country estate. It's an old tractor starting up! Just for a moment I was thinking battle fields. Wilfrid Owen. "*Only the stuttering rifles' rapid rattle*". Don't tell anyone. Especially not my posh Cheshire Set friends. They'd disown me. And certainly not my sister, who would be horrified.

'Listen. It's settling down into a regular rhythm now and it sounds nothing like machine guns. The shame!'

Ted was looking thoughtfully off into the distance. Trev was right. For a fleeting moment when the sound first began, it had sounded like rapid gunfire. Not at all the kind of sound a former soldier suffering from PTSD would want to hear.

* * *

DS Mike Hallam was doing his usual quietly efficient job with the gold bars fraud case. It was a Sunday, but he was at his desk getting paperwork in order. To date they'd only heard of one such scam on their own patch. Criminals posing as police officers, often with impressive fake proof of identity, were warning older people that keeping money in a bank account left them open to being robbed, whilst giving them the instructions so that they could do exactly that.

'You'd think, wouldn't you, boss, with all the publicity there's been over such cases, that people wouldn't still be falling for such things. It's not just on the news and in the papers, it's been on those fraud watch type programmes on the telly. But I suppose there's always someone who's not seen or heard about it before. Or who panics and forgets about what they've heard.'

'They're convincing though, Mike, that's half the problem. Remember our victim on the watch case, which was a similar thing? She was an intelligent woman and she was taken in. Anyway, the Super is going to ask if we can borrow Sal back, at least to pool information, if nothing else.'

'And what about Steve, boss? Can we have him for the computers, at least? There's a lot to wade through and it really would help. He'd be a lot quicker than any of us.'

'It's this weekend he's back from the States, I think, then he's taking another week's leave before he starts at Central Park. You know it's not up to me anyway, Mike, but I'm not even sure if it's a good idea. It might be better to send any computers which need his magic touch to him, rather than bring him here too soon. It could undo any progress he's made so far.'

* * *

The young man was sitting in his car, a newspaper open in front of him. His eyes constantly drifted to the semi-detached house diagonally opposite where he was parked.

A Sunday morning suburban quiet had settled over the road. Few people were about. One man was lovingly washing a shiny new car in a driveway several doors away from where the young man's car was parked.

A sudden loud sound jerked the watcher's eyes up above the top of the newspaper. A door slamming. A stockily-built man was striding out of the driveway of the target house, his face like thunder.

Despite the distance which separated him from the scene, the young man felt a sudden shudder of fear pass through his body. He jerked the newspaper higher, ensuring that the angry-faced man striding away down the road could catch no glimpse of him as he passed by.

Only after the man reached the end of the road and turned the corner, disappearing from sight, did the car driver lower his paper.

He checked the rear view mirror.

Once.

Twice.

Three times, to be sure.

Swivelled his eyes from one side mirror to another to make absolutely certain.

Only then did he get carefully out of the car, lock it, check all round him once more, then cross the road to the house the man had come out of.

He didn't expect an immediate response to his ring on the doorbell and there was none. He had to press the button twice more, then tap quietly on the glass panel, before he heard the Yale lock being turned and a crack opened in the door frame.

The face of a woman, probably in her late thirties to early forties, peered fearfully at him. Her hair was loose round her face but didn't quite cover the signs of bruising around one eye, the lids swollen and puffy. There was a split in her lip. Recent, the blood not yet fully clotted.

The two of them looked at one another in silence for a moment, as recognition started to dawn on the woman's face.

'I'm his son. Steve. Steve Ellis,' he told her. 'I knew he had someone else and I knew he wouldn't have changed. I've come to tell you that if you want to report him to the police, I'll come with you. I'll give a witness statement. I'll testify in court. I'm a police officer too, a DC. They'll have to take notice of me.

'Come with me now. I promise it will be all right. I couldn't save my mother from him, but I'll protect you. I'll do whatever it takes.'

Chapter Ten

Ted and Jo Rodriguez met outside the hospital before going together to the autopsy suite where Professor Nelson would be conducting the post-mortem examination on their victim. They'd arrived in different cars. Jo would be going straight to Ashton afterwards, whilst Ted wanted to touch base back at Stockport again before joining him there.

It wasn't the pathologist's usual early morning start because her students would be attending. Ted wasn't too keen on the idea but accepted that it was an essential part of their training. He also knew that Bizzie Nelson would have drummed into them the importance of total discretion, and there were no second chances with the Professor.

Because the students would be in the viewing gallery, Ted and Jo would be observing from another area, together with others whose attendance was required, including the coroner.

The students were already in place when Ted and Jo walked in. All of them knew better than to be late for the Professor.

The body was now naked and lying on a steel table in full view. Ted could immediately see that the man had been even thinner than the impression he'd formed of his build from seeing him fully clothed. He could also see that there was a large and distinctive abdominal scar which could correspond to the operation mentioned by the solicitor, John Alexander.

On the dot of the appointed hour, the Professor began by giving the basic details available.

'You can see that this is the body of a male person. His measured height is one metre point eight zero three four, or for anyone still using Imperial, five feet eleven inches. An average healthy weight for a male of that height would be around seventy-five kilos or a little over eleven stone, if you prefer. Our guest was a good bit less than that so we may be able to determine whether that was natural, pathological or due to how he lived his life. I won't pre-judge what we might find, but I will mention at this stage that alcohol abuse, for example, can sometimes be a factor in being underweight. But so, too, can other things not always related to diet.

'You can all clearly see that there is an abdominal scar. A prominent one. I received anecdotal evidence of a possible emergency appendicectomy. All I can think is that it was performed by someone very junior indeed, who had not yet read the relevant chapter in his or her medical text book.

'Closer examination of the scar shows an extremely wobbly start, which confirms my suspicions that this might have been someone's very first proper attempt with a scalpel on a living person.

'My glamorous assistant James,' she indicated her colleague as she spoke, 'and I have, as usual, done most of the preliminaries before your arrival, which included extensive X-rays of the body. They served to confirm my initial observations at the site where he was found, and that is that there was a clean break to the cervical vertebrae, just here.'

She indicated an area of the cervical spine.

'It will be our collective role here today to determine whether or not that was the cause of death, or whether there were any other determining factors. I can tell you, however, that a fracture in that location is sufficient, of itself, to have killed him, and rapidly, and that the initial examination would indicate that the injury was pre rather than post-mortem.

'For your information, the body was found close to a waterfall with a height of just over six metres. As you can see, there are no other injuries visible on first superficial inspection of the body. James and I will now carefully roll him so you can see both sides.'

The students were craning in their seats to look at the body, although the images were also being relayed via video camera to a monitor in the gallery for that purpose.

She encouraged comments and questions from them whilst she worked deftly, as well as giving a running commentary for the benefit of the police officers and others present.

She was as thorough as usual, both in her interaction with the students and her detailed examination of the body. Then she concluded, 'So, in summary, for all those present, in the absence of any other injury on the body, even superficial grazing, it is in my opinion safe to conclude that this man's neck was not broken as a result of a fall from the waterfall. That would tend to indicate that it was almost certainly manually broken by some as yet unknown third party.'

There was an immediate gaggle of questions from the gallery to which Bizzie Nelson held up an imperious hand for silence.

'Now, I have not made any study of manually breaking someone's neck. But the chief inspector here, Chief Inspector Darling, is something of an expert on martial arts, so I am hoping that he might be able to shed some light for us on how that might be done. I'm sure he will answer some questions, but please remember he is primarily here in his official role in connection with a suspicious death, not to give an impromptu lecture to my students.

'Chief inspector? Would you mind briefly walking us through the means of such an act, please?'

'First of all,' Ted began hesitantly, not remotely wanting to be lecturing to pathology students.

'Please speak up, chief inspector,' Bizzie told him. 'The video cameras will pick up and relay your words to your eager audience, but only if you don't whisper.'

'First of all,' Ted continued, a little more loudly, 'this is a real "please don't try this at home" technique. It shouldn't be being taught by anyone, except possibly to trained special forces. It's highly dangerous and can go badly wrong.

'Also, please, I'd prefer it if it was not so much as mentioned outside here. There are obvious confidentiality issues involved.'

'Oh, they know that, chief inspector. Places in my tutor group are limited and strictly controlled. There are also no second chances. At all. Even the most minor breach of the rules would incur my further and terrible wrath, which is not a sight for the faint-hearted.'

'Well, on that understanding, I can tell you the basics. It's not easy to do, for a start. Necks are stronger than you might think, and probably more resilient. It's also a move where you'll certainly have one chance and that's it. You have to get up close and personal, for one thing, which you certainly can't do with anyone who's suspicious of your actions.'

'Would it be too presumptuous of me to ask you to demonstrate? Carefully, of course. Perhaps your Inspector Rodriguez might volunteer to be your guinea pig?'

Anything like that was always Ted's biggest nightmare. Literally playing to the gallery. Especially with the coroner present, who was not his biggest fan at the best of times. Ted suspected, but could never prove, that there was a hefty dollop of homophobia behind the man's attitude towards him.

'How much do you trust me, Jo?' Ted asked him, since it was clear he wasn't going to get away with refusing.

Jo gave him a broad smile which showed off the shiny gold tooth, as he replied, 'Considerably less than I thought I did, in these particular circumstances, boss.'

Ted looked up at the students as he started to explain.

'Effectively, you need a two-way action. Well, three-way, in fact. One hand pushes the head one way while at the same time the other one then pulls the jaw the opposite way and sharply upwards at the same time. Opposing forces. Which can often produce a force far greater than the sum of the two contributory elements.'

He stepped closer to Jo as he moved to put his hands in place.

'You can all see that the inspector is a good bit taller than I am, which makes it slightly more difficult, though certainly not impossible. We're talking speed and technique here more than anything else. Although clearly I'm going to be doing things slowly, to demonstrate, and with none of the lethal force necessary.'

'I'm relieved to hear that, boss.'

'So, push with one hand, pull sharply and lift with the other.'

Ted made the demonstration slowly and with extreme care using Jo, then released him and made the same motion with his hands holding nothing more than air, to show the speed and timing which would be required to make the perfect lethal movement.

'Thank you very much, chief inspector. And Inspector Rodriguez, of course, very brave of you.

'Remember the warning about confidentiality on this, all of you. And I hope you will all have noticed, from the demonstration, that we can easily see, from having watched the theory behind what happened, that there is a strong probability of the assailant's DNA being deposited liberally on the victim, which is excellent news for the investigation.

'The much less good news, I'm afraid, is that there is currently a considerable back-log at the lab for such things so I cannot guarantee how soon you can have the results, chief inspector. Although, of course, I will as ever pull any strings I might be able to in order to expedite matters.'

* * *

Ted stopped by the front desk on his way to his office, hoping to find out an update about Steve. He waited while Bill Baxter dealt patiently and politely with someone wanting to report something which was not really a police matter.

Ted smiled to himself. Bill could be a grumpy old bugger when he wanted to, but he did an excellent job of filtering the serious stuff so it went straight to the right place, without alienating members of the public by appearing to give them the brush-off.

'What's the news on Steve?' Ted asked him, after the usual polite greeting.

'He flew in on Saturday. Found time to text me, then he was off again. He'd left his car at the airport for this trip he's gone on, wherever it is. He's a good lad. He knows I worry about him.'

Ted was about to go on his way when Bill pulled an envelope from under the desk to hand it to him.

'This was left for you, sometime over the weekend. Hand-delivered and put in the letterbox. It doesn't look particularly sinister. The handwriting's a bit childish, I would say, so threat assessment is low, I think.'

If there had been anything dodgy about the seemingly innocuous envelope, it wouldn't be the first time someone had made an attempt to harm a police officer with the contents of a letter or package.

Ted took it upstairs with him to his office. He was in need of tea after the post-mortem. The writing on the envelope meant nothing to him, but he could see what Bill had meant about it. There was something laborious and possibly juvenile about the carefully-composed address. He opened it warily, unfolded a single sheet of paper and read from the message composed in the same script.

'Dear Mr Darling,

It's Oliver Burdon with a D writing to you. You have al-

ways been verry kind to me.

I am getting maried. A nice young lady I met at the homeless caffe. Mary she is called.

Please will you be my best man? It will make me verry happy. I know you are buzy we can make the date when you are free.

You can bring a pluss one.

Please reply and please say yes.

Your friend

Oliver Burdon with a D'

Ted shook his head in surprise. The man had briefly been a suspect in a previous murder case. Because Ted had been kind to him, Burdon had rather latched onto him, although it was some time since he had heard from him.

He'd talk to Trev, who would be delighted at the idea, no doubt, although Ted had no idea what sort of an occasion it would be. He put the letter in his briefcase and promptly forgot all about it. He had a murder and a serious fraud to oversee before he could even begin to think about his social life.

* * *

It was past mid-afternoon by the time Ted was finally driving back to the Ashton station for an update on the case there. Jo Rodriguez had left his sergeant, DS Pete Ramsay, in charge whilst he was at the PM. Both he and Ted had had a quiet word with Rob O'Connell to tell him to be prepared to step in if DC Alan Burgess started his old trick of trying to take over and undermine Ramsay. On a serious crime case like the current one, there was no place for such behaviour.

His drive was interrupted by a phone call.

'DCI Darling? This is PS Jackson, sir, from Southampton. Sorry to bother you. Is this a good time for you to talk?'

Ted pulled his service vehicle over to the side of the road

and switched off the engine. He had no idea why a sergeant from Hampshire would be phoning him. But he had a vague memory of Steve Ellis having a connection with Southampton, so he would certainly make time to take the call.

'It is, yes, go ahead, please, sergeant.'

'Well, sir, this all sounds very wild and improbable but the young man was insistent I phone you and said you would vouch for him. I checked that there really is a DCI Darling at Stockport and he wasn't getting me to phone one of his mates.

'We had this young chap come in today. He was with a woman who's clearly had some recent injuries and seems very afraid. He says his name is Steve Ellis and he's a DC with your Serious Crime Team. Or he is usually, but he says he's currently on sick leave.

'The thing is, the two of them have come in with a wild story of serious assault, including sexual assault on her. Only the person they're accusing is a serving officer here. Sergeant Ellis. This lad Steve says he's his son.'

'I'm sure you know as well as I do, sergeant, that being a police officer does not automatically prevent someone from committing criminal acts, including serious assaults. What makes you convinced there can be no truth in the accusations? And please don't answer that by saying what a good officer PS Ellis is and how highly everyone speaks of him.'

'But they do! There's never been the whiff of anything about him, and I've known him for years. We were on the point of charging this Steve Ellis with wasting police time, because there's not a shred of evidence. Yes, the woman, who lives with Sergeant Ellis, says he gave her the cuts and bruises, but there's no proof, of course. No witnesses. So then Ellis said we should phone you and you'd vouch for him. And he said he'd testify as his mother went through the same and he witnessed it all.

'But we all know that the sergeant's first wife had a lot of emotional and mental health issues. She committed suicide on the day of the son's passing out parade. And this young bloke claims to be that son and says she was driven to her suicide by Rod Ellis's behaviour.'

'DC Ellis, sergeant,' there was a warning edge to Ted's tone now. 'Please use his rank. DC Ellis. He is not "this young bloke". He is on sick leave, that much is true, but he is a valued member of my team. An honest person, of high integrity.

'What I suggest you do is to forget that the person being accused of a crime is a serving police officer and proceed as you would for anyone else. Take detailed statements from DC Ellis and the woman. Get her seen by a doctor as soon as possible and make sure her injuries are photographed and carefully detailed, then open an assault case, as you would do for anyone else.

'Also think of a place of safety for her whilst your enquiries are ongoing. Possibly for DC Ellis, too.

'Please give Steve my best wishes, tell him I think he's doing the right thing and that it takes courage to do what he's doing. And assure him that I am at the end of the phone whenever he needs further support, or wants to talk to me.'

Chapter Eleven

'Have you got a minute before you go off duty, sergeant?' Ted asked Cai Thomas as the team members were getting ready to finish for the day. 'Only I have a few questions I wanted to ask you which I'm not yet ready to air in public as they might sound daft.'

'No worries, sir. Shall we find a quiet corner?'

He'd been hoping to get away. He'd been out going round his patch all day, not just on the murder case, but all the every-day crimes and grumbles he had to deal with. He'd had endless cups of tea but the quickly-snatched sandwich hours ago was now but a distant memory and, to put it mildly, his belly thought his throat was cut.

'I went for a walk yesterday, all round where the body was found, to see if that brought me any inspiration. Going on our earlier observations at the site, and the post-mortem findings, it seems more and more likely that the victim was killed else-where and taken to the waterfall to be dumped.

'You have the local knowledge, of course, but from what I saw I can imagine a quad bike being the most likely means of moving the body there. So which of the local farmers have quad bikes?'

'To be honest it would be quicker to tell you who hasn't. And off the top of my head, I can't think of anyone around there who doesn't have one. They're very popular. But on the subject of quads, sir, that does open up other suspects, possibly.

'One thing we're always getting complaints about is people

coming out from the towns with their quads on trailers, then taking them out off-roading and generally making bloody nuisances of themselves. Not all the tracks they use are open to motorised traffic. Restricted byways aren't, for one, but they ignore the rules.

'We've had a few horse riding accidents, including one serious enough to need a casualty airlift, where riders, who are allowed on the RB tracks, have come across quad bikers, who aren't. It's an ongoing problem, especially as it's another pastime for some of the organised crime gangs.'

'So that's another angle altogether which we'll need to consider,' Ted told him. 'We've all rather been assuming that the victim was killed within a relatively short distance of where the body was found. But factoring in that new information, he could have been brought in from outside.'

'Except we're back against the same thing as before, anyone strange coming into the area with a body to dump risked being spotted by someone.'

'Unless the body was inside the towing vehicle and only put onto the quad at the last minute. There'd be less risk of being seen that way. Then as my partner, who was with me, pointed out, something which looked like a silage bale on the back of a farm quad would appear natural enough. But if anyone saw a total stranger seemingly going out to feed livestock, someone might well spot and query that, I would imagine.'

'I should have thought to mention the quad bikers before, sir. Sorry.'

'No worries, although it does throw up yet more possibilities. Is there any reason you can think of to suppose that Brendan Doyle was involved with organised crime, or might have done something to get on the wrong side of them, for some reason?'

'He certainly wouldn't like them ripping up the countryside. To be honest, sir, Spike wasn't one of the really militant "Meat is Murder" lot, but he was an ardent eco-warrior. He tended to be slightly more tolerant of the farming round here because quite a bit of it is low density organic stuff, not so much factory farming. As long as there was no neglect or obvious ill-treatment of animals. One thing he didn't like was any hint of an animal welfare issue. I know he'd had at least one brush with Janice Burrows over the state of those skinny dogs of hers, for a start.

'What he hated with a real passion was any environmental damage. The reason he went on the warpath sometimes was anything which could harm the environment. And that included things like slurry seepage from farms getting into water courses and causing serious pollution, often with catastrophic damage to fish and other creatures in the rivers. Again, Janice Burrows' farm doesn't have the best housekeeping when it comes to slurry.

'What about things like planning applications, in that case?' Ted asked him. 'From my own recent experiences of the gang bosses, I would imagine not all of them go through the correct official channels to build their properties, both residential and business, for one thing. I think palms might be greased to give them what they want. All of which could potentially have a significant impact on the environment.'

'That's right. We've had cases where new builds have caused a lot of damage to surrounding areas and properties. Concrete going in for gates and fencing where it interferes with previous natural run-off and causes flooding where there's never been any before, for one thing. I'm sorry, I really should have mentioned this angle before, too.'

'Not to worry,' Ted told him, 'we're on it now. More leg-work next, to see if we can find any known cases where Doyle might have tangled with some unsavoury characters.'

'The more we look at this, the more possible motives we seem to come up with.'

'We'll just have to keep at it until we discover the right one. Now, some more of my thoughts which might sound completely off the wall, but they're just things which came to me on my explorations.

'Firstly, we heard a noise on our walk which, to begin with, sounded like machine-gun fire. My partner correctly identified it first, although not immediately, as being an old tractor starting up from cold. Does that mean anything to you?'

Thomas nodded and said, 'That'll be Diego Smith. He's a bit of a collector and dealer. He's currently got an ancient Nuffield he enjoys tinkering with. He does them up, takes them to shows and exhibitions, then sells them on. Makes more money at that than through his farming, and enjoys it a lot more.

'As you might possibly guess, his late father was a big football fan who actually believed the "Hand of God" story, so he saddled his son with Maradona's first name. Poor bloke got a lot of stick growing up, with a name like that.'

'How near does he live to Jamie Robinson? Would the sound travel from one farm to the other?'

Cai Thomas was looking at Ted in open admiration.

'I can see why they made you a DCI. I live in the middle of all this, every day, and that thought never crossed my mind. I'd never have even thought of a tractor sounding like gunfire, but now you say that, I can see that the old Nuffield starting up reluctantly could well trigger some bad memories for Jamie. He's already hypersensitive to sudden noise. You've only seen him the once and you might well have identified a trigger factor, excuse the pun, which had never occurred to me.'

'Pure fluke,' Ted assured him. 'I just happened to be in the right place at the right time. People living out here would know the noise of a tractor instantly, but it might sound like something completely different to someone with PTSD.

'Is it widely known in the area about Jamie Robinson's condition?'

'Very much so. One or two of the neighbours have had to pitch in a time or two to help sort out animals when Jamie's been particularly bad. Like I said, they're a closed lot usually, but the one thing that does bring them together is animals in need of care. Not so much for people. They don't like to interfere in their problems. But animals needing fed? Yes, any one of them would do that without a second thought.'

'Right, my next question and possibly the wildest idea. Might a farmer, or anyone who keeps animals, perhaps know how to break a neck in extreme circumstances, like where immediate euthanasia might be needed and they didn't have access to a gun, for instance? I've been getting hung up on the Armed Forces angle a bit too much, I think. But I did wonder what a farmer might do if they came across an animal out in the middle of nowhere which needed putting out of its misery quickly.

'This morning I was coerced, against my better judgement, into showing the theory about how to break a person's neck. That set me wondering if someone had, perhaps, ever had to do it on a farm animal so had at least had the practice.'

This time the sergeant's look was more sceptical.

'I'd say it was a possibility, yes, although an unlikely one. I'd also say it would be a beggar to investigate that line of enquiry. Anyone who had ever had to do that probably wouldn't want to talk about it. Despite what some of the militants may think, most farmers care about their beasts and that would be a very hard thing for anyone to have to do, even in dire need as a humane action. And then anyone who'd been practising on their own animals prior to trying the procedure out on an intruder would hardly be likely to admit to it.'

He saw the DCI's expression change and hurried on, 'But of course I'll get the teams asking around about that, sir.'

'Thank you, sergeant. It really does seem as if there might possibly be more potential motives behind the case than we initially thought.

'Tomorrow, if possible, I'd like you to take me round some of the other surrounding properties and introduce me to some of the people I've not yet met. Starting with Diego Smith.'

* * *

'You should try to eat something. We're quite safe here. No one knows where we're staying and they're not likely to find out. Have something to drink, at least.'

Steve Ellis was sitting opposite the woman, Barbara, who had, up until the day before, been living with his father.

She'd been in something of a daze from the moment she finally opened the front door to his insistent knocking and then, reluctantly, agreed to go with him to the police station.

Steve had borne the brunt of the cynicism as the son of a clearly well respected colleague of the officers to whom he was speaking. To his own surprise, he'd stood up to it well. He'd stayed assertive, refusing to be fobbed off.

He'd spent many hours talking it all through with his girlfriend, Océane, on his visit to see her in the United States. It was something they both agreed he needed to do, no matter how painful.

Steve's one wish was to get back to DCI Darling's team, the place where he'd felt the strongest sense of belonging he could ever remember. But then a domestic abuse case involving what he was still convinced had been a cynical murder dressed up to look like suicide had tipped him over the edge. He'd slipped into the darkest pit of despair he'd encountered in his short life.

Unable to bring himself to ask for help, he'd made an attempt on his own life, just as his mother had taken hers. He'd been thwarted by the intervention of Bill Baxter, his landlord, and Ted Darling, his boss, who'd rushed to the scene in response to Bill's phone call.

'Do you have someone you can go and stay with round here?' Steve asked her now. 'Any family you could go to? There'll be more interviews and examinations, I'm afraid, but now you've begun the process, it should get easier, and I'll support you all the way.'

She shook her head, trying to pick up the cup of tea Steve

had poured for her. They hadn't had much time for food so far that day, although they'd been kept supplied with drinks at the police station. Barbara's hand was still shaking from the ordeal so she needed several attempts to lift it high enough to take a sip.

'I don't have any family. There was only Rod, your father. I didn't realise, until too late, how much he controlled my life. Not until I realised I had no friends left. The few I'd had all dropped off gradually because of him and I was too stupid and gullible to see the signs.'

'You're not stupid, or gullible,' Steve assured her. 'Nor was my mother. You were just up against a total control freak. A sadistic bully. I promised my mother that as soon as I'd finished my training, I'd come back for her and take her somewhere safe so he could never hurt her again. But I was too late to help her.

'I kept in touch with a couple of people down here, but I never let them know where I was in case he got at them and made them tell him. Which is how I heard he was with someone new. I knew he wouldn't have changed. So I wanted to come and see for myself.'

'You've been living abroad, haven't you? Canada, was it? I think he said Canada.'

Steve frowned.

'No, I'm in Greater Manchester. Have been since straight after I finished training. They let me transfer our of the area after what happened.'

'I'm sure he said Canada. He said that was why you never visited, and I never saw him get any phone calls from you. He said because of the time difference you usually phoned him when he was at work. He led me to believe that the two of you were on good terms and that one day I'd get to meet you, when you came back for a visit.'

'He's a liar,' Steve told her with a note of bitterness in his voice. 'Everything about him is a lie. That's why they didn't believe us when we said what he was really like. He won't let any of that side of his nature slip out at work. Or only in rare glimpses. But there'll be something, somewhere. Once word gets out he's under investigation, people who've been too afraid of him to speak up will start coming forward. I'm sure of it.

'It's not going to be easy, but we're going to do it. We're going to beat him, I promise you. I know, from work, about the domino effect of cases like this. Once the very first person stands up and says something, gradually others will start to join in. They'll feel the safety in numbers.

'When I'm sure you're all right and you feel safe to stay here on your own a bit, I'm going to find the pub where the coppers from his station drink. I'm going to find someone who'll talk to me. And they will, you'll see, because we've knocked down the first domino.'

Her eyes filled instantly with tears and she reached out across the table to give his hand a squeeze.

'Thank you, Steve. Thank you. I didn't think I would ever get away from him. I thought no one would ever listen to me if I tried to tell them what he was really like, because of who he is. Even I didn't at first. I'm not a weak person, but he was so totally convincing and I was very vulnerable at the time. By then I was sure no one would believe me. But they'll believe you. You're his son, and you're a police officer. They'll have to believe you.'

Steve flushed and awkwardly removed his hand on the pretence of reaching for his scone.

'How did you meet him, if you don't mind me asking?' he said, seeking a way to change the subject.

'My husband was killed in a road accident. Roddy was the one who came to tell me the news, along with a nice young lady PC. He was so very kind and compassionate.

'My husband was a lovely man but he was hopeless with paperwork and accounts and anything like that. I didn't find out until after he died that the mortgage was in arrears. Significantly so. And that the life insurance he'd taken out wasn't worth the paper it was written on. So I lost everything.

'Your father was so kind. He came round endlessly to help me with all the paperwork. I would have been lost without him. He sorted everything for me. I don't know what I would have done without him. When the house was repossessed he suggested I move in with him. We'd become close and I had absolutely nowhere else to go. His offer was a straw and I clutched it with both hands.

'It wasn't until I was living with him and totally dependent on him for everything that I started to see what he was really like. A controlling, sadistic bully. But by then I was trapped. No home, no money, no job, nor any prospects. I had no idea how to get away from him. Who would ever believe me if I told them what he was really like outside work?'

'But now there are two of us, so they'll have to listen to us. And like you said, I'm a serving police officer, too. They can't ignore us. Especially when I find other people who know what he's really like. And there will be others, for sure. He's clever; he'll be careful who he picks on, especially at work. But I'll find them. Other victims.

'We're in this together, Barbara, and we're going to beat him. He's not going to get away with it any more.'

Chapter Twelve

'Motives,' Ted began at the start of the Ashton briefing the following morning. 'We may possibly have been looking too closely in one fixed direction - the Hippy Valley feud with the farmers - without considering the broader picture.

'We now know that money is another possible one. Sergeant Thomas, where are we up to in getting sight of the will? Have you had chance to speak again to the solicitor?'

'I have, sir, but he's still digging his heels in waiting for a positive ID on the victim. I think he knows perfectly well it is Spike but he's right, of course. From a legal point of view he does need more than his own viewing of a week-old corpse in order to make disclosure.'

'Jo, can you please chase up the lab and swear undying gratitude if we could get something back from the toothbrush soonish. We need to be cracking on and we've still not had any ID results from the PM.'

'Will do, boss.'

'Something else has come up, in the context of organised crime. Mr Doyle, if our victim is him, was passionate about all things environmental, not just animals. My team know, from our latest case, that gang leaders often have big posh houses which cost a small fortune. There's a strong chance, I would say, that sometimes planning laws could be circumvented, palms greased, in order to allow building in places where no one else would be allowed to erect a house.

'That might involve encroaching on habitat of endangered

species of animals or plants, for one thing, I imagine. And that might well come within the scope of the type of thing Mr Doyle was passionately opposed to and trying to fight.

'Some of us will remember activists in the past living in tunnels or up trees to try to block road developments, planned new railways and so on. But then imagine activists like those who might be going up against organised crime, perhaps without realising it. Peaceful protesters would be no match for the type of heavyweights we've had recent experience of through the drugs world, for example.

'Now this might widen the geographical scope of our enquiry considerably. Apparently some gang members and their guests like to come out to play in the countryside well outside their own area. Things like shooting deer, but also off-roading on quad bikes.'

'Chelsea tractors too, sir,' the sergeant put in. 'Those big four-wheel drives they love to roar round the towns and cities in. Occasionally they bring them out here and start off-roading with them, often where that's not allowed, and that can cause enormous environmental damage. Especially for things like ground-nesting birds, for instance, many of which are endangered species. That would be a red rag to a bull to Spike.'

'If that's who he tangled with and who killed him, we'll have a hard time finding any evidence. For those who don't know, we've had recent cases involving drugs gangs and they certainly do use Special Forces operatives, especially from Eastern Europe. Some of those might very well be trained in close combat techniques, like breaking someone's neck.

'The post-mortem confirmed that it was a clean break, no false starts, so it's either someone with the training, or who was incredibly lucky putting the theoretical knowledge into practice. We've previously rounded up some of the mercenaries we've had dealings with, and had them sent back to their own countries, but there will always be more ready to fill their boots.

'One thing which might get us somewhere in this context is looking at recent objections to planning applications. Who raised them, and who were the applicants? It's a long shot, but one we can't overlook. Rob, can I put you onto that, please? You'll need help, of course, so, Jo, what about your Civilian Investigator, Lee Wu? Could you spare her to help Rob? Her work impressed me before. It's likely to be a fair bit of digging which needs a methodical approach. Start with the closest planning authorities then work further out. Maybe Maurice, too, depending on how big a job it turns out to be.'

'Press reports for starters, perhaps, boss?' Jo suggested. 'If there's been some controversial planning applications, they might have made the local news.'

Ted nodded.

'Good point. Let's not talk to the press about it yet. We don't want them getting wind of that angle too soon. Internet searches first to see what, if anything, that throws up. Maurice, that's one for you to start on until Rob needs you.'

Ted turned again to Sergeant Thomas.

'Perhaps someone from your team can give Maurice a run-down of anything like that where any of the people from Hippy Valley have been involved. Or any of the locals, of course, if such an application could impact on them.

'Meanwhile perhaps you can take me round your patch again and introduce me to some more of the people on it. I'm not claiming psychic powers, but sometimes I pick up on things, so it's always worth a try.'

* * *

'Is it all right with you if we start with Jamie, sir? I'd like to check he's all right and functioning and that the animals have been seen to,' Sergeant Thomas asked Ted as they set off round his patch.

'That would be the logical thing to do, I agree. But would

you humour me and take me to see Diego Smith first, please? This tractor restoration he does. Is he likely to spend time on that most days, or only at weekends? Or does it depend?'

'Farmers don't really do weekends. Unless they're church goers, and I can't off-hand think of anyone round here who is. Most farming days are the same, seven days a week. Any reason you want to start with Diego?'

'I don't want to put Jamie at risk of another episode, but I'm curious about this idea of the tractor noise as a trigger. I'd be interested to see if there's any correlation there. And while we're out today, I'd like to ask everyone about any particular problems they've had recently, either with the occupants of Hippy Valley, or any incomers, like the off-roaders, causing trouble.

'It's just possible, from what I've heard about him, that Mr Doyle may have encountered some of them and tried to take them on over what they were doing.'

Smith's farm, set up on a hill, bore the brunt of any rain and wind. Ted thought it must be a bleak and desolate place in the depths of winter.

There was a tractor shed to the side of a large barn close to the house. From it they heard unmistakable sounds of an old and recalcitrant tractor being cajoled into life against its will, so far with no signs of success.

As the two men approached, they could also hear colourful swearing as a soundtrack to the mechanical noises.

'Now then, Diego, none of that language. Not when I've brought a senior officer round to see you,' Cai Thomas called out cheerfully as he and Ted walked over to the shed.

The man inside, leaning into the open engine compartment of an old tractor and cursing like a trooper, straightened up at their approach and grinned sheepishly at the sergeant. Whether it was a look the man affected because of his name or whether it was his natural appearance, he had curly, black, collar-length hair which, combined with his short, powerful build, was reminiscent of footballing legend Diego Maradona, after whom he was named.

'All right, Cai? Sorry about that. This old bugger is being a right bastard to start, even though I had it running at the weekend. And it would be this one, of course, because I've got someone interested in it who wants to come and have a look at it.'

'This is Detective Chief Inspector Darling. He's senior investigator on our latest case. You've heard by now about a body being found, I expect?'

The man nodded to Ted, his eyes appraising. Ted had abandoned his suit and was dressed for the countryside, which didn't go unnoticed.

'Aye, of course. One of the hippies, was it? I won't be a hypocrite and say I shed a tear. They're nothing but trouble for us, that lot. But that's not to say I would kill one of them, if that's what happened to him. I couldn't kill anything, me. Big softy.'

'So you don't slaughter any of your own livestock yourself?' Ted asked him.

He shook his head vigorously.

'Not allowed to, and I couldn't even if I was. Much too soft. You can only get it done on the farm these days for your own consumption and by someone with a WATOK or a CoC. Mine go off to the slaughterhouse when it's their time.'

'Welfare at the Time of Killing licence, or a Certificate of Competence to slaughter animals,' Sergeant Thomas translated helpfully.

'Tom Taylor gets it done on his place. Enough for family use, that is. With all those mouths to feed, and him eating like a bear, it makes sense to do it that way.'

Ted was looking at the tractor now.

'I think it was this I heard at the weekend when I was out nearby. Just as it was starting up, before it settled into a rhythm, it sounded a bit like rapid gunfire. I thought I was being warned off.'

He said it in a light-hearted tone and Smith laughed. Then his expression changed slowly. He looked stricken as he turned to Cai Thomas to ask, 'Bloody hell! Is that what sets Jamie off? This old bugger coughing and farting when she starts up, and he thinks he's coming under fire? Christ, poor bugger. I never even thought of that. She just sounds like a tractor to me, and a bloody temperamental one at that. Shit! I wonder if I should park her up a bit further away so she might not sound as loud to him? Mind you, I need her in the shed to get her cleaned up for potential buyers.'

* * *

'Genuine reaction, or Oscar-winning performance, do you think?' Ted asked the sergeant as he put the car in gear and they pulled away from the farm.

Cai Thomas took a quick sideways glance at him then said, 'You surely don't think Diego's doing it deliberately? To what end?'

'Not think, no. Just considering all options, which is what we need to do. There's no bad blood between them that you know of?'

'None at all. Diego's a decent bloke. I can't imagine him deliberately wanting to make Jamie's life any harder than it already is. They're not friends that I know of. A lot of these folk have no time for socialising with anyone because they're too busy. But I'd probably know if they were sworn enemies.

'So, shall we go and see Jamie and see if he's having a reaction to however many times the old Nuffy has been coughing and spitting like a machine gun today?'

* * *

They found Jamie Robinson in the barn. He had a few sheep in a small pen and was checking and trimming their feet whilst the dog, Nell, kept a watchful eye. Ted could see straight away how much the man's hands were shaking, but whether that was his normal state, he had no way of knowing. He was certainly being careful with his livestock.

'Now then, Jamie. You remember the DCI? We were just in the area so I thought I'd see how you were doing today.'

The man straightened up slowly and looked at them. His glance towards Ted was less hostile than previously, although still wary.

'Not too bad, thanks, Cai. Getting there. I'm back on the pills regular now, and Nell's taking good care of me. I heard them again, though. Just now. The guns. You must have heard them, too. They can't be all that far away.'

Sergeant Thomas's tone was gentle as he said, 'Jamie, we've just been up to see Diego. He was trying to get that old tractor of his going. She coughs and spits like a machine gun until she fires up properly and starts to run sweet.'

Robinson gave a loud scoff.

'I'm a trained soldier, Cai, don't forget. I know the sound of an AK47 well enough when I hear it. I've come under fire from them, plenty of times. Seen mates killed by them. No, it was definitely gunfire I heard. I didn't hear an IED go off, though. If those bastards think they're going to get me, they've got another think coming. I can still remember a trick or two from training.

'They're clever, though. They plant IEDs, then when they go off and kill a patrol, they wait for the rescue mission then pick them off with AK47s. Lost a couple of good mates that way, so they won't catch me out the same way.'

'That was in Afghanistan, Jamie,' Cai Thomas told him, his tone calm and reassuring. 'Not here, not recently. You're back on the farm now. There are no explosive devices here, no machine guns. You just get a bit confused with where you are.

'Remember what we talked about. Take the pills, and focus

on Nell. She helps to ground you. When you're with Nell, you know you're safe.

* * *

Steve Ellis knew the time of day that officers going off shift from the station where his father was a serving sergeant were likely to descend on the local pub for a drink after work. He was praying that his father wouldn't decide to join them. With what was going on, he had a feeling that if he did go for a drink, it would be with one or two of his closest mates rather than the rest of them, and far away from where the others were likely to go.

Steve was not much of a drinker. Never had been. Not a pub-goer by nature. But he'd lived in the area until he left to join the police and he could remember the names of the pubs his father frequented, and those he tended to avoid.

He was still taking an enormous risk and he knew it. If he did run into his father, or any of the officers who knew who he was and what accusations he'd made, he knew he'd end up down an alleyway getting the stuffing knocked out of him. But he'd decided he was going through with his actions, whatever it took. He needed to do it, to prove something to himself and to show everyone he was ready to go back to work with his old team. He enjoyed the computer work and knew he was good at it. But DCI Darling's team was where he felt most at home. Where he belonged.

Barbara had told him she'd much prefer to wait in her hotel room, watching television, until he got back and they could eat together in the dining room. The more he'd talked to her, the more convinced Steve had become that his father would not have changed. He'd always seen other women when married to Steve's mother and seemed to be still doing the same. Steve found it hard to believe that none of them would have seen what he was really like, but he knew he could turn on the charm when it suited him.

Rod Ellis liked them young, too. There was a strong possibility he might have tried it on with younger officers and used his rank and his bullying nature to make sure they stayed quiet.

As soon as he walked into the first pub he tried, he knew he was in luck. It was a younger clientele than his father's age group. He could easily spot the off-duty coppers, as one himself. He got himself a half of lager shandy and found a place at a small round table in the corner. He didn't so much as glance at the two young women at the next table. He was almost certain they were police.

He took out his mobile phone, selected something with a soundtrack and put one bud into the ear away from the next table, feigning total absorption in what he was watching.

Like many habitual keyboard users, Steve had the ability to remain totally focused on what he was doing on screen whilst still filtering background conversation for anything which might concern him. He did it often in briefings, when he appeared to be paying no attention at all but would always chip in at the appropriate moment. He was doing it now with the low dialogue from the next table.

' ... not surprised it's finally come out ...'

' ... own son who shopped him ...'

' ... look what he tried with you ...'

' ... bullying and intimidation ...'

' ... keep quiet ... lose career...'

Steve made a show of chuckling out loud at something on his phone, then swiped to close it, removing his ear-piece and taking a drink of his shandy. He took out his pocket book and wrote a careful note.

'I'm his son. Steve Ellis. I reported him. I need more witness testimony. I'll make sure any witnesses are kept safe. My car is outside. I'll wait in it for fifteen minutes. Here's my mobile number if you feel you could talk about it.'

He stood up to leave, dropping the note nonchalantly on the

next table as he did so, then went outside into a light drizzle and got into his car, parked nearby.

It was more than ten nail-biting minutes before his phone pinged with an incoming text.

'Drive round the back of the pub, then first turning on the left. Wait there. We'll come and find you. It's time someone stopped him.'

Chapter Thirteen

'You're ex-firearms aren't you?' Cai Thomas asked Ted as the two of them sat down with a drink while they waited for their food to appear.

They'd decided on a pub lunch in the area, rather than going back to the station. It would save time and it might even give them some useful gossip to go on, although the place was quiet on a mid-week lunchtime.

'Long time ago now, but yes, I started out at Openshaw. I was an SFO.'

'So I imagine you might have had a firearm pointed at you a time or two. Only while we're out this way, I really should take you to meet the charming Miss Burrows and she's bound to welcome us by pointing either her .22 or a shotgun at us. It's her habitual form of greeting.'

Ted took a sip of his drink before he asked a question. The pub hadn't run to ginger beer for his customary Gunner so he was making do with ginger ale and lime.

'So is she a potential suspect, would you say?'

'If our victim had been shot, she'd be my prime suspect. She's fired warning shots over trespassers' heads before now and I've had to have strong words with her about it on more than one occasion. But breaking a neck with her bare hands? I'm not really buying that, knowing her.'

'As PC Newton reminded us, you can never tell, by appearances,' Ted told him. 'We had to put away a teenage girl once, a serial killer. One of her victims was a little boy, just a toddler.

She drowned him in a river. I wouldn't want to meet another like her. She appeared to have no concept that what she'd done was wrong. She seemed to think it was funny. She laughed as she talked about killing the little boy. She even spent time flirting with me when I was interviewing her.'

'I read about that one in the papers. That must have been hard. The thing with Janice Burrows, though, is that I'm convinced she wouldn't think twice about shooting someone. She knows she'd stand a good chance of getting away with it as self-defence, living out there all alone as she does. And there's enough on record of her reporting intruders on her farm.'

Ted's phone interrupted them. Jo Rodriguez calling him. Ted picked up the call.

'Yes, Jo, any developments?'

'Identification from the toothbrush DNA has come through, boss. Our body is definitely Brendan Doyle, also known as Spike. He's been arrested a time or two so his DNA is on file.'

'Excellent, thanks Jo. Can you send me a text to confirm. I suspect his solicitor will want more than my word to go off, before he'll let us see the will or discuss the contents with us.'

As he ended the call, Ted looked at the sergeant.

'Positive ID from the toothbrush DNA. It is Brendan Doyle. So while we're out and about on our travels, can we call in on John Alexander and I can show him in text form that his client has been ID'd. I'm assuming he wouldn't simply take my word for it. And I'm definitely looking forward to meeting your Miss Burrows.'

* * *

This time there was no sign of the solicitor, John Alexander, when they arrived at Hippy Valley. No immediate signs of anyone, in fact. The site had a quiet, empty feel about it. The usual campfire was merely a mound of ash with the faintest hint of a wisp of smoke rising.

The door to the house stood open and the chimney indicated there was a proper fire burning inside there, so Ted and the sergeant walked in that direction.

The sound of the car doors being closed had brought the little girl out of the house, peering at the two of them from under her fringe.

'Hello, Ruby, you remember me, don't you? Is your mam about, love?'

A woman appeared in the doorway behind the child. There was no mistaking the waves of hostility from her as she glared at the two men.

'Ruby, I've told you, you don't talk to strangers. And you certainly don't talk to pigs.'

'Come on, Ali, that's not fair. You both know me well enough. And I had nothing to do with arresting Bruno. He thumped a policewoman, badly enough to put her in hospital, and he did it in front of the news cameras. He was never going to get away with a warning for that.

'Anyway, we're never going to agree on it, and that's not why we're here. This is Chief Inspector Darling. We need to talk to John. Do you know where he is, please?'

'If I knew I wouldn't tell you.'

The little girl piped up, a helpful smile on her face, 'They gone to The Stones.'

'Ruby, I told you, don't talk to pigs. Go back in the house.'

The woman pushed the child, none too gently, back inside, followed her and slammed the door behind them.

'Thank you, Ruby, you little belter,' the sergeant said with a smile, then, turning to Ted, 'That would explain why there's no one about. So, as they say, if the mountain will not come to Muhammad ...'

'Then you and I must go to the mountain, or wherever The Stones may be,' Ted finished for him. 'I'm assuming we're talking a stone circle, or standing stones or something like that?'

They got back into the vehicle and Thomas started the engine.

'It's not Stonehenge, for sure. Nor the Nine Ladies. And not even standing stones. A lot of experts say it's actually nothing significant at all, just a dozen or so big rocks whose purpose nobody really knows. My own theory is some farmer brought them in decades ago intending to make gate posts from them, but never got round to it. But our fun-loving friends from the Valley have decided there's a spiritual vibe to the place and they often go there. It's a greener option than Nine Ladies, for sure, as they can walk to the place easily enough from here. We'll take the vehicle, though, in case we're less than welcome and need to beat a hasty retreat.'

'So what was all that from the woman, about Bruno? Why does she hate the police so much? I know we have some bad ones but we're not all like that, so why are her views so extreme?'

'Her bloke, Bruno, was at a demo. They were blockading lorries taking animals for shipping overseas for slaughter. Now, I know there are strong feelings about that. The wife and I are having battles with our teenage daughter who wants to be a vegan, which is fine, we support her right, as long as she researches properly and eats a sensible diet. What we're not so keen on is the endless screaming rows when she calls the two of us murderers because we're not vegans, nor even vegetarians, so she refuses to eat with us.

'Anyway, Bruno. This wasn't on our patch, it was down near the Channel ports. They were blocking the road to stop lorries driving onto the ferries. It got very heated, and more than a little nasty. I'm not claiming that all the officers present behaved perfectly. Tempers got very frayed; there was wrong on both parts. Some officers were disciplined, others less so. But what Bruno did went way beyond the bounds. He had a metal pipe, like a scaffolding pole, and he hit a young woman PC in the face with it. Broke her nose badly, gave her a nasty concussion and left a lot of scarring.

'He was damn lucky. The defence made a big thing of the lack of intent. Not pre-planned, heat of the moment, strong sense of self-preservation when it all blew up, grabbed the nearest thing to hand. We've heard it all before.

'Ali wanted to try to appeal but we both know what that costs, and he wouldn't really have stood a chance. Not with the TV camera coverage.'

'And is this Bruno the father of Ruby?' Ted asked him.

'Who knows? Like I said, it's a bit fluid there with regard to relationships. Bruno and Ali were certainly together when he was arrested.

'Right, if we park here and walk up this track, it takes us straight to these legendary stones. Although as I said, don't expect anything all that impressive. Unless you're into the woo yourself and pick up on these supposed vibes.'

They walked in companionable silence up the track, which rose on a gradual incline. Ted could see what the sergeant had meant about the damage done by the off-roaders, despite the 'Private Property - No Right of Way' sign at the bottom. Tyre marks carved deep gouges which heavy rain had worn away to make into much deeper ruts. He was glad of his good walking boots.

The track opened out into rough grassy upland, with a bowl-shaped depression at its centre, for which PS Thomas set course, Ted by his side. They paused for the moment at the top. Ted could clearly see The Stones now, randomly scattered as if cast aside by a petulant giant. He agreed with Thomas's theory. They looked for all the world as if they had been intended as gate posts in the distant past and abandoned where they were for some reason.

There were about a dozen people sitting in a circle at the centre of the hollow. Ted spotted the Homburg hat of John Alexander amongst them. One person was playing a guitar, another a flute. Ted recognised the tune, being played mournfully. The famous TV theme. It was a peaceful scene.

Nevertheless, Ted turned to Thomas and said quietly, 'I don't know if you've ever seen the film *The Wicker Man*, sergeant, but it's made me rather wary of being the police officer who tries to break up any sort of Pagan gathering.'

Thomas chuckled at that.

'I've seen that film too, sir, and I often get that feeling when I go out to the Valley on my own. Especially me being a Uniform sergeant. Are you a religious man?'

'Not remotely.'

'That's a shame. I'm not either and from the film, I remember the copper praying fervently at the critical moment. We'd better try not to get on the wrong side of them, then.'

They moved closer but stayed silently in the background, waiting for John Alexander to notice them. He was sitting, quietly contemplative, taking no notice of them, as if he'd not even seen them. It was hard to tell from his posture and body language. None of the others there so much as acknowledged their presence.

Finally the solicitor's eyes landed on them, seemingly seeing them for the first time. He stood up to move towards them, not making any noise or gesture to disturb the quiet meditation of any of the others.

'We're saying our goodbyes to Spike,' he said when he drew level with the two men. 'He came here often, both with us and alone. It's a special place for us. It's where he wanted his ashes to be scattered, which will be done once the body has been released.'

'You accept that he's dead, then?' Ted queried.

There was amusement in the man's eyes at the question.

'Well, clearly I do, having seen his body for myself. But then as I'm not a relative and he has a brother, who is his real next of kin, my identification of him alone doesn't suffice, in my humble legal opinion, to make full disclosure of his affairs to you without DNA confirmation.'

'Which we now have, from analysis of the toothbrush taken from his home,' Ted told him, holding out his phone with the document Jo had sent him. 'Now that we have that, are you prepared to disclose who inherits, under the terms of the will? And could you give us at least an idea of what sort of amount of money we're talking about.'

'Because in your world, money is always a motive for murder, I imagine. Whereas to someone like Spike, it had no more value or significance than that toothbrush.

'I take it you went to the Valley before coming here, since you clearly knew where to find us. In which case you would probably have encountered Spike's sole beneficiary.'

Cai Thomas frowned as he asked, 'Ali? Spike left all his money to Ali?'

John Armstrong smiled as he shook his head.

'Not Ali, no. Ruby. She inherits everything he owned and all his future royalties for seventy years. Not forgetting the various shares and investments he's made over the years and never touched. That little girl has suddenly become a very wealthy young lady indeed.'

* * *

The time taken to get a reply to his text had been tense for Steve Ellis. Sitting waiting to see if the two young women would turn up to find him in his car was nothing short of agonising.

He had had a sudden irrational moment of panic. What if they'd known all along who he was? Perhaps they were actually in league with his father and this whole thing was a set-up. Suppose they didn't turn up at all but had instead phoned his father who was on his way right now with some of his mates.

He tried to control his breathing. Remembered the 5-4-3-2-1 coping skills which Océane had patiently taught him.

Five things you can see:

Man walking dog.

Hands on the steering wheel.

Smudge of a squashed fly on the windscreen. That needed cleaning.

Newspaper in the foot well where it had fallen.

Woman walking two dogs.

Four things you can touch:

Gear lever.

Mobile phone.

The panic was rising again. Can't have steering wheel, he'd already used that.

Upholstery. The feel of the car seat.

Windscreen wiper lever. That might get rid of the dead fly.

Three things you can hear:

Traffic.

Footsteps.

A tap on the side window.

His heart leapt into his mouth as he turned and looked, but it was just the two young women, on their own. And they were smiling at him.

He released the central locking and the two of them slid into the back seat.

'I'm Kathy, this is Linda,' one of them told him. 'And would you mind if we drove somewhere else before we talk to you? Only it could be very difficult for us if we were seen doing so. You know better than us how controlling your dad is, and he has a lot of mates who watch his back.'

'Yes, of course,' Steve started up the car, glancing at them in the rear view mirror. 'Another pub? Can you suggest somewhere?'

'Nowhere public, for sure,' the one called Kathy told him. 'Don't worry, I'll direct you somewhere quiet we can park and talk and it won't look odd.'

She saw the quick anxious look he gave them in the rear view mirror and leaned forward to give him a gentle reassuring pat on the arm.

'Don't worry, Steve, we're on your side. We know what he's like, and now you've started the ball rolling, we honestly want to help.'

He followed their directions to a car park next to a public open space. They talked for so long that Steve had to break off to phone Barbara to say he would be late back and to tell her to go ahead and eat, without waiting for him to join her.

Kathy told him that she was a PC and Linda, who was younger, was a PCSO. It was Linda who'd had the trouble with Sergeant Rod Ellis.

'I tried to ignore the inappropriate comments. I don't like anything like that but I know some older blokes say such stuff and really don't mean any harm, nor realise how inappropriate it is. I did try saying I didn't appreciate it but he just laughed and said I was being over-sensitive and not to take him too seriously.

'Then we all went to the pub together one evening. Farewell drinks for someone who was retiring. Your dad had a bit to drink and he was getting a bit loud. I bumped into him in the corridor when I was going to the ladies and he was just coming out of the gents. That time he tried to get physical. He pushed me up against the wall and was leaning against me with his whole body.

'I tried standing up to him, not letting him intimidate me. I told him I'd report him. But he's a big strong bloke. You know that, Steve. He grabbed me by the boob and squeezed, really hard. He had me pinned so I couldn't get a knee up to stop him. Then he told me if I said anything to anyone he'd see my career was ended before it began. I was too scared to take the risk, until I heard his son was prepared to testify against him. So I will, too. Of course I will. And once I do, I think you'll find others will join in, because I can't believe I'm the only one.'

* * *

Steve was smiling to himself the whole way on the drive back to his hotel. It had all gone better than he could have hoped for. It felt like the beginning of the end, after the dark times of feeling totally powerless.

Linda had even agreed to let him record her making a very brief statement, so that he had something more to go on. He'd go back to the station the following day to pass on the additional evidence. That would add powerful weight to his own and Barbara's statements.

He parked his car in the hotel car park then walked inside to meet her in the dining room, as he'd arranged on his second phone call. He was looking forward to telling her the latest news over something to eat. He realised suddenly how hungry he felt.

He was so absorbed in thoughts of the latest development that he appeared not to notice the vehicle which had crept quietly into the car park behind his and paused, without the engine being turned off. The driver stopped for long enough to see Steve go into the hotel foyer, then drove round the car park and left the way they had come in.

Chapter Fourteen

'Right, then. Let's go and find Miss Burrows. And don't say I didn't warn you,' Sergeant Thomas told Ted with a smile as he let off the handbrake and pulled away.

'We're not likely to find her at the house at this time of day. She'll be out in the fields seeing to her stock, most probably. But wherever she goes, one of the guns goes with her. Oh, and you mentioned being wary of dogs. You'd do well to be on your guard with hers. They're as bad-tempered and unpredictable as she is, but at least she has good control of them, and most of the time they'll obey me, if I sound fierce enough. Just don't say anything to get on the wrong side of her.'

'You're filling me with confidence,' Ted told him, grinning. 'I shall stand firmly behind you and leave you to do all the talking.'

The sergeant laughed at that.

'That's fine, but remember that working sheepdogs always start by going round behind whatever they're sent to round up.'

They had to do a fair bit of driving around before they tracked down Miss Burrows. Her quad bike was parked in an open gateway while she and her dogs drove skittish young cattle from one field to the next.

The two men got out of the vehicle and started to walk into the first field. They could both see clearly that the woman had a shotgun, in the broken position, tucked firmly under one arm while she worked.

'She's got the old Purdey with her today, I see. That means

she can take out the pair of us at the same time,' Cai Thomas remarked pleasantly. 'We better not go any closer until she's secured her beasts. We don't want to start out by making her angry.'

'We certainly don't,' Ted agreed with feeling. 'And you might not believe me, but it really is the dogs that worry me the most.'

Once the cattle were through the far gate, the woman shut and secured it, then turned to see the two men standing waiting for her. In a fluid movement which spoke of frequent practice, she flipped the gun up to re-engage both barrels which were now pointed at Ted and Cai as she started to walk towards them.

At the same moment she uttered an indistinct command to the dogs which flew away from her, becoming stiff-legged and bristling with raised hackles the closer they got to the perceived intruders.

'Let's hope she doesn't trip and fall, carrying that gun pointing straight at us,' Cai Thomas remarked, his demeanour showing little concern. He'd clearly seen it all before.

'I'm hoping she tells those dogs to stop, sometime soon,' Ted told him.

'Oh, don't worry about those two,' Thomas told him cheerfully, then he gave the dogs a steely-eyed look as he snapped out a command at them.

'*Lawr!*'

Both dogs instantly dropped, bellies to the ground, chins on paws, though not for a second taking their eyes off the two men.

'Why did you speak Welsh to them?' Ted asked the sergeant, keeping his own eyes warily on the two dogs.

'Like a lot of the best sheepdogs, they came from Wales. They arrived not knowing any English commands. The whistles are universal, of course, but they were used to Welsh verbal commands for close work. Miss Burrows actually had to swallow her pride and ask me to teach her the main ones, which is probably why she hasn't shot me. Yet.'

He added the last word as the woman had now walked to within a few yards of them. The muzzle of the old gun was lowered slightly, but not enough to miss them altogether if for any reason she decided to pull the trigger.

'Now then, Miss Burrows, this is Detective Chief Inspector Darling, from Stockport. Please don't shoot him. It would be an awful lot of paperwork and I'd have to arrest you for it.'

She gave a snort like a startled horse, then said, 'I'd like to see you try that, Cai Thomas. And I couldn't know he was a copper. Look at him. He looks nothing like one.'

'I'll happily show you my ID, Miss Burrows, but only if you lower your firearm,' Ted said quietly. 'You really shouldn't be pointing it at anyone, even if you don't know them. And Sergeant Thomas is in Uniform, so you can certainly tell he's a police officer.'

Shrewd eyes scanned him. She detected something about the softly-spoken short man which led her to lower the shotgun slightly more, though not completely.

'Thank you. You know by now, no doubt, that we're making enquiries into a suspicious death. I understand that you've had a fair bit of trouble with uninvited visitors to your property, and that you feel not enough has been done about them.'

'Not enough?' she barked. 'Nothing. Nothing has been done. Bugger all.'

'I keep trying to explain, by the time we can get anyone out here, any intruders are long gone,' Sergeant Thomas told her patiently. 'And we simply don't have enough officers to keep a watch in case someone comes bothering you.'

'Yet if I shoot one of the bastards, I can guarantee you'd be here in record time.'

'If you want to make a formal complaint about lack of response to your phone calls, Miss Burrows, I can assure you that I will personally see to it that it's thoroughly investigated.'

'And then binned. I know how you lot all watch each others' backs,' she spat at him.

Ted's voice was even quieter as he locked eyes with her to reply.

'Not me, Miss Burrows. Not me. I investigate anyone who does anything at all out of line, whatever their occupation.

'Now, is it all right if I ask you some questions about our current case, please? The suspicious death. You've no doubt heard by now. A body was found near the waterfall not far from here.'

'Make it quick, I have work to do. And I already told the others I don't know anything about it. That useless Colin Nield, who couldn't catch a cold never mind a criminal.'

'I've seen his report of his visit. You weren't able to give much of a description of the people you've been having trouble with,' Ted told her patiently. 'That makes it slightly harder for us to do our job and speak to any of them. Can you give us anything more specific, at all? Something more detailed, even if it's only for one of them.'

She was studying him closely. Weighing him up. Sensing his determination, which could well mean he wouldn't be fobbed off as others had been.

'I keep saying, they all look the same. Hairy. Long hair. Beards. Hippy clothes. There was one sniffing round recently. Not as hairy as the usual lot. Shortish dark hair, or maybe tied back perhaps. Stubble rather than a beard. Short and stocky. A bit cleaner than usual, too. Better clothes. I caught him trying to let some of my sheep out of one of the outbuildings. Good runner, though. I set the dogs on him and he ran off at a good rate. I've not seen him since.'

'You didn't shoot him, did you?' Sergeant Thomas asked her.

'Why waste a cartridge when the dogs could do the job?'

Ted took one of his cards out of his pocket and held it out for her to take, still keeping a wary eye on the dogs in case they misinterpreted his movement.

'Thank you, Miss Burrows, you've been very helpful indeed. If you think of anything else at all, or if anyone bothers you again, here's my contact number. Please don't hesitate to call me, any time.'

* * *

'Was that helpful, did you think, sir? Her description didn't ring any bells with me, and I probably know the Hippy Valley lot better than most, I think. Plus anyone else who lives or works on our patch.'

'Oh, very helpful, I would say. Sometimes, when someone has previously refused to give any useful information then suddenly appears to do so, you have to wonder why. What their motivation is. She'd previously told DC Vine and PC Nield that the ones she has trouble with are all hairy and bearded. Suddenly we have one who is the direct opposite.

'I've admittedly seen very few of the Valley residents, and you say the population there is fluid. But I certainly haven't seen anyone fitting that description. Does it mean anything to you?'

'Nothing at all. I can't offhand think of anyone like that, not from Hippy Valley. Not currently, not even someone who's been and gone. If the person bothering her fitted that description, I've certainly never seen them in the Valley. And if they were doing things like letting her stock out, it's likely that they were some part of the anti-farming brigade. Unless they were perhaps looking for stuff to nick and just left the gate open so the stock got out, I suppose.'

'I think it's unlikely you would have seen someone of that description. I may be wrong but I've found often that when someone is volunteering a lot of detail, especially when they haven't done so before, it may not necessarily be true. It could perhaps be the exact opposite of what they say. Short, stocky, no beard and short hair is the diametric opposite of Brendan Doyle, for instance. He was tall, thin, bearded and long-haired.'

'Tom Taylor is like that for sure. He'll always give you way too much detail for it to be probable, and he feeds off body language to see if any of it is close to what's wanted. But Janice Burrows isn't usually like that. She's normally a woman of few words. That was out of character for her, now you mention it. In fact it's the first time I've heard her volunteer anything at all, which is why we can never help her with her complaints, although we do try.

'Her description does sound a bit like Diego Smith, and he's interested in her old tractor. But she knows him well enough, so she'd say if it was him.'

'So our next question needs to be why? Why did she do that? What information does she not want us to have? Is it purely coincidence that the person she described could in no way be Brendan Doyle?'

Sergeant Thomas took his eyes off the road for a brief instant to look towards Ted.

'You suspect Janice Burrows of killing him? Of snapping his neck? Shooting him, yes, I'd believe that easily enough. But in cold blood like that? That I would find harder to believe, even by someone as unpleasant as she can be.'

'I like Hercule Poirot's method. Suspect everybody till the last minute. And with that in mind, can we please get someone onto in-depth background checks on everyone, and I do mean everyone. Plus anyone they've ever been associated with. Let's see if that throws up anything interesting.'

* * *

Trev was at karate when Ted got home. Ted had warned him it was highly unlikely he'd get there himself, so Trev had put their supper in the oven on a low light and left him a note to tell him to eat if he was hungry, otherwise they could eat together when he got back.

Ted wanted to wait and used the intervening time to go through the copy of Brendan Doyle's will which John Alexander had sent through as promised. When he opened his briefcase to take it out, he realised he hadn't yet done anything about the letter from Oliver Burdon. He put it to one side on the table whilst he went through the fine print of the will.

As he'd expected, it was watertight. Everything was left to Ruby, to be held in trust until she came of age, and there was no way he could see for anyone to get at any of it before then. Not even Ruby herself, if he had read it correctly.

Trev was talking on the phone as he bounced in through the front door. Welsh, so clearly speaking to Ted's mother. His use of the language was improving all the time. Yet another one he mopped up with ease. He was clearly in high spirits. Karate must have gone well.

'Speak to your mam,' Trev ordered, thrusting his mobile phone into Ted's hands. 'I'll sort the supper. I am absolutely starving.'

Ted always got the guilts at how infrequently he spoke to his mother, Annie. He always intended to, but work got in the way, as it did with so much of his personal life.

To please her, he tried a few tentative words of Welsh to say hello and ask her how she was. It was about all he could remember now from what he'd learned as a small child.

She sounded delighted as she replied briefly in her native language then switched back to English, knowing his limitations.

'I've got yet another murder case on at the moment, but as soon as I can get away, I promise we'll come down and see you again,' he told her.

'I'll look forward to it, *bach*, but I know how busy you are. Cariad would love to see you, too, never mind me. She kept looking for you after you went home last time.'

To his own surprise, Ted had found himself at ease with

Cariad, the little Corgi his mother had inherited when her friend died suddenly and suspiciously.

Trev was looking at the handwriting on the envelope, which Ted had left on the table, when his partner finished the phone call.

'What's this? Do you have a secret admirer? Should I be worried? They must be very young, going on the writing. A schoolgirl crush?'

Ted shook his head.

'No, it's that hospital porter, Oliver Burdon. With a D, as he says every time. I told you about him. He was a suspect, briefly, in the Blue Eyes case, and because I released him without charge, he seems to have rather latched onto me. He's getting married and he wants me to be his best man. I'll have to tell him I'm too busy.'

'Oh, Ted, you can't do that, he clearly thinks the world of you if he's asked you. And I feel awful now for making fun of the handwriting. I remember you saying he could barely read and write. Can I read it?'

'Of course. But do you really think I should accept?'

Trev was scan-reading the letter now.

'Yes, of course you should. It would be a kindness. And look, you can take a plus one, and you know how much I love weddings. We'll need to get them a gift. What does he like?'

Trev had put the letter down now and was busily dishing up their supper.

'I have honestly no idea,' Ted told him. 'I barely know the man, although I saw him a time or two when I had that stay in hospital. All I can remember about him is that he likes white chocolate.'

'Oh, that's perfect. Write back tonight, tell him you'll do it with pleasure and tell him I'll bake a cake for the reception. A white chocolate wedding cake. What fun that will be to do.'

He finished dishing up the supper and moved oven

dishes and utensils over to the sink, at the same time as massacring Wagner's *Lohengrin* at the top of his tuneless voice, causing some of the cats to decamp to the sanctuary of the next room.

* * *

'So that's another person, a serving police officer, who's also prepared now to testify against him,' Steve told Barbara as the two of them ate together in the hotel dining room. 'Another domino, you see. And I think there will be others, now the ball is rolling. I just have to find them.'

'Do be careful, Steve,' Barbara told him, her expression anxious. 'We both know what he's like. He's going to fight this - and us - every step of the way. And he has a lot of friends who, even if they suspect for a moment there might be some truth in the accusations, would be very reluctant to come forward and say anything.

'Are you absolutely certain he can't find out from any of his mates where we're staying? Should we perhaps think of changing hotels? Of not staying too long in one place? Is there any way he can get at the paperwork to find where we are? I wouldn't put it past him to try. He's certainly been trying to phone my mobile, no doubt to cajole or threaten me into not testifying against him, so I wouldn't put anything past him. I've been ignoring all his calls.'

Steve shook his head.

'It would be a very serious matter indeed if anyone gave him that information or made it available to him. By rights he should have been suspended from duty while he's investigated because these are serious charges, but they may just give him the benefit of the doubt for now.

'With an investigation starting up which has serious potential consequences, I wouldn't be surprised if some of his old mates started to distance themselves from him, until it's all sorted out.

'We should be safe enough staying here. He won't know where to find us.'

Chapter Fifteen

'Any signs of a breakthrough yet, Ted? Anything at all? Only the hours are mounting up with not a lot to show for it yet.'

Detective Superintendent Sammy Sampson was tapping papers with a pen as she spoke to Ted in her office. She had a divisional budgetary meeting coming up and was looking for something positive to input at it.

'I wish there was. We've no witnesses, or certainly none who will admit to having seen anything. Plus we have rather too many motives to make it easy. There's a lot more money than I imagined, for one thing, and we both know how much of an incentive to kill that can be.

'We never expected to find money behind Spike the hippy, but Brendan Doyle the songwriter was very wealthy, and now this little girl Ruby is set to inherit the lot.'

'Five Day Johnny would have solved it by now,' Sammy told him with a smile.

Ted frowned at the nickname, although it rang a distant bell.

'Five Day Johnny?'

Sammy chuckled.

'Met officer on the Jack the Stripper case in the nineteen sixties. You must have heard of it. The killer targeted prostitutes, like Jack the Ripper did, and left them naked, hence the nickname. They called the Super that because that's how long he usually took to crack a case. You'd think I'd have enough of crime in my job, but my guilty secret is watching and reading all sorts of stuff on historic crime.

'So what's yours? Guilty secret?'

'It won't be a secret if I tell you. But it's reading Agatha Christie. She was excellent on the psychology of the criminal. Just as well, with nothing like DNA in her day. And speaking of which, there's still a delay at the lab so we've not had any results from the body yet, although we did get the ID from the toothbrush, at least.

'I'm not optimistic of the body having kept any traces which will help us, given the state of decomposition and the adverse weather, but there's a slight possibility it could tell us something.'

'You don't need me to tell you we need something, anything, and soon, before the press and media start hanging us out to dry.

'What of the gold bars case in the meantime? Any progress on that? I'd like something to wave at this meeting to show we're all earning our keep.'

'At the risk of repeating myself, the team need that computer forensics person, and soon. It would speed things up enormously. And it's next Monday that DC Ellis is back at work so ...'

Sammy opened her mouth to speak but Ted went on determinedly.

'I know, he needs to be cleared to do anything but routine CFI work tied to a desk at Central Park. But there's been a development. A significant one, which might go to show how far Steve's come in dealing with his issues.

'I had a phone call from a sergeant at Southampton to say that Steve had been in with a woman, who now lives with his father. He's a serving sergeant there and from the little which Bill Baxter and I have managed to put together about Steve's background, leading up to what he did, he's a nasty piece of work who subjected his wife, and Steve, to years of serious physical and psychological abuse. Steve and the woman have now made official complaints about Sergeant Ellis. About both physical and sexual assaults.

'They weren't initially taken seriously until a sergeant there phoned me and I set him straight.'

'Has he, now? That must have taken an enormous amount of courage on his part. Especially as there was a strong possibility that he wouldn't be believed. You say his father is still serving there despite such serious allegations? He's not been suspended from duty, or put on restricted duties pending investigation?'

'Apparently not.'

'Right,' Sammy said decidedly, scribbling a note on her jotter. 'Who have you spoken to, down south? If they won't listen to a DCI perhaps they might sit up and take notice of a Det Sup, and remember that they're supposed to investigate all crime impartially, whether or not it's one of their own.

'First, though, as I don't personally know DC Ellis, can you reassure me that what he says is likely to be true? I'm not implying I don't trust him simply because he's suffered from mental illness. But if you can assure me that illness is not likely to have affected his judgement, then I'm more than happy to mount my white charger and ride into battle on his behalf.'

'It was a Sergeant Jackson who phoned me, sounding very sceptical and saying they were thinking about charging Steve with wasting police time. I've always found Steve to be of the highest integrity. I honestly doubt he could lie. He could blush for England for the slightest reason, for one thing, which would make it hard. But even if he isn't telling the truth for some reason, the complaint should still be investigated, whether his father is a serving sergeant or the Chief Constable, surely?'

'Absolutely so. Leave it with me. If it's not properly investigated, heads will roll or my name's not Sammy Sampson. So off you go, Ten Day Ted, get me a nice result on this murder before the top brass start to grumble.'

* * *

Jo Rodriguez was in the incident room when Ted got back there, talking to Rob O'Connell and Lee Wu. There was a buzz of anticipation about them.

Jo looked up as Ted entered the room, a smile on his face.

'Boss, early days, but something interesting showed up once we started looking at planning applications.

'There's an ongoing dispute over plans to build a big house out in the country, surrounded by high fencing which would make Fort Knox look easy to penetrate. The application is from this man, Greg Whittaker.'

Jo pointed to a photo which had been put up on the board on the wall behind where he was standing. There was a map of the area surrounding Hippy Valley and the place where the body had been found.

'As you can see, it's out in the country, beyond the fringe of any existing development, and according to the objections, it's a vital habitat for,' he checked his notes before continuing, 'great crested newts, and pennyroyal, whatever that is. Oh, and some rare birds too, which nest in trees in line for felling to make way for the development. I'd no idea there were so many planning restrictions because of things like this but apparently so, and quite stringently enforced, too.

'If you look at the map, the development site is not all that far as the crow flies from Hippy Valley, so unsurprisingly, one of the objections raised came from a collective of the residents there. And they certainly know their stuff as they were all over the whole endangered species thing.'

Ted moved closer to the map, put his reading glasses on, then tapped a spot on it.

'It's even closer to a place they call simply The Stones which they seem to think has some spiritual significance to it. Sergeant Thomas is convinced the actual stones in question are just ones which were intended as gateposts and never erected and he could well be right. That was the place where he and I found the Hippy Valley dwellers, with the exception of the woman called Ali and the little girl Ruby, the heiress, saying their goodbyes to Spike.

'So who is the person behind the application, this Greg Whittaker? In terms of is he known to us for any reason?'

'No convictions on record, boss, no. He's a scrap metal dealer who also does waste disposal and various other such things. There's a hell of a lot more money in that than you might imagine, it seems. Nothing official against him but he's suspected of all sorts of stuff, including illegal fly-tipping. Although not him personally, the people he employs.

'He's also thought to be behind various thefts of farm machinery in the area, although again he wouldn't soil his own hands with anything like that.

'That's the trouble with him; he's as fly as anything. Nobody can ever pin anything on him personally. From time to time he does a token sacking of a couple of the people who work for him, although the suspicion is that he simply moves them to a different part of his empire and employs them there, sometimes with a name change.'

'Where's the planning application up to now?'

'Stalled,' Jo told him. 'There has to be all sorts of surveys done regarding the protected species and the application in general, with no end of official bodies having to be involved. The person Rob spoke to says there are widespread suspicions that Whittaker is desperately trying to grease palms to get it moving, because he seems to have set his heart on that site. Or perhaps it's his wife pushing for it because it seems to be an open secret who wears the trousers in that marriage.'

'So has there been any sort of open aggro with the protesters? Or is it all just on paper?'

'Apparently there has, yes. When the planning authority went to do their initial survey on the site following the written objections, several of the folk from Hippy Valley turned up and staged a peaceful sit-in. But then it all got a bit heated when Whittaker and some of his people arrived, too.'

'We need to find out if Brendan Doyle was there,' Ted told him. 'And we need a much more recent photo of him. Ask Sergeant Thomas to see if anyone at Hippy Valley has one. John Alexander at least seems to have technology and a decent phone, so let's see if he might have had occasion to take any photos.'

He was looking at the board. The only photos they had of their victim were one pulled from the internet, taken at the height of his fame a good few years ago, the post-mortem picture, and an old police one from when he'd been arrested at a protest but later released with nothing but a Public Order caution.

'Jo, I think you should be the one to go and pay this Mr Whittaker a visit. The presence of a DI should show him we're taking this seriously. Take someone local from Uniform with you, see if you can get any more details about him. Not just anything official, we can do that easily enough, but also what the gossip is about him. That might well be revealing.

'Rob, can you do a deep background check on him in the meantime. Not just him but employees, colleagues, friends, all of that. We need to know the kind of people he has working for him. That could be significant.'

'I've heard of some odd motives for murder in my time, but killing someone in a row over newts is a new one on me,' Jo told him. 'But if this planning application is really the background to the murder and it somehow manages to go through despite the environmental objections, at some point someone will definitely need to start looking into council and other palms being greased along the way.'

* * *

Steve was smiling and humming to himself as he drove from the police station back to the hotel. He was starting to feel more confident than he could remember being for a long time.

He checked his rear view mirror several times to see if he could spot his tail. It wouldn't be his father. Not yet, anyway. It would be one or more of his mates, taking turns to see where Steve was staying and if he had changed the venue to throw them off the trail.

He hadn't, and he didn't intend to. His entire plan was based on his father knowing exactly where to find him. It was risky - very risky - but with Océane's support, and the help of her new police friends in the States, he felt ready. He felt more in control of his life than he ever had before.

At the station this time, he'd been ushered into the office of the Duty Inspector, a man named Dutta. He'd been formal, polite, reassuring, but had refused to answer Steve's question as to whether or not his father had been suspended from duty pending investigation.

He'd listened in silence while Steve recounted what he had been told by PCSO Linda McCrae, then played the brief statement she had recorded for him.

'I'm not in any way trying to tell you how to do your job, sir,' Steve told him, 'but in light of what PCSO McCrae has told me, there might possibly be other people within the station with similar experiences who have previously been too afraid to come forward.'

'There will be no cover-up on my watch, DC Ellis, if that's what you're implying.'

The man visibly bristled as he said it. Steve hurried to reassure him.

'No sir, I wasn't implying any such thing. It's simply that I know better than most what a bully my father is and how he can intimidate people into keeping quiet.'

'I hear what you say. But these are as yet unfounded accusations which need thorough investigation. As a serving officer yourself, you know that we can't simply accept your word for it. You will be kept informed of any developments, and especially if any charges are brought when your presence at court could be required to testify.

'Are you staying in the area for now?'

'Until the weekend, sir. I start back on duty next Monday.'

'We have your contact details, I think?'

He was looking at papers on his desk and mentioned the name of the hotel where Steve and Barbara were staying.

'That's right, sir. Clearly Barbara doesn't feel safe to return to the home she shares with my father at the moment, so we're both staying at the hotel.'

Dutta rose to his feet, the interview clearly at an end in his eyes.

'Well, thank you, DC Ellis, you can safely leave this new information with me. And rest assured, there will be a full investigation without fear or favour. You'll be kept informed.'

If it was a brush-off, it was certainly one of the politest Steve had ever heard. It had contributed to his good mood. He had at least believed that Inspector Dutta would look into the matter. Whether he would come up against a brick wall of silence remained to be seen.

When Steve approached the final roundabout before the turn off for the hotel, he checked his mirror again, smiled to himself and decided on a bit of mischief.

Instead of driving straight ahead, he went round the roundabout to the last exit, appeared to dither, drawing some angry blasts of the horn from drivers behind him, then went round again to take the correct road. Another quick check in the mirror showed him his pursuer having to do the same manoeuvre and getting the same reaction from other drivers.

It wasn't his father, he knew with a certainty, although he'd never been able to get a proper look at who was driving. Sergeant Ellis wouldn't be stupid enough to risk being seen anywhere near his accuser. Not yet, anyway. He'd have called in favours owed, and probably still had enough mates who'd be dismissing the allegations as wildly exaggerated, if true at all. Steve knew his father well enough to know the totally different persona he could portray outside the home.

The following car turned into the hotel car park and hovered just long enough to see Steve park his own vehicle then get out and walk up to the entrance.

Steve paused to look up at the discreetly hidden security cameras, not easy to spot unless you were close to them. He'd chosen the hotel for exactly that reason. Phoning up to book, he'd spun them a story about having previously stayed in a hotel where the cameras were very visible and had been vandalised, leading to his car being damaged.

The hotel receptionist had hastened to reassure him that they did have cameras and that they were deliberately placed so as not to be an easy target, ensuring they worked properly at all times.

Steve's plan depended in part on reliable cameras covering the car park. The plan was risky, especially for him, although he'd gone over it endless times with Océane and her friends in the States.

CCTV footage from the hotel car park would be the clincher. The final nail in the coffin of his father's career, and possibly the end of his liberty.

So much was riding on those cameras working when he needed them to.

Chapter Sixteen

Jo Rodriguez chose PCSO Fiona Murray to go with him to speak to Greg Whittaker. She knew the area well and most of the main people in it. They went in a marked police vehicle, with Fiona driving, because Jo wanted to make it clear to Whittaker from the start that although this was initially a fishing exercise, it was official.

The man had told them to come to his house rather than his business premises, which Jo thought might well have been significant.

Looking at the size of his existing home and mentally trying to put a price tag on it, Jo wondered what sort of a mansion he had planned for the new site, if planning permission was ever granted there. Not to mention why he felt the need to move.

Three shiny, latest model, high-end cars were parked in front of the house on the immaculate gravel driveway. Jo wasn't much of a petrol-head so could only speculate on what they might have cost. His own choice was limited to a functional eight-seater people carrier to accommodate his large family, and he used his service vehicle for work.

The man who appeared as soon as they pulled up was short and stocky, clean shaven, with collar-length curly dark hair. He had on a golfing sweater with a logo which Jo recognised but could never afford even if he'd wanted to. Waves of expensive cologne assailed the nostrils of the two officers as they got out of the car and walked towards Whittaker, who was beaming towards them as if at valued guests.

'DI Rodriguez,' Jo told him. 'We spoke on the phone. And this is PCSO Murray. Thank you for agreeing to see us, Mr Whittaker.'

'Greg, please. Do come into the kitchen and have some coffee. I'll show you the way.'

He led the way into a bright kitchen at the rear of the large property, one whose footprint was not much smaller than the ground floor of Jo's house, even without the enormous conservatory he could see beyond it. Everything looked new, state-of-the-art. Jo wondered whatever was planned for the proposed house which could top this one.

'The wife's out at one of her classes, if you wanted to speak to her for any reason. Now, coffee?'

He was standing in front of a machine which wouldn't have been out of place in a decent restaurant.

'This beast can make almost anything you want, so fire away with the orders.'

'Just an espresso for me, please,' Jo told him as he and PCSO Murray perched on the high bar stools the man indicated.

'Coming right up. And what about you, dear?'

Fiona Murray gave Jo an exaggerated eye roll behind the man's back as he turned to the machine but stayed professional as she said, 'A cappuccino would be very nice, sir, please.'

'Greg, please. You're guests in my house, no need to stand on ceremony.'

He busied himself with setting the machine in motion then sat down opposite them across the marble work surface.

'Now, what can I do for you? You mentioned something about the planning application for the new house. What did you want to know?'

'That's right, Mr Whittaker,' Jo told him, again stressing the formality. 'I understand planning permission has been delayed because of concerns about endangered species and fragile habitat. And that these came to light as a result of objections to the application.'

For the briefest instant the mask slipped and dark fury flickered across the man's face. Then he regained control and was all smiles once more.

'Oh, that,' he said dismissively. 'Bunch of hairy, hippy tree-huggers kicking up a lot of fuss about a few flowers and some birds. They started being obstructive. We're not environmental vandals, inspector. We won't start any work until nesting season is over. The birdies will soon find a new place to lay their eggs. And we'll be planting more trees, of course, as part of landscaping the gardens, so they won't be short of somewhere to nest.'

'They won't be the right sort of trees though, Mr Whittaker,' Fiona Murray told him. 'And not mature enough for nest sites. Those birds have been nesting in those trees for years and because they're an increasingly endangered species, they are protected by law.

'And then there's the newts. Your planning application calls for draining a pond where they breed successfully, and again, they're a protected species, with a diminishing population.'

Whittaker banged their coffees down in front of them none too gently.

'Bloody newts! I told them I'd build another pond in the garden. The wife fancies keeping koi carp. The newts could go in there.'

'It doesn't work like that, unfortunately, Mr Whittaker,' PCSO Murray told him patiently.

Jo got out his pocket book and made a show of looking at notes. He'd found through long experience that there was nothing quite like a police officer reading from a notebook to concentrate the mind of an interviewee.

'Turning to the incident at the planning site meeting, Mr Whittaker,' Jo began. 'You said it was the environmental protesters who started the trouble. But wasn't it the case that you brought some of your workers with you to the meeting? Was that strictly necessary?'

He looked again at the open page in front of him, carefully hidden from Whittaker's view as he said, 'Six of them, in fact. Up to that point, I've been told, the protesters had simply been sitting peacefully, singing and playing music. There was no aggression, and they weren't blocking anyone's access to the site. According to council officials, it was your employees who immediately went on the offensive and tried to remove them.'

He looked up directly at Whittaker as he asked, 'Why did you take half a dozen of your men with you to a simple site meeting, Mr Whittaker?'

'We were going on somewhere to do a job,' the man blustered. 'I can't remember now where, but it made sense to go together then go on from there. We weren't expecting the site meeting to take long.'

'I see,' said Jo, again looking down at his book, then back at Whittaker. 'And yet you were in separate transport, according to my information. Your men were in a crew cab and you were in a car. Presumably your private one. So would it not be a waste of your employees' time to have them accompany you and then hang around waiting? Their time presumably costs you money. Could they not have met you on site for the job, and done something else constructive in the meantime?'

'They didn't know the way there,' Whittaker said in a rush, then visibly winced when he realised how transparent the lie was.

'And the crew cab doesn't have sat nav, nor do any of their phones?' Jo asked smoothly. 'That's unusual, these days.

'Well, setting that aside, again according to witnesses, and to the police who had to be summoned to restore order, the aggression and violence came from your employees rather than the protesters, who remained passive throughout. Your men instigated it by trying to forcibly remove peaceful protesters. Why was that thought necessary?'

'They were being provocative. And they had no right to be there.'

'Technically speaking, they had as much right to be there as your employees did, Mr Whittaker,' Jo told him, his tone neutral. 'But moving on, is that the only trouble you've encountered with the environmental protesters? Have you had any dealings with them before or since? Any one of them in particular you, or any of your employees, may have had a run-in with?'

'I don't bloody know one from another of them. They all look the bloody same to me. Dirty and hairy. They're a pain in the arse trying to block this application. No one else gives a shit about it, or they didn't until they turned up poking their noses in. The wife's got her heart set on the new house on that plot, but fuck knows if we'll get the application through now they've stirred up all this crap.'

* * *

'Is that enough of a motive for murder, would you say?' Fiona Murray asked Jo as she drove them away from Whittaker's property. 'He's certainly not happy about the big spanner the hippies have thrown in the works of his wife's dream home.'

'I'm not sure. Whatever he is, Whittaker is no fool, although he's rubbish at thinking up lies on his feet. He must realise that the objection still stands, whether or not Spike is still alive.'

'Unless killing Spike was a threat? A warning to the others that it's not wise to cross him and that they might like to rethink and withdraw their objection, perhaps?'

'I think it's too late for that, and I imagine he knows it. I suspect now that all this environmental stuff has been flagged up officially, unless he's planning on doing some serious bribery, the process can't be stopped. We're no longer talking just the local authority now, but statutory bodies like the Environment Agency too, I expect. Hopefully some of those types are beyond bribery and corruption, although you never really know these days.'

'So very possibly a threat, then, knowing a bribe would be harder to pull off? And not a very veiled one. If people, even decent incorruptible ones, think they might be the next in line for a snapped neck, they might be more inclined to turn a blind eye.'

'So far, though, don't forget, this latest development isn't out in the public domain. Now, if an investigative journalist were to get wind of the connection between our victim and the planning dispute, it would probably make a big story. But at the moment I don't know if anyone would join up the dots.

'That's the first time you've met Whittaker in person, you said. So what did you think of him?'

'I'm trying not to be prejudiced by the patronising way he called me dear but he really is the stereotypical wide boy, isn't he? He's clearly made a lot of money out of what he does. Did you see those worktops? They probably cost more than my entire kitchen. In fact, more than my house, I wouldn't mind betting. And in my admittedly limited experience of business, people don't make that sort of money by playing nice.'

'That pretty much sums up my feelings, too,' Jo told her. 'And that's yet more background checks we need to be doing. I want to know what sort of people he employs. If any of them have the skills to bump someone off with their bare hands. Or any form at all for violence. Because whether or not he believed it would cancel out the planning objection if one of them died, I didn't get the feeling that our Mr Whittaker has a benevolent forgiving side which would easily forgive anyone who got between him and something he wanted.'

* * *

The hardest part of the whole plan was always going to be to persuade Barbara to trust him enough to go along with it. Steve had known that from the moment he'd started thinking about it, which is why he hadn't mentioned it until the end of the week.

He'd spent the intervening days letting her get to know him and, most importantly, to trust him. And that was always going to be a big ask after what he knew she would have been going through living with his father.

Before he left to return north, he was going to drop her off with a friend of hers who lived well away from Southampton. Someone from her past about whom Steve's father didn't know enough to trace her there. Steve had reassured her she could continue to stay at the hotel, as his guest, in the meantime. He knew his father would have left her with virtually none of her own money.

He'd gone with her to the house so she could collect some more of her things. He'd done it carefully and by the book. He'd phoned Inspector Dutta first to tell him of their intentions and to get his assurance that at the time they were planning to be there, Steve's father would be on duty so should have no valid reason to go anywhere near his own home. Barbara did at least still have her own key.

He'd also managed to establish that his father was off duty the following day, Saturday, which fitted perfectly with his plans. Now all he had to do was to win Barbara over.

He decided to tackle the subject over dinner. She always enjoyed a glass or two of wine with her meal, so she might feel more relaxed in such a setting. He still didn't expect it to be easy, and he was right.

She listened to him in wide-eyed silence as he spoke quietly, explaining everything, as her face gradually flushed redder. Whether that was the wine or the strong emotions evoked by what Steve was outlining to her, he couldn't tell.

She spoke as soon as he had finished.

'Steve, are you mad? He'll kill you. He'll kill both of us. You know how out of control he gets when you cross him. This is going to drive him right over the edge. It's far too dangerous.

And how do you even know he'll turn up? Is he stupid enough to risk everything by showing what he's really like?

'You know how he's pulled the wool over everyone's eyes for so long. *"What a great bloke Roddy Ellis is. Such a good copper, and so unlucky to have a hysterical wife who'd do a thing like that, and on the day of their son's passing out parade as well."* That's what they all say. I've heard it often enough. Let's face it, I believed it, to begin with, when he was being so kind to me to win my trust.'

'Barbara, believe me, I know how hard it is to trust anyone after you've been with him,' Steve told her earnestly. 'I still find it hard, after all this time. But I need you to trust me on this. We are so close to getting there. To showing people what he's really like. He could go down for what he's done, and he deserves to.

'You'll be quite safe. You'll be in the car with the central locking activated. He can't get at you. You'll have two phones. With one, you can just point and press to film exactly what's going on. At the same time with the other you can dial 999, then when you get the prompt you tap 55 to show you're in danger and can't speak. That means you won't need to break your concentration for filming what's happening, and the nearest available unit will be sent.'

'But what about you? Steve, he'll do you serious harm. He could even kill you. It's far too dangerous.'

'No, he won't,' Steve told her quietly, surprising himself with his self-assurance. 'While I was in the States I had a friend of my girlfriend show me a trick or two. Bruce, he's called. He's FBI. They don't mess about, and they use some take-down and restraint techniques that wouldn't be allowed here. Bruce was a good teacher. He made me practise over and over, with him coming at me, getting more aggressive every time. And he was a big man. But I did it. I got that I could do it every time, without thinking about it. My father won't be expecting anything like that. Not from me.

'There's a pair of handcuffs in the glove box of my car. As soon as I give you the signal that it's safe to approach, I want you to get the handcuffs and come over to pass them to me, still filming all the time. He won't be able to move, I promise you. The restraint technique I was shown is excruciatingly painful if you do try to struggle against it. Believe me. Bruce put me in that position a good few times so I'd know how effective it is and would feel more confident.

'Once he's safely down and handcuffed I can phone the police as well, give them my police details and report a serious assault taking place. They'll have to respond, and promptly.

'And don't forget, the hotel has good working CCTV cameras pointing straight at the car park. As well as the film you shoot, they will show everything which happens.'

'But how do you know he'll come? And how do you know it will be tomorrow?'

'Because I was careful to tell Sergeant Jackson that I was leaving first thing on Sunday morning to go back to Manchester. And it was clear from the way he was with us that he's a mate of my father and would do anything to watch his back. So he'll have told him, for sure.

'I also told him that before I left I would be dropping you off at a place of safety, which I wouldn't disclose, and that you would only be contactable by phone.

'So he'll come, all right. The only question is what time of day he'll choose. And I have a plan so that we can control that, as well.'

Chapter Seventeen

Jo Rodriguez and Fiona Murray reported back on their visit to Greg Whittaker when the team got together at the end of the day to discuss any developments.

'I think we definitely need to dig a little deeper into Mr Whittaker, boss,' Jo told Ted, 'and certainly into the background of the types he has working for him. From the info I've had from attending officers at the site meeting, they were definitely the ones causing the trouble, and they were pretty handy types. They took some restraining. The Hippy Valley folk were simply sitting passively and singing the songs of their people.'

Sergeant Cai Thomas was frowning as Jo spoke, his eyes on the photo of Whittaker which Jo had added to the board as a person of possible interest. It was taken from his company's slick and professional-looking website.

'Sir, this is going to sound daft and it hadn't struck me before. We rather assumed Janice Burrows' description of a so-called intruder at her place was just something to show willing, and/or the direct opposite of someone she had seen, to throw us off the trail. But the person she described could well have been Greg Whittaker.

'I know him, of course. I've had occasion to speak to him a time or two about his men fly-tipping. Always very charming and promising to sort them out. But then I have no idea why he would be up at Miss Burrows letting animals out of the stock sheds, like she said.'

'Unless, of course, the animals were not his target,' Ted replied. 'You mentioned theft of farm machinery, and dealing in scrap metal. Could that have taken him out there? Does Miss Burrows have anything that might be of interest to him?'

'She does have an old tractor at the back of one of the sheds which Diego Smith keeps trying to buy off her. She's having none of it. But Whittaker doesn't usually get involved in any transactions like that himself. That's what his employees are for.'

'Does she know him for any reason? Is there a connection between them?' Ted asked. 'There's a tendency sometimes, if someone is inventing a suspect, for them to model the description on someone they've seen before. Can we at least look into that as part of the background checks on everyone?

'Come to that, on that basis, her description also fits Diego Smith himself, as you said before. Is there bad blood between the two of them? Over the tractor, for instance, if he wants it and she's not selling. Is she trying to implicate him in something, for some reason, without giving his name? Or is she trying to deflect attention towards him from something she's up to herself?'

'Maybe she has shot someone, sir, and we've just not found the body yet,' Cai Thomas put in dryly. 'I wouldn't put it past her. She's a wily fox and no mistake.'

'Where are we at with the in-depth background checks? Is there anything at all in her past to suggest we should be keeping a closer eye on her?'

'Still a work in progress, boss,' Jo told him, then seeing Ted about to say something, he went on, 'And yes, we'll make it a priority over the weekend. A bit of intensive dirt-digging on everyone.'

'Please do. I feel we're missing something obvious and it's slowing progress. Jo, I also agree, in-depth background checks on all of Whittaker's people are essential, too. On paper at least, there's a strong possible motive there. Certainly as a warning to others who might be thinking of standing in his way. Let's cross-check him against Mr Doyle to see if there's any history between the two of them in particular which we don't yet know about.

'If Whittaker had had Doyle killed, he might well have got his men to dump the body near the farms if he'd heard about the feud between the farmers and the Hippy Valley dwellers.

'We also need to go back to John Alexander and ask him about any possible direct connection between Doyle and Whittaker. I wouldn't mind betting he'll have been consulted on the drafting of the objection to the planning application. Find out, for instance, if it was signed by any one person in particular, or if it was a collective and if so, whether all the names were listed. Look for any reason why Brendan Doyle might have been singled out, of all of them, if that is our motive.

'Thank you, everyone. Jo, I'll call in at some time over the weekend, but you know where to find me if there are any new leads.'

Ted wanted to drop by the Stockport station on his way home, to see if there were any developments on the case there, although he knew Mike Hallam would have updated him if there'd been a breakthrough. He was hoping for something to wave at Sammy Sampson next time they met.

He was surprised to find another hand-written envelope left for him on his desk, writing he now knew to be that of Oliver Burdon. He scanned it quickly, groaning inwardly to read that the man wanted a meeting, which he promised would be brief, the following evening at a pub he named. Not one Ted usually drank in. He'd extended the invitation to Ted's 'pluss one' so he could at least take Trev along, then take him somewhere nice for a meal afterwards. They hadn't had much quality time together for a while. It would ease Ted's conscience, if nothing else.

Trev seemed genuinely pleased at the prospect when Ted showed him the letter once he got home and mentioned going on for a meal after the meeting with Oliver Burdon and his bride to be.

'Ted, this is lovely,' he told him, tapping the letter as he read it. 'It's clear Oliver thinks the absolute world of you, so he is obviously a man of great taste and discernment. I like him already. And don't you dare forget that it's Sunday of next weekend that we're going to the baptism of Aspen Jade. Note the we. We are both invited and we are both going to be there. The Paps will be out in force, for one thing, to get shots of Willow and Ebony together on such a glamorous occasion. Failure to turn up for that is definitely grounds for divorce, no matter how many bodies turn up on your patch.'

* * *

The one place Steve could be sure that even his father, arrogant though he was, wouldn't dare to approach him or Barbara was at the police station. Which is why he chose to make a trip there in person, with Barbara as a passenger, to let them have a contact telephone number for her, to use from the following day, when she and Steve would be leaving Southampton.

He could have phoned them, easily enough. But he wanted to manage the whole encounter with his father so that it happened on his terms and gave him the best possible chance of a positive outcome. That meant drawing him out and giving him the opportunity to follow them back to the hotel.

He spotted the car tailing him from the minute he pulled out of the hotel car park. He couldn't easily make out the driver, not without breaking his concentration, but it was a different car to the previous one.

Barbara had the visor down on the passenger side and was using the vanity mirror to see if she could make a positive identification.

She kept up a running commentary, her voice noticeably trembling with mounting anxiety.

'It's his car, I'm pretty sure. And it looks like him driving. I can't be a hundred per cent certain without turning round to look, and that would give the game away, wouldn't it?

'Steve, are you sure this is safe? What if he decides to attack us before we get back to the hotel? You know what he's like when he loses his temper.'

'One thing he isn't is stupid. And don't forget he knows the system inside out. His one hope is to deny our allegations completely and continuously. Our statements don't amount to any material proof and he knows that. He's never been in any trouble at work and even with the testimony of PCSO McCrae, the CPS might yet decide that it's too flimsy to stand up in court.

'There's always a chance they would advise against charges and he'd get away with a warning to mind his behaviour. And you and I want more than that. We want to see justice properly done.

'We don't yet know if Inspector Dutta has found anyone else to back up our allegations. Or even if he's made any effort to do so. I got the feeling, speaking to him, that he was fairly by the book, so he should have done. But there could be all sorts of reasons why no one else is willing to speak up.

'The very last thing my father can afford to do is to approach the two of us anywhere he's likely to be seen doing so. Anything like that could hang him out to dry far more effectively than any witness testimony. Now, unless he knows our hotel well, he may not realise the car park is under surveillance. It's impossible to see the cameras unless you get very close to them. I am taking a gamble, I admit that. But I'm doing it based on knowing not only my father but also how a copper's mind works.

'I know you still don't know me well, Barbara, but I have to ask you to trust me on this. Worst case scenario, I've got this wrong and he does approach us somewhere else. But you've still got the two phones. You can still film what happens and call for help.

'This is going to work, Barbara. Trust me. Please.'

* * *

Steve had kept his voice positive but he had to admit to himself that inside he was having serious doubts. He hadn't been exaggerating when he'd told Barbara that he'd reached the point of being able to put Bruce down on the floor, every time, no matter how hard and fast he had come at him. But this would be different.

This time it would be his own father. The person who had bullied, abused and terrorised him all his life. The person who had driven his mother to take her own life. Someone in the face of whose anger he had always buckled and snivelled like the coward the man had constantly accused him of being.

As he drove back from the police station towards the hotel, he checked his rear view mirror frequently, anxious not to lose the tail. He was sure his father would follow them straight to the hotel, but he wanted to know where he was at all times. He didn't want to be taken by surprise by his father doing anything unexpected and distracting. He needed to keep his focus, at all costs.

He'd had a long Zoom chat with Océane the previous evening. The fact that someone like her believed in him meant the world to Steve. Hearing her tell him that he could do what he was planning to do motivated him to want to succeed. As well as that, behind all of this as a driving force, was the thought that it might show DCI Darling and his old team that he really did deserve to have his place back amongst them. Even if it didn't happen immediately, like some sort of miracle.

He checked his mirror once more as he found a parking space, put the handbrake on and switched off the engine. He reached gently for Barbara's hand and gave it a reassuring squeeze. It was trembling in his grasp like a captive bird.

'We can do this,' he told her, filling his voice with a confidence greater than he was feeling, now that he was facing the reality of his plan. 'Remember, hit the central locking as soon as I get out, then start filming what happens, then dial 999. And don't forget the handcuffs when I give you the signal.'

He got carefully out of the car, standing tall. He heard another car door slam shut at the same moment as he closed his door quietly, immediately hearing the clunk of the central locking. He gave a reassuring smile through the window to Barbara who was holding up the phone to film, the tremor of her hand at odds with the determined look on her face.

He heard footsteps, a heavy tread, coming fast across the car park. Heard his father's rasping breath behind him. Steeled himself not to react until the last possible moment, to maintain the vital element of surprise.

'You little piece of shit! Did you seriously think you could get away with slandering me with your lies, and those of that tart? You'll never get away with it.'

It was the loud, sneering, hectoring tone he remembered so well.

Steve held his nerve to the very last second. Then he whirled on the balls of his feet and went into action.

The first part of the plan was the hardest. He had to let his father land a punch. Something which would mark but not incapacitate. And Steve had spent so much of his early life learning to avoid any blows which rained down in his direction that it had become a reflex action.

He had to keep his focus. To remain confidently calm. To get the evidence he needed, recorded on camera. Then, and only then, could he think of retaliating.

Instead of the angry, puffy, red face of his father, he saw only the black face of Bruce, heard his strong Brooklyn accent telling him to do the move again. And again. Until the timing was right.

And this time it was. Perfectly.

He felt the punch graze his cheek as he rode it with split-second timing. Felt but then ignored the brief pain, soon drowned out by the flood of adrenaline which came racing to his aid.

He saw the second punch coming as if in slow motion. Only then did he go into action. Before he had any time to react in self-preservation, Sergeant Roddy Ellis suddenly found himself face down on the tarmac of the car park, one arm held stiffly up straight, the wrist bent at such an angle that the instant he tried to move so much as a muscle, he screamed with pain.

Steve lifted his face towards the car, unable to stop the broad grin of triumph which split it wide as he nodded to Barbara to bring the handcuffs.

She jumped out, still filming with one hand, holding up the restraints. She too was now smiling. She felt no fear as she approached her former partner and passed Steve the means to immobilise him completely.

'I phoned, just like you said. And I filmed everything.'

Roddy Ellis was swearing between clenched teeth, his face still pressed down to the ground.

One or two people were starting to appear, including one of the hotel staff. Cautiously, not knowing what was going on. Not even sure of who was the goody and who the baddy in the scene they were watching.

Steve deftly applied the handcuffs, pinning his father's hands behind his back, using a knee between his shoulder blades to hold him there, knowing he would be feeling vulnerable and powerless, and hating it.

Then he took out his warrant card and flashed it round at the onlookers.

'It's all right everyone, I'm a police officer. Nothing to see here. Reinforcements have been summoned. Thank you all for your concern.'

Then, looking down at his father, he said, 'Rodney Ellis,

I'm arresting you for assault. You do not have to say anything. But, it may harm your defence if you do not mention when questioned something which you later rely on in court. Anything you do say may be given in evidence.'

Chapter Eighteen

Ted was planning on working for part of the day on Sunday, though not to make too early a start. Even without Sammy Sampson chivvying him, the lack of solid progress to date was disheartening. It would help if he could narrow down the list of potential suspects.

He went over some paperwork at the kitchen table, then took Trev up a mug of tea before leaving for Ashton station via a quick call at Stockport.

Trev yawned and stretched, his movements as feline as the cats piled around him on the bed. Only little Adam had abandoned him and followed Ted downstairs as soon as he stirred.

'I need to go and visit a few more places this afternoon, so I wondered if you fancied coming with me, for the run out?' Ted asked him, putting his tea down in reach.

'Aah, more tours of the murder scenes of Cheshire. What larks, Pip. How could I refuse?'

Ted smiled at that.

'Not murder scenes, this time. Just possibly places significant to the current case. I'm too close to it. I feel there's some connection there I'm just not seeing and you sometimes have a way of spotting things I've missed. If you're up for it?'

'Yes, love to, why not? Anything to spend some time with my husband. I really enjoyed last night, though, thank you. A lovely meal and so nice to meet Oliver and Mary first. He certainly has a big man crush on you. But Mary is going to be so good for him. Isn't she funny? I haven't laughed so much for far too long.'

Oliver's intended had turned out to be a tiny, bird-like woman who had never stopped smiling and cracking funny comments the whole time they were together, many of them self-deprecating about her size, especially in relation to the much taller Oliver.

It was to be a Register Office ceremony followed by a reception at the dining room for the homeless where Oliver volunteered and where he'd met Mary. There wouldn't be many guests as neither had any family, but there would be a handful of friends and the regular cooks there were putting on a spread for them. They were both delighted at Trev's offer to make the cake, Oliver visibly touched that Ted had remembered his fondness for white chocolate.

'Right, I need to go in to the nick first, but I'll text you when I'm on my way and I'll pick you up. It'll be after Stockport dinnertime.'

Trev laughed at that. When they'd first got together he'd teased Ted gently about their different backgrounds, highlighted by the difference in what they called the midday meal. Dinner, for Ted, lunch for Trev.

'Morning, boss,' Mike Hallam greeted Ted when he walked into the main office. There was only him and Gina Shaw in, still plodding through the mountain of paperwork any kind of fraud case automatically brought with it.

'Progress?' Ted asked him.

'Slow but steady, but good news in that I've had confirmation that we can borrow Sal Ahmed from tomorrow, but only for a couple of days. We'll whiz through the paperwork a lot faster with his knowledge to point us to the shortcuts.'

'I won't feel slighted to take a back seat on this one, boss,' Gina Shaw told him with a smile. 'I'm doing my best, but I'm the first to admit this sort of stuff is all new to me, so I'm worried I might be missing something obvious simply by not knowing what to look for.'

'Don't worry about that, Gina, I'm feeling exactly the same with the Ashton murder case. Rural crime is certainly different to what I'm used to. I'm sure there's an obvious angle there I've not yet explored, but for the life of me I can't pin down what it is.'

'Any further news on borrowing Steve, too, for the computers, boss?' Mike asked. 'That would really tie it up neatly for us.'

'I've put in a request, and it is tomorrow he's due back at work. But remember he'll need return to work interviews and all sorts before he's cleared to work anywhere, particularly here. So that remains a definite don't hold your breath.'

* * *

'So I want to go and look at this planning application site for myself. It's somewhere we know our victim went to protest and he had a run-in there with a possible suspect, plus the men who work for him, who by all accounts are a bit handy.

'I've not seen the site yet so I'm hoping doing so might make the little grey cells spring into action. It's about time they did. Of course there's always the chance that this planning application has nothing at all to do with our case, but I need to explore every angle.'

'Is this you clutching at straws?' Trev asked him.

'It is a bit,' Ted admitted. 'We've got rather too many suspects and an abundance of motives but still no prime suspect or suspects. It doesn't help that there's a delay on DNA results from the victim's body which might give us a steer towards who killed him. So let's see what an outsider to the case might spot which I haven't.'

He parked the car well away from the site. They strolled down a country lane with not a house in sight, only meadows and woodland. When they came to the plot which was the subject of the disputed planning application, they stopped at a modern metal gate and looked over it.

'Well, initial thoughts would be why on earth would anyone imagine for a minute they'd be granted planning permission to build here? It must be green belt, surely? Or greenfield, at the very least. There's no development anywhere near, and the person who owns it must surely realise that. Unless they've found some old evidence of building here, but looking at the maturity of the trees and other plants, that doesn't seem likely.

'If they've even applied, does that suggest they're confident they could pull strings? Or grease palms? Or maybe something more sinister than that? Is that what this is about? Someone's been killed as a threat over a planning application?'

'It's possible,' Ted said evasively.

'If someone even thought for a moment that they could get it through, they must wield a lot of power, or think they do. I seriously doubt if the Mafia could pull off getting planning permission on a site like this. It must be protected, surely?

'How am I doing so far, Miss Marple?'

'Pretty spot on. You're confirming what's been going through my mind. More so since I've seen the site. To even think of getting permission here seems to me to smack of some pretty widespread corruption. Your second opinion at least convinces me that time spent digging into the application won't be entirely wasted.

'Right, for your next mission, how's your woo detector? This isn't really for the case, it's just something that's intriguing me.'

'Woo detector?' Trev queried.

Ted laughed at his puzzled expression.

'I don't want to say too much. I want to take you to a place so you can tell me what you sense there. What feelings you get, if any.'

He drove out to the track where Sergeant Thomas had parked when he and Ted had walked up to The Stones. If nothing else, it was a pleasant walk of a Sunday afternoon.

When they reached the top of the hill and walked down into the shallow depression, Ted stayed silent, watching his partner and waiting for a reaction.

Trev looked all around him, turning a slow circle so he saw all of his surroundings. Then he turned to face Ted, his expression still showing bewilderment.

'I must be missing something because I don't get it. It looks as if someone had a load of stone gateposts nicked and abandoned. Or they lugged them up here to use but the effort killed them. Either way I can't see how it's Serious Crime, which is what you'd be investigating. So what am I not seeing?'

'Whatever it is, I'm not seeing it either. That was my immediate thought when I saw this supposedly sacred site. You're not feeling any mystic vibes from them or anything like that?'

'Well, there's a first time for everything but I never thought I'd hear you, of all people, asking about vibes, mystic or otherwise. Perhaps I should have brought dowsing rods.'

'You know how to dowse?' Ted asked him in surprise.

Trev laughed.

'Not remotely. But purely to humour you, I'll have a wander about and see if I get the feels from the place, or whatever it is I should experience.'

He walked all round The Stones, laying a hand on each in turn, sometimes closing his eyes. Then he walked back to where Ted was waiting, shaking his head as he approached.

'Well, whatever woo there is to this place is evading me. All I see is abandoned gateposts. Admittedly they don't yet have holes for the hinges, but that's exactly what they look like to me.'

'Me too,' Ted admitted. 'Yet this place seems to hold special significance for our friends from Hippy Valley. I wonder if there's anything to that? I'm sure they'd be much more sensitive to anything like that than I ever would, with the best will in the world.

'So what other reason could bring them up here for significant occasions? Or am I just drowning under so many red herrings that I'm seeing them everywhere, including where they don't exist?'

* * *

'So on the face of it, with so many people having a possible motive for killing Brendan Doyle, can we spend some time on establishing alibis for anyone and everyone who's come to our attention so far?' Ted summed up at the start of Monday morning briefing at Ashton.

He saw Jo Rodriguez's expression and said, 'I know, it's a lot of work, a lot of hours off the budget. But unless someone is going to obligingly come in and confess, we really need to start narrowing down and hopefully eliminating the suspects. And the best way to do that is by looking for alibis.'

'Sir, I don't want to start off by sounding negative here,' Sergeant Cai Thomas began, then hesitated until Ted nodded for him to continue.

'I agree that any one of the farmers in the area could have a serious grudge against Spike for his attitude towards farming and animal welfare, and his actions. I still think all of them would be more inclined to shoot him in the heat of the moment than get up close and personal to kill him the way it was done. But getting an alibi out of them is like pulling teeth. Always.

'I can guarantee that the answer from all of them is always going to be "I was out round the stock", and it could well be true. But they'll have no way of proving it. Unless they were in a tractor with a GPS Dome, possibly. No CCTV anywhere and probably only a dog or two for company.

'Plus, and again, I'm trying not to sound too negative, sir, but we haven't got a definite date and time of death. All days are pretty much the same, in farming.'

'We have a rough idea in terms of the date, so let's at least try that and hope there was something significant happening which will jog a few memories.

'We also definitely need to talk to the little girl Ruby's mother, Ali. We all know what a powerful motive money is, so we need to know what she knew, or might have guessed, about the terms of the will. It would be useful to know, too, if Ruby was Mr Doyle's daughter, or if he might have believed she was.

'And then there's this whole planning issue with Greg Whittaker ...'

He was interrupted by his mobile phone, on vibrate, going off in his pocket. He pulled it out to glance at the screen. Assistant Chief Constable (Crime) Russell Evans calling him. It gave Ted an uneasy premonition.

'I have to take this. Jo, can you carry on, please. Alibis. For everyone we've mentioned, plus their other halves and anyone else close to them.'

He picked up the call as he strode out of the incident room heading for Jo's office.

'Russell Evans, Ted. Have you seen the local scandal sheet this morning?'

The premonition grew stronger as Ted reached the office and pulled up the relevant page, using Jo's computer.

'Not yet, sir, I'm just doing that now.'

'Well, be warned, the Chief is doing his nut, to put it very mildly. He was accosted by this bloke Greg Whittaker at his sports club over the weekend and he doesn't take very kindly to anything like that, as you know. And it was your name which came up in conversation, as SIO.'

Ted frowned as he looked at the screen. He'd found the article, by-lined by their local reporter, Penny Hunter, about the trouble over Whittaker's planning application. It made the link with the incident between the Hippy Valley protesters and Whittaker's own men having been at the site meeting. A quick scan of the article confirmed Ted's immediate thought, which he put into words.

'Sir, I can't think how Whittaker would have known that I'm SIO on this case. It was Jo Rodriguez who went to interview him about it. We've not gone public with anything much about Mr Doyle, and certainly nothing yet about any possible link between the death and the planning issue.'

'When you read the whole thing in detail, insubstantial though it is, you'll find the phrase "a source close to the inquiry". You've got a leak, Ted, it seems, which is something else the Chief isn't happy about. Someone on the team, or close to it, has loose lips. That needs sorting, and sharpish.

'And it goes without saying that the case needs winding up, speedily, without further delay and any other phrase to convey he wants it done yesterday. It's taking you longer than usual. Out the mole and get us a nice result sharpish, so the Chief can have a bit of peace in his own club. Yes?'

'Yes, sir.'

Ted was angry. Not about the rebuke. He was SIO so his head was always first on the block. It went with the role. But he was furious at the thought that someone within the expanded team had been talking to the press.

Now he'd have to waste valuable time trying to find out who had the loose lips instead of getting on with the job. But first he needed to make sure his temper was under control before he went back to the incident room.

He put his phone back in his pocket, closed the press page on Jo's computer, then whirled fast on the balls of his feet and threw a lethal punch at the nearest wall.

Split-second timing from years of training stopped the blow scant centimetres from the wall. Ted held his hand still for a moment longer, breathing deeply, until he felt suitably composed to go and talk to the team. Then he left the office and strode back to the incident room to ask some searching questions.

* * *

'So, Steve ... are you comfortable with Steve?'

Steve nodded agreement and the man continued.

'As you know, after any long period of sick leave, we need to have a talk before you start back to work, one of the primary objectives being to make sure you return to a suitable role.

'I know we've had a note from your own GP pronouncing you fit for work in their opinion, and that since that date you've had a holiday in the States. That sounds good. How was it?'

'Excellent!' Steve beamed at him, more at ease than he'd expected to feel. 'It was a holiday, but I also learned a lot.'

'Good, that sounds very positive. So, shall we start by tackling the elephant in the room? Because we need to touch on it at some point, I think. Would you like to tell me about it, in your own words?'

Steve had been dreading this return to work interview because so much was riding on it, as far as he was concerned. It was something else he'd talked about at length with Océane. He knew the person he would be speaking to would be on the look-out for answers which were too off pat and sounded rehearsed. Océane had encouraged him to be frank and open.

'I made an attempt on my own life because I'd let things get on top of me, and a current case reminded me painfully of my own childhood. My mother and I were subjected to years of abuse from my father, a serving police officer, who everyone else thought was wonderful.

'My mother did kill herself and for a long time I blamed myself for not protecting her. I've realised since that as a boy, there was nothing I could have done.

'But I'm older now, and stronger. Physically and emotionally. And on Saturday, I arrested my father for assaulting me.'

He touched the slight graze, still visible on his cheekbone, as he spoke.

'He's now suspended from duty pending investigation and possible charges.'

The man must have heard all sorts of details in the many

such interviews he had carried out. He usually managed to retain a professionally bland expression, but on this occasion, he couldn't prevent the sudden arching of his eyebrows. He looked down at his pad to scribble notes as Steve continued speaking.

'All I want to do now is to get back to work and hopefully, at some time in the future, to be allowed back to my old role on the Serious Crime Team at Stockport.'

Chapter Nineteen

Jo Rodriguez knew the boss well enough to read the change in his body language the minute he came back in through the door. Although controlled, his anger was palpable. Whoever was in for a massive bollocking, Jo fervently hoped it wasn't him, although he couldn't offhand think of anything he'd done or not done to warrant one.

He noticed the other members of Ted's own team sitting up straighter and knew they too would be wondering who was in the firing line.

Ted went to stand at the front of the room with Jo where he could see everyone present as he spoke. His voice was no louder than usual, but the intonation grabbed everyone's attention.

'Right everyone, listen up,' he began. 'I've just had the ACC on the phone. Apparently the local press have somehow got hold of the possible connection between our victim and the Whittaker planning application.'

There was a low murmur from those listening. No guilty expression he could spot so far.

'That's bad enough, but the article is citing "a source close to the enquiry" for what they've quoted.'

He looked slowly round at all those present, a flash of green to the normally warm hazel-eyed gaze. One or two of the officers shifted slightly in their seats, though whether or not that indicated guilt, or discomfort at his evident anger was hard to tell.

'I shouldn't have to say it, but I will. Nobody speaks to anyone connected to the press or media, at all. Not about this case, nor any other. Any queries you might encounter, you refer to me or to the Press Office.

'You don't discuss this or any other case at all outside the station, not between yourselves in the pub, not even with your nearest and dearest at home.'

Even as he said it, he felt a stab of hypocrisy at the thought that he'd done exactly that the day before. But he knew Trev would never say anything. Someone had done, though. He made a mental note to try to have a word with the reporter, Penny Hunter. She would never reveal her sources, but he could perhaps try to smooth things over and remind her that the official channel was through the Press Office. Always.

It was strange that she hadn't so much as tried to contact him about it, though. He never told her anything, but she had always phoned him first, for form's sake. He'd try inviting her for a drink to try to smooth things over.

'Another thing, Jo, before I forget. As DC Vine previously reminded us, we're in danger of gender stereotyping on this one, focusing too much on possible male suspects. It's theoretically possible for a woman to have inflicted the fatal injury, if she'd had training, or practice. Or even got lucky. So let's not forget to look into any women connected to the case.

'Hasn't Tom Taylor spoken about how upset his children are when their pet lambs and puppies have been targeted? That might be enough of a motive for their mother to take drastic action, possibly. So full background checks, alibis and so on for everyone. Wives, girlfriends, anyone we know of.'

'Sir, should that include Mrs Whittaker?' PCSO Murray asked. 'It was only a feeling, but I did sense, from our visit to see her husband, that she was very much the driving force behind this proposed new build.'

'Good point, thank you. And let's not forget the woman who reported finding the body in the first place. DC Vine, can you follow up with her, please? Go on the excuse of checking her initial statement, seeing if she's remembered anything since. It wouldn't be the first time a killer has reported finding the body of their own victim, purely for the attention, and we're going to look like complete idiots if we haven't at least explored that possibility.

'And Jo, can you please get someone chasing up the DNA results from the PM?' Ted saw Jo open his mouth and cut across him, 'Yes, again. Please. It's slowing us down and costing us time we don't have. It's taking much longer than usual, so let's at least check that it's not simply a case of someone forgetting to forward results they've been sitting on for days.

'Right, thank you, everyone, let's crack on. And remember, no word about the case leaves this room. I don't want to have to mention this again.'

He took Jo to one side as the others were leaving the room.

'Jo, you and I need a get-together at the end of the day with Sergeant Thomas, DS Ramsay and Rob O'Connell. I'm not one for encouraging officers to tell tales but we need to jump on this leak, right away. If anyone knows or has a suspicion who it might be, one of those three should.'

* * *

Jo decided he'd better be the one to make the return visit to Greg Whittaker, this time requesting to meet his wife at the same time. He chose Jezza Vine to go with him. She was astute. If anyone could spot who was wearing the trousers in the marriage, and especially who was behind the planning application, or anything else of use to them, she would do.

There was much less of a smiling welcome this time. Whittaker was stiff-faced and formal as he showed them both into the kitchen and introduced them to his wife, Lynda. Her face seemed to be set in sucking lemon mode, and there was no offer of coffee this time, from either of them. The officers weren't even invited to take a seat.

'All this nonsense about some link between our planning application and some hippy getting himself killed is just ridiculous. How dare anyone suggest such a thing!'

Jo noticed that it was the wife who went on the offensive to start the conversation, before her husband chimed in with, 'I've already spoken to your chief constable about it, and I'll be speaking to my lawyers too. You lot had no business releasing my details to the press. None at all. It was slander.'

'Libel, if it was in writing,' Jezza said helpfully, smiling sweetly at them both. 'And none of that information came from an official police source, Mr Whittaker.'

'But now that the details are in the public domain, can I ask you both if the name of the deceased man, Brendan Doyle, means anything to either of you? He was, of course, one of the signatories on the objection to your planning application, which you will have seen.'

There was no mistaking the look of disgust on Mrs Whittaker's face as she replied to Jo's question.

'He's definitely not the sort of person we would have anything to do with. Either of us. Not from what we've heard about him.'

Her husband was nodding in agreement.

'When that lot turned up at the site meeting, I didn't even know which one was him.'

Jezza pounced, before Jo had chance to speak.

'But you know he was there?'

Mrs Whittaker scowled. Mr Whittaker blustered.

'Well, I assumed one of them was him, since he was one of them who signed the objection. But I didn't know which one.'

'Out of interest, Mr Whittaker,' Jo began again, thinking of what the boss had told them earlier about the disputed site, 'on the face of it your application would seem to be rather optimistic. There's no other residential development close by, I understand, so how confident are you that you will ever get permission to build there?'

'My people know what they're doing,' Whittaker told him dismissively. 'They surveyed the land very carefully before I bought it and they found evidence that there's been farm buildings there in the recent past, so the planning authorities have to consider the application.'

'Agricultural buildings aren't necessarily a green light for residential development, though,' Jezza told him. She'd been doing her homework on the whole planning issue before they visited the Whittakers.

'We want to relocate there,' Mrs Whittaker told them, as if that alone were sufficient reason to grant permission. Then her nose wrinkled in distaste as she said, 'It's getting very built-up round here.'

Jezza, with an upbringing and an eye for such things, estimated the footprint of their current property at around two acres. Nearby houses were barely visible, but clearly the woman had set her heart on something else. The question was what lengths the two of them would go to in order to make her wish become reality.

* * *

'Well, what did you make of those two?' Jo asked her as Jezza drove them away from the Whittaker's house. 'Could you see either of them being behind a murder?'

'She certainly wouldn't soil her hands with doing it herself. Did you see those nails? Must have cost a fortune, so even though they clearly have money to splash about, she wouldn't want to ruin them with anything sordid or manual in any way. But I could definitely see either one of them issuing an order for someone to be got rid of if they were standing between them and what they wanted. And Mrs W certainly seems to have set her heart on the move.

'Jo, have we time to swing by the site ourselves quickly, before we go to Hippy Valley to ask about the will? Nothing scientific but I just fancy a quick shufti in case something occurs to me, while we're not all that far away.'

* * *

'You should have given me time to get into costume for mingling with hippies,' Jezza told Jo as she parked the car near to the entrance to Hippy Valley and they got out to walk down there.

They'd had a look at the site of the disputed planning application, but other than unknowingly echoing Trev's first thoughts, Jezza hadn't been able to add much. Perhaps she might be able to pick up on something new from the Valley dwellers.

Her formidable acting talents had come in useful on several enquiries when she'd needed to blend in and look nothing like a police officer. She didn't most of the time, except on the rare occasions when she and others from the team were asked to dig out and don uniforms to help out in the front line.

'You're our token female, Jezza,' Jo told her with a teasing wink. 'We need a woman to speak to the seemingly prickly Ali, mother of the heiress-child, in her native tongue.'

'How do you fancy a nice bracing walk back to the nick, Jo? Just the thing in your stylish town shoes. I didn't realise winkle pickers were still a thing.'

Jo laughed.

'Now, if I could only master saying "DC Vine" in that tone the boss uses ...'

Jezza grinned at him then said, 'I spy a man in a Homburg hat sitting by a campfire and my finely-tuned detective senses tell me it must be John Alexander, Bachelor of Laws.'

They walked closer to the man, both holding up their ID, as Jo said, 'Mr Alexander? Detective Inspector Rodriguez,

Detective Constable Vine. Thank you for providing a copy of Mr Doyle's will. I wonder if we might ask you a few more questions about it?'

'Would you like some coffee? I've just made it.'

John Alexander saw Jo's expression and laughed.

'Don't worry, inspector, I have clean mugs, and it is only coffee. No prohibited substances. Please, pull up a log and sit down.'

'The will, of course, names the little girl, Ruby Howard, as the sole benefactor ...' Jo began.

'I know, I drew it up,' Alexander said drily, pouring coffee into mugs and handing one each to the two officers.

'Yes, sorry. Is Ruby's mother's name Howard, or is it that of her father? And do you know who her father is?'

The team had already established that the man Bruno, Ruby's mother's latest partner, was called Williams.

'I have no idea. It's not remotely relevant to me, and it doesn't affect the will in any way.'

'Who knew about the contents of the will, before Mr Doyle died?' Jezza asked him.

'Nobody, from me. I can't say who Spike might have told. Possibly Ali. They were friends.'

'Friends, or something a bit more? Could Ruby be his daughter, perhaps?' Jo asked him.

The solicitor looked from Jo to Jezza and back again.

'I noticed the two of you laughing and joking together as you came in through the gate. Looking like friends, sharing a laugh. So are you sleeping together?'

'Point taken,' Jo conceded. 'I'm just trying to build up a picture to help with our investigation into Mr Doyle's death. And while we're here, we'd also like to speak to Ruby's mother, if she's at home.'

'I'd better come with you, when we've finished our coffee, in that case.'

'There's really no need, Mr Alexander. It's just a chat, not a formal interview.'

The man gave him a knowing look.

'No, I'd better come with you for your own protection. Ali doesn't like the police. Not at all. She is at home. She's cooking and baking. Which might mean pans full of hot liquid to hand. It would be altogether safer if I come with you.'

'Visitors, Ali,' John Alexander called out as they neared the entrance to the small house, its door standing wide open, smoke rising from the chimney.

The little girl, Ruby, was sitting in the minuscule porch, making an intricate design on the floor from twigs, leaves, pebbles, the odd feather.

'That's amazing,' Jezza said, with genuine admiration. 'Did you make it?'

With no trace of shyness, the little girl nodded her head and said, 'It's my 'dala. I made it myself. For Gracie.'

'It's beautiful. It's the best mandala I've ever seen. Well done you!'

John Alexander was already inside the house, introducing Jo to the woman. Jezza joined them just in time to hear Ali spit, 'What are you doing bringing pigs into my house, John? Get them out of here!'

'Come on, Ali, be reasonable. They just want to ask you a couple of questions then they'll be on their way. I'll personally see them off the premises.'

The woman was kneading bread on an old stripped-down pine table in the middle of the kitchen. The ferocity with which she slammed the dough onto the surface, pulled it apart with the heels of her hands, folded and punched it before starting again increased visibly in intensity at the presence of those she perceived to be the enemy in her living space.

Jo threw Jezza a beseeching *"you try, she might relate better to another woman"* look, realising he would almost certainly be wasting his time even trying.

'Ali, I'm Jezza. DC Vine. I really do only need to ask you a couple of questions and then we'll get out of your way.'

The woman slammed the bread even harder and sneered, 'Spare me the clichés. I don't like pigs, of either gender.'

Jezza knew better than to even try to persuade her otherwise. Instead she said, 'Yeah, whatever. But my boss is a pain in the arse and he's going to expect me to go back with something more than "I don't talk to pigs". So gimme a break, eh? I know you know the contents of the will now. Mr Alexander has already confirmed that. All I need to know is did you know before, and if so, how long ago?'

The woman paused briefly in bashing the bread to study Jezza with clinical detachment.

'So posh middle-class rich bitch assumes that the idea of a bit of money is enough motive for me to kill Spike. Well, let me tell you something you'll find hard to believe, no doubt. I fucking hate money. It's behind all that's wrong with the world today and it does so much damage. I don't want it for me and I certainly don't want it for Ruby. Not now, or in the future. I've already talked to John and there's no way to break the will. Ruby will inherit when she comes of age, so it will be up to me to persuade her to give the lot away, as soon as she's old enough to.

'Save the Children, save the whales, save the polar bears. I don't care what she does with it, but I don't want her to have it, and I hope in time she'll decide for herself she doesn't want it, either.

'Did I know about it? No, I bloody didn't. But I'll tell you this, posh lady pig. If I had known, before he'd talked to John to get it drawn up, I'd have gladly killed him myself, to stop him doing it. So make of that what you will, and now get out of my house.'

As they strode back up the track to where they'd left the vehicle, Jo turned to Jezza.

'Well done, Jezza. Well done for keeping your cool in the face of all that and getting anything at all out of her.'

'What did you make of what she told us?' Jezza asked him. 'Personally, I thought it was sincere. I believed what she said. It's refreshing, in a way, to find someone who doesn't appear to be motivated by money. What about you? What did you think?'

Jo chuckled.

'Looking at the way she was strangling the life out of that dough, especially when we walked in, I wouldn't have any difficulty at all believing she'd killed a man with her bare hands. But I didn't fancy our chances of asking her about an alibi for the likely day that Mr Doyle died.'

Chapter Twenty

'So both Tom Taylor's and Diego Smith's wives would seem to have watertight alibis for around the time of Mr Doyle's death, as long as the approximate date we're working on isn't too far off the mark. Mrs Smith works as a classroom assistant in a local school, and outside those hours she drops her own children off at school then picks them up again afterwards.'

Jo Rodriguez was summing up at the end of the day, based on the information which had been fed back to him when Jezza dropped him off at Ashton, before she went off to talk to the woman who had reported finding the body.

'It's still a possibility for her to have been involved, if he was killed sometime outside those hours, but that would have involved getting Diego to see to the kids if his wife was off somewhere killing someone. He was asked about that - not the killing suggestion, of course - and he couldn't recall any time recently when childcare had been an issue. There are no family members close to for handy babysitting emergencies, and they're too young to have been left alone, so he would surely have noticed and remarked if that had happened.'

Sergeant Cai Thomas made to speak then, getting the nod from Jo, he went on, 'Sorry, again, Jo, I always seem to be contradicting everyone or throwing cold water on suggestions. But if the kids were in the house and Diego was off round the farm somewhere, or even with his head stuck down under a tractor bonnet, he probably wouldn't have noticed them being left alone. Unless they'd managed to burn the house down, or something like that.'

'Fair enough,' Jo acknowledged, 'but as a father of six, I know that if I'd abandoned mine for even five minutes when I wasn't supposed to, I would have been reported to the mother of my children immediately on her return by my kids, the faithless brats.

'Maggie Taylor's alibi for the day we think we're talking about is a lot tighter. She had to take the twins to the Royal Manchester. They both have some sort of condition which affects their hearing and therefore impacts on their speech. It's a rare one, so they get the VIP treatment there and are well known. So again, as long as the date isn't too far off, she probably ceases to be a person of interest at this stage.'

'It's good to be able to rule some of them out, at least,' Ted told him. 'I've said before that one of our main problems is too many possible suspects.'

'Boss, there's something Jezza mentioned when she was driving me back to the nick after we met Ali. It might well be worth looking into.'

Jo gave a brief summary of their conversation with the woman and her seemingly genuine violent objection to the will which left her daughter an heiress.

'Now, we don't know whether Ruby was Doyle's daughter or not, but we were told he and Ali were on good terms. She told us she didn't know about the terms of the will before he died and we were both inclined to believe her. She actually said she would have killed him to stop him making the will, if she had known, and she sounded like she meant it.

'But here's the thing Jezza picked up on. I think, boss, that both you and Sergeant Thomas said it was the full complement of people who currently live in Hippy Valley who were up at the supposedly mystical stones to say their goodbyes to Spike. But Ali wasn't there. Why not?'

PCSO Murray put forward a suggestion.

'It could be as simple as Ali not wanting to take little Ruby there to a solemn and possibly sad occasion, and having no one to leave her with, of course.'

'That's true enough,' Ted conceded, 'but there's something about that place which is niggling at me. What is it about it that draws them there? I know you can't really tell by the naked eye but those stones look modern to me, somehow. So why there? They do indeed seem to treat it as some sort of mystic site, but for what reason?

'Jo, I know, it will be yet more hours clocked up with possibly no answer so they might be wasted, but can you at least get someone to check on the history of the place. Do we know an archaeologist or a historian or some such person who might be able to tell us definitively if it is a significant site? Another long shot, but it might be worth exploring. And do we know who owns the land up there? Sergeant Thomas?'

'D'you know, sir, now you ask, I don't know for sure. I'll make it a priority to find out.'

'I feel sorry for that little girl, Ruby,' Maurice put in, sounding glum. 'Is she there all the time on her own, with just a mam who seems to be teaching her to hate the police? All of them. Are there no other kiddies up there for company for her? Poor lass doesn't even have a puppy or a kitten to play with.'

Cai Thomas shook his head.

'No other children that I know of at the moment, although, like the rest of the population, they come and go. Maybe she'll get to meet some if she goes to school. But they're such a closed lot up there her mam might decide to home school her.'

'Who's Gracie, sarge?' Maurice asked him. 'The bairn showed me a colouring she'd done. A good one, too. She said it was for Gracie. Is she an imaginary friend? Wouldn't be unusual for a kiddy on her own all the time to invent someone.'

'She mentioned Gracie to Jezza, now you come to mention it. She'd made a mandala and said it was for her,' Jo told him.

'The name Gracie means nothing to me,' Cai Thomas replied. 'And I go up there a lot. But I'm always in uniform, and you'll have discovered Ali is bringing up that little girl to hate all police officers on sight. Ruby will try to talk to me, and I have heard her mention a Gracie, but Ali stops her, every time. I've tried with her but I get nowhere so I don't force the issue. I assumed Gracie was an imaginary friend, too.'

'What if something happens to that little lass one day and she needs help? Who would she go to if her mother keeps telling her all the time we're the enemy?' Maurice grumbled. 'There are some bad coppers, of course, but most of us are decent enough.'

'It seems likely that Gracie might simply be someone the little girl's made up. It might not be another child, of course. It could be an adult we haven't yet encountered. But can we at least look into it, please? In case it's a person of interest we don't yet know about,' Ted told them.

He wasn't about to admit to anyone that growing up as an only child, with no mother present and only his disabled father with a drink problem, doing his best for his son, he'd had an imaginary friend. Andrew. He hadn't thought about him for years and now was not the time to take a walk down that particular Memory Lane.

Once they'd caught up with everything - still, worryingly, nothing which took them forward very far - Jo and Ted adjourned to Jo's office with the three sergeants to discuss who might be behind the leaks to the press.

Ted had sent Trev a quick text to warn him he might be later than planned, as once he left Ashton, he'd arranged to meet the local journalist, Penny Hunter, in The Grapes in Stockport. He wasn't optimistic of getting anywhere, but he needed to be seen to be doing something to placate the top brass.

'So, this is entirely between all of us. Anything we say stays in this room. That should go without saying.

'We're probably all going to say we can't imagine anyone from our own team doing anything like talking out of turn to the press. But someone has, clearly, and all I'm asking for is, if any of you have any strong suspicions about anyone, please share them with me, in confidence, and then I can arrange for a watch to be put on any suspect. Because the job's hard enough, without the press being one step ahead of us all the time.'

Nobody spoke for a moment. They all looked uncomfortable, not liking the idea that someone they worked with, perhaps closely, was behind the leak.

Eventually, DS Pete Ramsay, one of the Ashton team, said reluctantly, 'Sir, you know well enough that when we first met, I was in the pub with DCs Alan Burgess and Milo Sharp. We weren't actually talking shop like I told you. We were skiving, to be honest with you. I just said we were to cover our backs.

'Anyway, I have to say that Al Burgess is a bit inclined to run his mouth off in public. I've had a word with him a couple of times, so he's more careful when he's with me. But goodness knows what he's like out on his own, especially if he's had a pint or two. Maybe the press got wind of him being loose-lipped and got in touch with him? Should I have a word with him, sir?'

'I'll give another general reminder tomorrow morning so we're not at this stage singling anyone out, I think. I'm off to talk to Penny Hunter shortly. She won't tell me her source, for sure, but there's always a chance I might pick up on something.'

As they all stood up to leave, Ted called Jo back for another quick word.

'Just a heads-up for the weekend, Jo. Trev and I are invited to a posh Catholic christening on Sunday. He's a godfather.'

Jo's eyebrows rose when Ted mentioned the church in question and the venue for the reception afterwards, then went on, 'So I am under fair warning of slow and painful death if I'm a no-show. Trev knows that there may be a valid reason to stop me attending but I'm counting on you to hold the fort if you can.'

'Baptism, boss,' Jo told him. 'I know you're not into religious terminology, but us left-footers tend to say baptism rather than christening. And I'll do my very best, of course. It sounds as if it's going to be some impressive occasion. I hope you get to enjoy it, and I'd far sooner cover for you than have to get out my black tie to attend your funeral. Not to mention having to arrest your Trev.'

* * *

Ted stood up as Penny Hunter walked into the bar of The Grapes, pulling out a chair for her at the quiet table he'd chosen in the corner. It wasn't empty show. His dad had brought him up to be polite to everyone and the habit had lingered.

'Thanks for coming, Penny. Let me get you a drink. What would you like? And do you want something with it? Crisps, nuts?'

He went off to get her order. He wouldn't bother with another Gunner for himself. He wasn't intending to linger any longer than he had to. Although she was a good journalist, Penny was not a natural at small talk so it could be hard going making conversation with her, especially when his own stock reply to anything she asked was, 'Talk to the Press Office.'

Somehow he needed to find the key to communicating with her. He smiled to himself, remembering how Steve had suddenly opened up and lost his shyness one time when he'd started on the subject of the Star Wars films. He could do with finding out what Penny's interests were outside work so they might have something neutral to talk about.

He put her drink and packet of nuts down in front of her and resumed his seat, putting on his most disarming smile. Time for a serious charm offensive.

'Penny, I wanted to meet up with you in person, rather than speak on the phone because I owe you an apology.'

Penny Hunter's face was a picture at his words. Whatever

she'd expected the discussion to be about, she was clearly not anticipating that.

'You have a job to do and I don't make it any easier, always appearing to fob you off to the Press Office. I'm often busy when you catch me, but that's no excuse. How about if I promise that when you call, if I possibly can, I will personally speak to the Press Office and get them to call you with the information you need. Would that help?'

Even as he said it, he was wondering how it would even be possible, but he needed to do some damage limitation. If the Chief Constable was as annoyed as the ACC had suggested, Ted could expect an invitation to a squash game which would leave him suitably humiliated in defeat, to make a point of the Chief's displeasure.

'That would be very kind, chief inspector. I understand you're a busy man, but I'm only trying to do my job.'

'I appreciate that, of course.'

He decided to take a gamble on a hunch, as he went on, 'The trouble is, if you rely on people like Alan Burgess for your information, it might not be all that accurate.'

He was rewarded by a sudden flush which appeared up her neck as she reached for the packet of nuts and suddenly became intensely concentrated on picking the right one.

Bingo! He'd hit home with his first shot.

'You have no way of knowing just how "close to the inquiry" your informant might be, and in that particular case, the answer is not very. I know you're a journalist of integrity, Penny, so I'm as anxious as you are that you get accurate information for your piece, rather than relying on third-hand gossip.

'So that's my promise to you. If it's remotely possible, I'll always try, in future, to get you the most reliable source, if you phone me first.'

He finished his drink then said, 'And now, if you'll excuse me, I'd better get home to my partner, not to mention a houseful of lying cats who will no doubt pretend they haven't been fed.'

The reporter's face lit up instantly at his words. Her eyes wide, her expression beaming.

'You have cats? I love cats! I have a Burmese called Jasmine. Would you like to see a photo of her? What do you have?'

* * *

'I honestly thought I was never going to get away,' Ted told a laughing Trev when he finally got home. 'I'm sure I must have seen every photo of Jasmine from the day she was born.'

'But that's so sweet! I love the idea of the two of you bonding over pussy cats. Did you show her photos of all our boys and girls?'

'In the end I had to. I didn't want to, I wanted to get back home, but she was very insistent. And, bless her, she didn't want to tell me who her contact was, and in fact she didn't. But her body language gave the game away, so at least I know whose backside I need to kick tomorrow. No surprises there. It was who we thought it would be, so he's in the firing line first thing.'

'I love it when you get all masterful,' Trev told him teasingly, putting the last touches to their evening meal. 'So which of our pussies did she like best?'

'Well, Adam, clearly. No contest,' Ted smiled, cuddling the little purry cat with the wonky ears and the mismatched eyes. 'But then I admit I might just have pushed her in that direction.'

Trev was dishing up now, bringing laden plates to the table and pushing inquisitive felines out of the way. He looked directly at Ted as he asked, 'And you genuinely didn't, not even for a minute, think it might have been me who spoke to the press?'

'No, of course not!' Ted told him with complete sincerity. 'I know you well enough for it never to have crossed my mind. I probably shouldn't have taken you to the sites, I suppose, technically speaking. But I would never for a moment suspect you of doing anything like that.'

'So you didn't think it was my fiendish way of financing a new bike myself, rather than waiting for you to get your cheque book out? Flogging info to the gutter press?' Trev asked him, grinning.

'Point taken. I haven't studied the books yet and I'm sorry. Go ahead and order it, though, if it's what you want. I'm sure we won't starve as a result.

'But speaking of the sites we visited, there's still something about those famous stones which is bothering me, and I can't for the life of me figure out what it is.'

Chapter Twenty-one

The door to the Serious Crime main office at the Stockport station opened and a familiar figure walked in, photo ID round his neck.

'Did someone here order a takeaway computer analyst?' DC Steve Ellis asked, his face beaming with evident delight.

Virgil looked up from his desk, saw who it was and jumped to his feet, his smile even wider than Steve's.

'Steve, mate, are we glad to see you.'

He crossed the room, his hand outstretched to shake Steve's, then at the last minute he said, 'Oh, bugger that, come here you,' and threw his arms round him to crush him in a hug.

The Steve Ellis of old would have blushed bright red to his roots and tried to wriggle out of his grasp. The new Steve looked pleased and hugged him back almost as hard.

Mike Hallam had also risen to his feet and came over to give Steve a pat of welcome on the back before saying, 'This is Gina Shaw. I can't remember if you've met?'

'And I'm particularly pleased to see you, Steve. I've heard so much about your skills with a computer. I've had no real problems with the victims' one. They're an elderly couple, who don't seem to know about keeping things safe and confidential. Our suspect is something else entirely. Stuff is hidden and protected everywhere and it looks like a lot of useful stuff has been deleted.'

Steve grinned at her and rubbed his hands in evident delight.

'Ah, but if you know a few tricks, sometimes even deleted files are there for the finding. I can't make any promises, but let me see what I can do for you.'

'I'm doing a preliminary interview with our prime suspect tomorrow afternoon,' Virgil told him. 'If you could get me anything at all to confront him with, and preferably something which would rattle him, I would be forever in your debt. Oh, and if you could write it up in terms even someone like me can understand, that would be even better.'

Steve could see where the computers had been placed awaiting examination and made his way over to them. He'd just taken a seat to make a start when the door opened again and Ted walked into the room. Steve shot to his feet.

'Steve!' Ted exclaimed, crossing the room, smiling, his hand out to shake Steve's. He made no mention of what had gone before, saying only, 'I hope you might be able to give us a steer, at least, on the gold bar scam. We could certainly do with something on that.'

Ted had started the day at Stockport. He'd wanted to let Superintendent Sampson know he'd at least discovered the source of the leak to the press so had met with her first thing, before going upstairs for an update.

'What do you intend to do about him?' Sammy had asked him. 'That should be a disciplinary matter.'

'Oh, I have something in mind which might be just as effective but without all the paperwork. And at the same time, give him a chance to redeem himself. I'll put him somewhere he won't hear much of anything about the case but might still come up with something of use to the investigation.'

'Colour me intrigued,' Sammy told him. 'What do you have in mind?'

'Obviously the lack of a prime suspect is concerning, so I'm going with the "no stone unturned" approach on this one. We're looking not just at likely possibles in the area but also anyone connected with them. One of the farmers who has a real beef -

excuse the pun - with the militant vegans, Janice Burrows, has a missing father. There's not likely to be any connection there to the current case, but it remains an unsolved Misper and it forms an important part of her own background check. I don't see it as a waste of hours as there's just a chance something more about the feud may show up there. So that's what I'm going to put him on, at least for the time being, which will keep him shut away in some dusty basement for much of his time.'

'I like it. It's fiendish. It gets my approval,' she told him, then added, 'You can be surprisingly devious at times, Ted.

'Now, before you go, I have to give you the statutory reminder about time, and hours and lack of results and so on. I know you know, I'm just covering my own rear by reminding you. Seriously, though, we could do with a breakthrough, as soon as you can, if not sooner.

'Oh, and when you go back upstairs, you'll see I've arranged a little surprise delivery for you. So don't say I never listen to your requirements.'

* * *

When he got back to Ashton, Ted caught up with Jo first thing.

'Anything?' he asked him, more in hope than anticipation.

'*Nada*, boss. Nothing. Sweet Fanny Adams. We're still digging, all of us. And yes, I have tried chasing the lab results again, and once again I'm getting nothing but apologies. I'm starting to have a nasty feeling something has gone badly wrong with the system and they've lost them.'

'Has the body been released yet? Worst case scenario, could they be done again? The ceremony up at The Stones wasn't them scattering his ashes there, so it may still be possible to repeat the tests, if it comes to that.'

'I should have checked. I didn't. Sorry, I'll do it now.'

'Can I borrow your office? I want to have words with Alan Burgess. I plan to stick him out of harm's way on cold cases for a bit. Penny, of course, didn't betray her source by anything she said, but she blushes as much as Steve does. Oh, and speaking of Steve, he's back at Stockport for the time being, working on the computers.'

'That's good news. How is he?'

'He looks a lot better than the last time I saw him, that's for sure. He's matured somehow, too. He didn't turn pink when he shook my hand, for one thing.

'Right, on your way out, can you point DC Burgess in my direction please, but don't tell him why he's summoned. Let him stew a bit first, wondering.'

Jo went on his way chuckling to himself.

It was certainly a wary knock on the door which followed shortly after Jo's departure.

Ted called out a brusque, 'Come in,' not looking up until Burgess was standing in front of his desk like a spare part. Then Ted lifted his head and considered him, thoughtfully, over the top of his reading glasses.

'DC Burgess, you've been talking to the press,' he began, then, as the man started to bluster, he went on, 'Please don't insult my intelligence by denying it. I know it was you.

'I could make this official and you would face serious consequences. However, rather than throw you off the team, I'm going to give you another chance. But to keep you from temptation, I'm going to put you somewhere you'll have nothing of interest to sell. Cold cases. Missing Persons, to be specific.'

'Mispers, boss? Seriously?'

'I'm very serious, DC Burgess. As you know, one of our potential suspects, Janice Burrows, has a missing father. There may be no connection at all to our current case. But there's just a chance there is, and we're not in any position to leave stones unturned, no matter how unlikely they might appear.

'So I want you to find the files on the missing man. I don't even know his full name, for one thing, and I need to. I need to know everything there is to know about him, including when and by whom he was reported missing.

'You'll most likely find the files buried somewhere in the archives. Maybe down in the basement? You can work on them wherever you find them. That should keep you out of harm's way when it comes to any more leaks. I don't imagine there's much of a mobile phone signal down there, for one thing. And for now you report to me and only to me on this. Bring me your first report this afternoon and I'll decide what to share with the team. Is that clear?'

Burgess's curt, 'Sir,' was as sulky as a teenager being told he was grounded. Ted didn't care. It might just remind the man of the importance of confidentiality.

* * *

Ted hadn't realised quite how far advanced the afternoon was when there was a knock at the door of Jo's office, where he had spent much of the day wading through paperwork looking for inspiration or errors. In response to his invitation, DC Alan Burgess appeared.

Burgess was holding photocopied sheets plus his own handwritten notes on a jotter. For once, he looked focused on what he'd been doing.

'Sir, it may be nothing but there's a possible inconsistency in this report about the missing man, Janice Burrows' father. Fred, he's called. Only Sergeant Thomas said Janice had to leave her job and come back to the farm because her father had disappeared.'

'That's right, he did. Is that not accurate?' Ted asked him.

'It could still be, I suppose. Only now I've looked more closely at the files and at the timings, Janice Burrows was already at the farm when her father was reported missing. She was the one who reported him as having disappeared.'

Ted nodded to the spare chair and told Burgess to sit down. This was promising. It may be something and nothing, but it did show he'd done as he'd been told and spent the day down in the archives going through the files.

'But Sergeant Thomas also said the mother had mental health issues. Perhaps she wasn't capable of making the report herself. It would have been natural for her to phone her daughter to come to the rescue if her husband was missing. I'm assuming there's no one else in the family? No brothers or sisters?'

'No, she's an only child. But the dates still don't add up. Janice Burrows reported her father missing on a Monday morning, from the farm, and said that she'd just arrived back that day. But she told the officer who took the details that Fred had gone missing the previous Friday. Now from all the details in the file, it looks highly unlikely that Mrs Burrows could have managed anything at all by herself for a whole weekend. She couldn't have fed herself, never mind all the livestock. So it looks as if Janice Burrows must have gone home sooner than she let on, but not reported her father missing immediately. She may even have been there when he went.'

'We know that can happen, though, with a missing adult,' Ted told him. 'By all accounts there was no love lost between Miss Burrows and her father so it could simply have been a case of good riddance and hoping he wouldn't come back.'

'So why bother to report him missing at all?'

'She worked in accounts, didn't she? She must have realised there could possibly have been all sorts of financial implications if he wasn't officially reported missing. It might have caused problems with things like bank accounts. She'd have seven years to wait for a presumption of death, for one thing, so there could have been significant delays with financial matters without a date to work from. For that reason alone, the sooner she reported him, the better it would be.'

'Fair enough, but I want to check next when she gave in her notice at her work. That might tell us something. If she was just going back to make sure her mother was all right if the old man had gone walkabout, she wouldn't do that, would she? Resign, I mean. Why would she assume she wouldn't be able to get back to work once he turned up?

'But then supposing she knew full well he wasn't coming back. Then she'd know she wouldn't be going back to work, if she was taking over the farm, wouldn't she?'

'Are you saying she killed her father for the farm? I'd need to ask Sergeant Thomas about such things but would there really be enough of a motive there? I can't imagine it makes a lot of money, and it seems like a lot of hard work for not much return.

'Plus she must surely have known she couldn't inherit, even if there was money in it, without a long wait and a lot of back-breaking work in the meantime.'

'There's something else, though, sir. Like the sarge said, the mother didn't last very long. She'd had a long history of ill health and there were strong indications the husband used to knock her about. And worse. She'd been having those mini-strokes - what do they call them ...?'

He consulted his notes then continued, 'TIA's. Anyway she died from a fall downstairs which broke her neck. There was an inquest, of course, but the finding was accidental death. A TIA made her fall down the stairs and the fall broke her neck.

'But what if it wasn't accidental, sir? What if the daughter got fed up and shoved her? Perhaps even broke her next first and staged an accidental fall? Should I at least try to find out what the farm's worth, to see if there is a money motive there? For getting rid of both the parents, I mean.'

'There's still the seven-year rule, though. She'd surely have known she wouldn't inherit until then, especially working in accounts. She must have been aware of that condition, I imagine. And it would need to be a substantial financial gain to go through all of that.

'Good work, though. Check the value, certainly. We know prices around there can be high, so it might be worth a bit of money. Find out about when Miss Burrows left her job and what reason she gave. It's an anomaly so it needs squaring away with some answers.

'Right, let's go and see what anyone else has that may be of any use to advance us with this case.'

Sergeant Thomas wasn't with the rest of the team when Ted and Alan Burgess went to join them. PCSO Murray explained. There was no mistaking the anxious look on her face.

'Sir, Sergeant Thomas asked me to pass on a message. Only PC Nield, Colin, is currently unaccounted for. Nobody's heard from him for a while. The sarge is just seeing if he can track him down. He's not answering his radio or his phone, but of course he could be in a black spot somewhere.'

'Can you trace the vehicle?' Ted asked her.

'It's stationary, pretty much in the location he set out for, but it hasn't moved for some time.'

'What was his last location? And is he on his own?'

'He is, sir, yes, he was the only one available at the time and there was nothing of concern about the report. It was some animals straying on the road so he'd gone up there to sort it. It could be yet another case of the hippies letting them out, or they might just have broken through the fence.'

'And where was this taking place?'

'Up by the road that leads to Jamie Robinson's place then on further to Diego Smith's, sir.'

'So not down in a dip anywhere there? There shouldn't be a problem with a signal up there, surely? Is there anywhere you know of close to which would be a comms black spot?'

She shook her head.

'Now you come to mention it, no, sir, I've never had any problems out there.'

'And would PC Nield routinely stay in contact?'

'Any of us would, going up there, sir. It's not that we think the people are any more dangerous than anyone else but all kinds of accidents can happen around farms, with animals and heavy machinery and so on. It's completely out of character for him not to be in touch.'

They were interrupted by Ted's mobile phone. Sergeant Thomas calling him.

'This is Sergeant Thomas now,' Ted told those present as he picked up the call.

He listened in silence, his face impassive, then responded with a brief, 'We're on our way.'

Then he turned to those assembled and told them, 'Right, we have a serious siege situation underway. Jamie Robinson has taken PC Nield hostage and is holding him at gunpoint. PS Thomas says he appears to be having one of his psychotic episodes but this time he isn't listening to reason. He's shut his dog outside and she's usually the one who can calm him down when he gets bad, so that's not an encouraging sign.

'I'll go up there now to make an initial assessment. Rob, you come with me. Jo, we'll need a negotiator as a priority, preferably someone with some experience of PTSD. Can you sort that, please?'

'Firearms, boss?'

'They'll need to be on stand-by, of course, but I don't want them anywhere he might get a glimpse of them. Make sure they know he's a trained soldier, with serious issues, and that he has access to firearms of his own.

'This situation has the potential to go very badly wrong if we're not careful.'

Chapter Twenty-two

PC Colin Nield was grumbling to himself as he drove out to the area where livestock had been reported straying on the road. Most of the time he enjoyed working in rural crime, but the prospect of trying to round up a flock of stubborn sheep without the aid of a working dog wasn't greatly appealing, especially as it could well involve him being late finishing his shift. He'd promised to take the wife out for the evening so if he didn't get back on time, he was going to be in the doghouse. Again.

He found the sheep wandering and browsing on the B road down below the farms. There wasn't a lot of traffic there, but a flock that size could still cause a serious accident, with the twists and turns in the road and drivers going too fast to brake when confronted with such an obstacle.

At least they were between him and the turn-off they must have come out of. If he put the flashers on and crawled slowly along behind them, he might just be able to chivvy them in the right direction and at least get them off the road.

They may possibly even do the decent thing and turn off up the farm road, where they'd either find their way back to their own field, or go up to one of the farms there and he could leave their welfare to either Jamie or Diego, depending on where they decided to go. You could simply never tell with sheep. Not the most cooperative of beasts.

He hoped Jamie was up to sorting them out, but if not, at least his dog Nell could pen them easily enough. She was a cracking little dog, Nell. Many's the time she'd helped out with livestock straying when Jamie wasn't up to managing.

Whatever supreme being there was must have been smiling down on Colin because the sheep did obligingly turn off up the farm access without any action required by him.

Even better, as if by a miracle, who should he spot coming trotting purposefully down the hill in a low, stalking crouch, but Nell herself. Of Jamie there was no sign, but Nell was a strong-eyed dog who knew her job inside out. Not one of the ewes challenged her authority with so much as a stamp of a hoof. Instead they all wheeled off the lane through the open gateway and started wandering away across the field, heads down to start grazing.

Nell shot into the entrance to the field behind them and paused, one front paw raised, to deter them from changing their minds while Colin Nield got out of the car and swung the gate to with a grateful, 'That'll do, Nell,' in the dog's direction.

It wasn't until he'd secured the gate and was turning back to get in his car that Colin Nield came face to face with Jamie Robinson.

But it was not the Jamie he knew. This one's eyes were cold, hard and distant, his face an expressionless mask.

Worse than that, both engaged barrels of his shotgun were pointing directly at the centre of the police officer's chest.

* * *

Rob O'Connell drove, fast, with occasional use of the blue lights to give him clear passage when he needed it. Ted spent the journey time on the phone.

He'd been reading up on Jamie Robinson's background as part of his desk time earlier on, and he wasn't reassured by what he'd read. Ex-Pathfinder Platoon, from the Airborne Brigade. He knew little about them but what he did know was not encouraging. He'd encountered a couple of them on Mr Green's training courses and understood that their role was to penetrate enemy territory to secure potential drop zones for Airborne assault, often at great personal cost. Hard men.

More than that he didn't know, and he needed to. He reached for his phone, called a saved number and crossed his fingers for a better reception this time. At least his call was answered by an audible voice. He wasted no time with small talk.

'Pathfinder Platoon. Should I be worried?'

'Run away, Gayboy. Well out of your league,' Green told him cheerfully.

'I've got an ex-Pathfinder soldier with PTSD holding a police officer at gunpoint. What do I need to get the officer out of there in one piece?'

Green snorted.

'A lot of luck. One thing you should know about their role is they're considered expendable, not expected to return home. Mortality rate in that unit is always high, so there's not much you can threaten him with that's going to worry him.'

'So what can I do to defuse the situation and get the two of them out of there as safely as possible?'

Another cynical noise.

'Good luck with that. They're trained to dig in and hold out in the most arduous hard routine for ten days minimum, but there are credible legends of some of them spendings months in a hole in the ground without resupply. You certainly can't starve him out.'

Green was being surprisingly talkative, although none of it yet was helpful, other than to make Ted even more worried than he had been before.

'Something else you need to know, Gayboy, before you even think of going charging in there. These blokes are also trained to make things go bang. Highly trained. They can make an IED out of things you wouldn't believe. So if he wants to keep you out of where he is, he's likely to have booby-trapped the entry points.'

'I've requested a trained negotiator ...'

He got no further before Green scoffed.

'Appealing to his better nature isn't going to work. Not if he's in the state you say he is.'

'He has a dog he thinks the world of. She usually keeps him on an even keel. He's shut her out of the house, which is very unusual. Is that significant?'

Green might have sworn, but it was in a language Ted didn't recognise.

'Significant, and very bad news. It means he's not expecting to come out of this alive but he doesn't want any harm to come to his woofer. That makes me think more and more he's wired the entrance points.

'You need the Army for this one, Gayboy. Bomb Disposal for a start. For god's sake don't send anyone in without their say-so. And you need someone he might possibly listen to. You want a hard-bitten Warrant Officer to bark some orders at him. He'll be so conditioned to that it might just work, even in the state he's in. Not guaranteed, though.'

'Someone like you, you mean?'

Green made a noise Ted didn't recognise in his context. It might almost have been a chuckle.

'There is no one like me, Gayboy,' he said, then cut the call.

'Boss, I was trying not to listen in, but do I gather it's not good news?' Rob asked him.

'Not good at all,' Ted told him frankly. 'That was my military contact. I knew the firearms situation would be difficult but I hadn't factored in that our man is almost certainly trained not only in disarming Improvised Explosive Devices, but in making them, too. So there's a good chance the place is booby-trapped. I need to let Sergeant Thomas know that, as a matter of urgency, before we get there. Then I need to call in the military.

'First thing you do when we arrive on site, Rob, is to put your vest on and stay well back, out of range.'

'I'll stand behind you, boss, because of course, you're going to stay well away from the danger zone, aren't you?'

Ted grinned at the jibe then hastily made the necessary phone calls. He called Jo Rodriguez first to update him, then he called Sammy Sampson. She was his immediate boss and had the rank to summon up the Army. He explained Green's rationale behind that suggestion.

'Makes sense to me. It's certainly worth a try. I'll sort it now,' she told him then, 'and I hope I don't have to remind you, Ted, that I take a dim view of Tactical Firearms Commanders phoning me to complain of my DCI acting like a bloody cowboy. So don't do it. Clear?'

'Ma'am,' Ted replied meekly. 'On the subject of protocol, who takes overall command in a case like this? Us, or the Army?'

'I've honestly no idea, off the top of my head. I'll find out and let you know. I'm not even sure where the nearest bomb disposal unit is based. I've a feeling it may be Yorkshire, so it might take them a while to deploy. Unless they come in by helicopter.'

'If they do, please make sure they know he's armed and dangerous. We've no idea what arms he has at his disposal, either. He could conceivably have something which would pose a risk to a helicopter over-flying too close. It's incredible what some ex-servicemen manage to bring home with them. Plus he may well have the materials and skills to make something.'

'Understood. Just try hard not to piss anybody off before I get the definitive answer. And seriously, Ted, be bloody careful with this one. It's a no win situation which can hang us all out to dry if it all goes pear-shaped.

'You've got enough on your plate there so I'll call DI Rodriguez to tell him to make sure DC Burgess is kept safely down in the bowels of the earth where he can't tip anyone off about anything. The last thing we need is any screaming "*Armed police shoot dead war veteran*" headlines.

Which was exactly what had been going through Ted's mind as well. What he wanted more than anything was to resolve the situation with no adverse publicity, no casualties and certainly no loss of life.

They'd reached their destination now, and Rob was pulling up behind where PC Nield's area car was parked next to a field gate, with Sergeant Thomas's 4x4 just behind it.

'I'm assuming you don't want me to drive any closer, boss? I thought probably the fewer cars he sees approach, the less he's likely to be spooked into hasty action.'

'Exactly.'

Sergeant Thomas was walking down to meet them, Nell trotting happily enough at his heels. Ted had phoned ahead to let him know they'd arrived.

'What's the situation?' Ted asked him, although he could tell from the sergeant's face that it wasn't going to be good news.

Thomas shook his head.

'Bad, sir. I've never seen Jamie as bad as this before. He's not listening to reason at all, and the fact that he's shut Nell outside is very worrying. She never normally leaves his side.

'He doesn't seem to recognise Colin, and he knows him well enough. He won't accept he's a police officer. He's very confused. He keeps saying Colin's an insurgent, an infiltrator. He also seems to think he's the one behind letting the stock out and the other things that have been happening. He's got him holed up in an upstairs room. I can see them well enough from the yard, but he's threatening Colin if I go any closer.'

'Threatening to shoot him?'

'Worse, sir. He's got it into his head that Colin is also one of the "*meat is murder*" lot. Jamie's got a big Army machete as well as the guns and he says if we try to approach he'll start hacking bits off and eating him. And to be honest, sir, the way he is at the moment, I'm inclined to believe him.'

'How close did you get to the house?'

'Not close at all, sir. I don't profess to be a hero. I was also thinking about Colin. He can be a lazy sod at times, but I didn't fancy having to watch him being eaten. I thought I was probably safe enough, as long as I stood well back, with Nell next to me. But I got nowhere.'

Ted nodded approval.

'I think it's best to proceed with extreme caution. As you say, Jamie is clearly very unstable at the moment. No point in taking unnecessary risks.

'I've been speaking to a military expert who said it's likely that Jamie will be trained in making explosive devices, so he raised the point that he could have wired the entrance points to blow if anyone tries to go in. He said that might well be why he left the dog outside. He doesn't want her to be killed or injured if anyone triggers the devices.'

'Bloody hell! Sorry, sir. That didn't even occur to me. I was too busy looking at the shotgun pointing in my direction. I know he has a .22 as well, but I've no idea what else he might have.'

'Do you by any chance have binoculars with you? And what about a loudhailer? I could at least try talking to him, but I'd prefer to do it from further away than point blank range. If you've got bins, I could at least scan the place to see if I can spot anything suspicious. I've done point of entry explosives training, although not recently.'

'Got both, sir. I keep the bins handy for checking on rare birds' nesting sites.'

'Right, we'd better go and have a look. The Super is summoning help from the Army, because my contact suggested there's just a chance Jamie might still respond to the sight of an officer in uniform. It's a long shot, but they're all we have at the moment. She's also liaising with bomb disposal just in case he's rigged up any nasty surprises for us. They might well bring explosives detection dogs, I imagine, but I've never dealt with this sort of extreme situation before, except on training courses.

'I'll just remind you that I'm also firearms trained, Sergeant Thomas, and that is up to date, always. So unless you are too, then please trust me to gauge safe distances to approach, and stick to them.'

'I'm not, sir, so I'm more than happy to be guided by you.'

'Tell me one thing first. In view of this development, has it altered your opinion of whether or not Jamie might have been capable of killing Brendan Doyle?'

'I've honestly never seen him this bad, sir. This is Jamie the soldier, the damaged one, not Jamie the farmer. Looking at him today, I could easily believe him capable of killing. By any means.'

Ted led the way, carefully gauging distances, looking for lines of sight.

They stopped well short of the house, taking refuge behind substantial stone gate posts. The sight of them confirmed Ted's theory about The Stones. To the naked eye, they looked virtually identical. No doubt some sort of testing could be done to see if they came from the same source, should that be necessary. Something was still mithering him about that site.

He used the binoculars first, keeping low and as much out of sight as he could. There was no sound or sign of movement in the house. Sergeant Thomas ordered the dog to lie down and stay. Nell did as she was told but whined and trembled, clearly anxious to be back with her master.

'I can't see anything of concern from this distance, but given his background, I can't take the risk of allowing any of us to go closer until the site is checked out by explosive experts, and it could take some time for them to get here. We'll just have to try to keep the lid on things here until the experts arrive.

'Above all our priority needs to be to see that nothing untoward happens either to PC Nield, or to Jamie himself. He needs to be treated as a vulnerable person, at this stage, not just a murder suspect.

'I'll try having a quiet word, to see if that achieves anything.' Ted smiled at the other two as he went on, 'One of the advantages of being short is that this nice big gatepost is taller than me. I should be safe enough behind it, but you two keep well down, just in case.'

'Mr Robinson? Jamie?' Ted began, through the loudspeaker, keeping his voice quiet and calm. 'This is DCI Darling, Jamie. We've met before. Do you remember?'

He got no further before there was the crack of a rifle shot, then a whine as it hit the top of the gatepost, making a stone chip fly off it.

Rob and Cai Thomas both ducked instinctively, swearing under their breath.

Ted appeared unruffled as he remarked, 'Well, that's taught us two valuable lessons to start with. One, these pillars are nice and solid. And two, we're not about to bring this siege to an end by ourselves. We'll just have to sit patiently and wait for reinforcements.'

Chapter Twenty-three

They heard a Land Rover lumbering down the track at best speed, from the direction of Diego Smith's farm higher up the hill. Cai Thomas was closest to its approach. He glanced anxiously at the DCI, hoping he really did know about range and line of sight, then on his nod, crouching as low as he could, he scuttled towards the oncoming vehicle and dived behind it, pinning the driver's door shut with his bulk.

Nell was shadowing his every movement, latching anxiously onto the person she knew best in the absence of her master.

Diego opened the side window, his face concerned, and asked, 'What's going on, Cai? I thought I heard a shot so I came to make sure Jamie was all right. I've been wrestling with that old bitch of a Nuffy again so I was worried that might have set him off.'

'It's not good. He's taken a police officer hostage and he took a shot at us when the DCI tried to talk to him over the loudhailer.'

Diego was sharp, observant. He had the situation summed up in a glance.

'And he's not got Nell with him, I see. Bloody hell, that's worrying. Is there anything I can do to help? Is it worth me trying to talk to him?'

'Not a chance,' the sergeant told him. 'The DCI wouldn't let you anywhere near because of the risk. He's called up the cavalry, but it was Jamie taking a shot at him which you heard.

There's no reasoning with him at the moment.'

'So what can I do to help? Bring down some flasks of tea or something, while you're waiting? I'd like to do something. I feel partly to blame because of that bloody noisy old tractor. I won't do any more with it, at least until all of this is sorted out.'

'I don't reckon any of us would say no to a cuppa. I've a fancy we're in for a long wait before we can get away from here.'

'Righto, I'll go and sort that now. What about the stock? They're going to need feeding and seeing to at some point. Can I do anything there?'

Cai Thomas shook his head.

'I don't think anyone's going to be allowed anywhere near for now, not with an officer being held.'

'Who is it, that he's got as a hostage? Anyone I know?'

'I can't tell you, Diego. I know you're not about to sell the story or anything but the DCI would hang me out to dry if he knew I'd said anything. I've said too much already, really.'

'Fair enough. I'll go and get the missus to make some tea and perhaps some butties. I imagine you've got a long night ahead of you.'

Still crouching patiently behind the gatepost, Ted hadn't missed Rob O'Connell constantly checking his mobile phone.

'Are we keeping you from something, Rob?' he asked him eventually, his tone dry.

Rob gave a guilty start and put the phone back in his pocket.

'Sorry, boss. Only it's tomorrow Faye is coming to stay. Our first foster child, and Sally's been fussing all day about getting the room perfect. I've booked tomorrow off as leave. If that's still going to be possible.'

'Phone her,' Ted told him. 'Tell her I'll let you go as soon as I can but there are no promises. You know that. But phone her, at least, although clearly don't say anything about what we're doing here. I'd better phone Trev, while I think of it. Let's just hope Jamie doesn't decide to take another pot shot at us while we're on the phone to our other halves. That might give the game away.

'I just wish there was a safe way to let PC Nield know that we're doing our best to get him out of there in one piece, but I think I'm better off not trying to talk to Jamie just now. Let's wait for the negotiator.'

They both spoke quietly into their phones. There was not much privacy, crouched as they were to either side of the farm entrance.

'I'm guessing this is you calling to say you're going to be late,' Trev responded when he answered Ted's call. His tone was good natured enough, though. 'What's your excuse this time?'

'Nothing too serious. We've got a bit of an incident out at one of the farms, to do with a rural case. I've no idea what time I'll get away but I may be some time.'

'Don't say that!' Trev told him in mock horror. 'Captain Oates said that in Antarctica and they never so much as found his body. Are you doing something dangerous?'

Ted thought about the earlier rifle shot but said, 'No, nothing much. I'm mostly waiting around for someone else to come in and run this one. I'll try to keep you posted, but don't worry.'

'Now I am worried. I really start to worry when you tell me not to,' Trev told him, but he still sounded light-hearted enough. 'Don't do any heroics, and I'll see you when you get back.'

They were in for a long wait. Ted issued instructions that no one should try to contact PC Nield, either via his radio or his mobile phone. He suspected Jamie might have rendered either or both of them unserviceable, but he didn't want to take the risk of a sudden noise from either of them acting as a trigger to a man already in a volatile state.

Firearms arrived first. Following instructions received, they left their vehicles down on the road out of sight and notified

Ted of their arrival. Things were currently quiet in the farmhouse, which he hoped was a good sign, so, with strict instructions to Rob and Cai Thomas not to move without further orders, he hurried down to brief the officers from Firearms.

Their commander rolled his eyes in mock horror as he saw him.

'Oh, bloody hell, that's all I need. Kung Fu Ted,' he said ironically.

Ted gave a guilty laugh. Inspector Bridger was clearly not ready to let him forget their most recent encounter. Then he switched to professional mode as he briefed the man on the current situation, summing up, 'So basically, we're all in for a long wait until we're given the all clear to go in from the military bods, and we have someone here to ensure Jamie Robinson's welfare.'

'Bloody hell,' Bridger said again but with more feeling. 'The lads are all fired up and ready for action, and you're telling me they have to crawl around in the cow pats before they can do anything? Not to mention playing second fiddle to the boys in khaki. Can we at least start a recce of the site?'

Ted shook his head.

'Too dangerous. With the skills our suspect has, if he has been making IEDs, he could have planted them anywhere. We'll all simply have to sit and twiddle our thumbs. The priority is to preserve lives, especially that of the officer stuck inside with him. Until then, all we can do is wait.'

* * *

Ted had seen it happen so many times before, both in training exercises and in real situations. After hours of anxious waiting, long delays while negotiations were attempted, there was suddenly a frenzy of activity. Then it was all over in a flash, with no casualties on either side.

Ted had been relieved to discover he was still the senior

officer on the incident. A young-looking and briskly efficient Army captain by the name of Toolin had reported to him and included him in all stages of the planning.

'It's all gone quiet in there recently,' Ted told him. 'Curtains closed, lights off, no sound of movement at all. We've not pressed him.'

'Excellent,' Toolin told him. 'I'll try having a word, explain his options to him, and try to get a peaceful result that way. I have to say, I'm not optimistic of that succeeding, from what you've told me. I think it's very unlikely that he would meekly surrender at this stage, so we're going to need to go in hard and fast to get your officer out as safely as possible, with the least risk to the Lance Corporal.

'It's only fair to warn you that with his skills, he might have prepared some worse surprises than an IED or two. Petrol in the microwave, set to blow, for one thing. And with the addition of washing-up liquid, it can burn like napalm.'

He sounded cheerful enough as he said it, then went on, 'I can have one try at talking to him, but I think we need to prepare to go in. For that I need as much detail on the interior of the house, and its surroundings, as I can get, so we can get in there as safely as possible. For all concerned. It won't be all that pleasant for your officer - we'll need to use percussion grenades, CS gas, that sort of thing. But if the intel is good and the talk-through detailed enough, we should be able to get them both out alive.'

Toolin was right about negotiation no longer being an option, although he did make one attempt at ordering Robinson to stand down. With that off the table, he was true to his word. His men were swift, efficient and ruthless. Police Firearms officers assisted, providing distraction cover at the front of the house while the military unit stormed in from the rear. Jamie Robinson made a token attempt to turn his gun on Colin Nield but was too incapacitated by the gas to succeed.

The siege was over.

Ted could well imagine that poor PC Nield would be needing a change of underwear after all he'd been through. He'd been in the house, once the all clear was given, and had seen for himself the formidable machete. It must have put the fear of god up Nield to be threatened with a slow and painful death from that.

Both Nield and Jamie Robinson would be taken straight to hospital, separately, to be checked over. For form's sake Ted cautioned Robinson but made no attempt to do any more. He wasn't convinced the man was in any fit emotional state to understand what was happening. He also had a quick word with PC Nield in the back of the ambulance where he was receiving first aid before being taken to hospital.

'Sorry we couldn't be any more supportive, Colin. I take responsibility for that. I took the view that anything we said or did was likely to escalate the situation, so we had to sit tight, say nowt and hope you didn't think we'd abandoned you to your fate.'

'Fair enough, sir. I understood that, although I don't mind admitting I was shitting myself. I'll tell you what, though. I wasn't sure I believed it before, but after all that, I could well see Jamie snapping someone's neck if they got in his way. I swear I didn't move a muscle the whole time I was in there with him. I'm not even sure I breathed some of the time. But I think we've got our man now, sir.'

Ted went to find Cai Thomas to tell him he'd drive PC Nield's car back to Ashton, where he'd left his own vehicle. As soon as it had been clear there was nothing useful Rob O'Connell could do, he'd let him go, which left him without a lift.

The sergeant was liaising with Diego Smith about the animals and what needed doing with them. The neighbour had hovered on the fringes to the bitter end, still clearly feeling guilty about any contribution he had unwittingly made with his tractor. It was clear that whatever the outcome of the investigation, Jamie Robinson was not going to be in a position to run the farm himself for the foreseeable future.

It would complicate things that the farm was now a crime scene which would need Forensics on site to sort through it. There had been a small explosive device set to blow at the slightest touch to the front door. Small, but lethal enough to have killed anyone trying to walk in. But the welfare of the livestock was also important. They would need seeing to, before CFI could come in and set up.

As much as anything, Ted was hoping they would find him some traces of Brendan Doyle's presence in the house itself. It would be circumstantial, but it was hard to think of any reason for Doyle to have been making a social call on Robinson. It would be useful evidence against Jamie for Brendan Doyle's murder, if he was ever fit to be charged and sent for trial.

'You'd best leave Nell with me, too, Cai,' Diego told him. 'She gets on fine with my dogs and she knows her work here better than anyone. Don't worry, we'll look after her.'

Much to Ted's relief, the presence of the military had helped to keep a lid on the story as far as the press and media were concerned. On the pretence of a secret exercise taking place, all road entries to the area had been closed. When an enterprising private helicopter attempted to overfly with a photographer on board, they were swiftly given their marching orders by Air Traffic Control.

Ted was bone weary by the time he arrived home, although he knew, from experience, that he'd be unlikely to sleep after an operation like that. Too much adrenaline still coursing through his veins.

The only time that Trev could be woken from his usual comatose state of sleep was when Ted had been out at an incident, especially one where he was sparing with the details.

As soon as Ted slid under what was left of the duvet on his side of the bed, putting his head on the small space left on the pillow by Adam, who was curled up on it, Trev stirred.

He reached out a possessive arm and pulled Ted closer. His

voice was sleepy as he said, 'Hey, you. Are you safely in one piece? And did you catch the baddy?'

'Not so much the baddy as a sad and very broken man, I think,' Ted told him. 'I don't know for sure if he could be our killer. We're still waiting on DNA results. But from what I've seen today, it could well be the right person.'

Trev was already snuggling back down and sounding drowsy.

'Good. That might mean you won't let me down on Sunday now. Night-night, sleep tight.'

Ted smiled to himself in the darkness, eyes wide open, staring at the ceiling. He knew there was no chance of sleep. Not while his mind was busy mentally writing reports, justifying every decision, asking himself over and again, had they got the right person? Or was it all a little bit too easy?

* * *

There was a buzz of excitement in the incident room the following morning, with news of Jamie Robinson having been taken to hospital and being currently under armed police guard there.

'He was in no fit state to be questioned or charged,' Ted told them. 'We're going to have to wait for a psych evaluation before we can even think of getting to that stage. I'm going to need to liaise closely with CPS about how they want things to progress. But for now we need to proceed on the basis that Jamie Robinson is our prime suspect for the murder of Brendan Doyle and we need to start building a case on that assumption.

'Let's see what we've got and if it's enough to prove that to the satisfaction of CPS first, then of a court. But keep in mind it might just be the case that Jamie won't be in any fit state to stand trial, at least not in the immediate future. This might end up being one of those frustrating cases where we're pretty certain we have our killer but we can't bring it to court.'

'Sir, I was going to suggest we send a card or something to Colin Nield, poor sod. He's going to need a few days off to recover so I thought he might appreciate knowing we're thinking about him,' Cai Thomas said.

He looked as rough as Ted felt after the long night of high tension and not much sleep.

The sergeant gave a wicked grin as he added, 'We could buy him some new kecks because he looked like he needed some when he got out of there.'

There was good natured laughter round the room. They all felt for what Colin Nield had been through. It could have been any of them. And they were feeling the euphoria of a case coming close to its conclusion.

Jo Rodriguez reached for his mobile as it pinged. He glanced at the screen, then said, 'I'd better take this, boss, it might be useful.'

He wasn't gone long and when he returned, his face was solemn. He motioned to Ted that he wanted a word in private. Ted followed him back into his office.

'That was the lab, boss, full of apologies for the delays. They've emailed me the DNA results, but they gave me the outline details over the phone. Baffling, and it means we're no nearer to closure than we were before the siege.

'The last traces of DNA on Doyle's body are female. That DNA isn't on record anywhere, but when they widened the search, they found a very high percentage match for someone who is on the system, as a Misper.

'The results show a very close to one hundred per cent likelihood that the last person to have physical contact with Brendan Doyle was female and related to Fred Burrows. So that means his daughter, Janice Burrows. Not Jamie Robinson at all.'

Chapter Twenty-four

Ted decided to go in person to inform Superintendent Sampson of the latest development in the case. There could well be ramifications to the news, which he'd prefer to deal with and in person.

'Well, it has the potential to be a bit of a PR disaster, but we already knew that. The press office have had the vultures circling and they're not yet ready to go away. Roadblocks and so-called Army manoeuvres were always going to risk that. I'll update the ACC for you. One less job for you. I predict a bit of high level flapping like budgies, though.

'Please tell me this woman Burrows isn't likely to start another armed siege with threats of cannibalism? She's not some white-haired old dear who's going to get the sympathy vote from the public if you arrest her, is she?'

'Fifties, and she does have grey hair. But I can't somehow see her attracting a lot of sympathy. She has what you might call an attitude. There is one slight problem, though. I'm going to have to request Firearms back-up again, based on my risk assessment, to bring her in for questioning.'

'Please tell me this is a joke in bad taste on your part, Ted. You've just headed a joint service operation, at god knows what cost, to pull in a poor, broken war veteran who, it turns out, hadn't done anything at all until he thought he was being infiltrated by the enemy. I'm imagining the headlines already: "*Did police harassment drive veteran to drastic action*?" '

She made exaggerated speech marks in the air as she said it.

'Now you want another armed operation to bring in a woman suspect just for questioning? Based solely on having touched a man later found dead, which she's no doubt going to say she did in legitimate self-defence when he broke into her property. And she'll no doubt claim he left there alive and well. You can see how it's going to look, especially as I presume she's in the same sort of area as the last raid?'

'She is, yes, not far away. But whichever way I do the risk assessment, there's no getting away from the fact that she is licensed to own and carry firearms and by all accounts she's never seen anywhere without one or other of the ones she owns.

'If we simply phone her and ask her to come to the station to give a voluntary statement, I don't imagine she'd take any notice. She might well hang up. So someone is going to have to go out there and issue the invitation in person. And in my opinion, that poses a significant threat to whoever does so.'

'Can't they just appeal to her better nature?' Sammy asked him hopefully, thinking, as always, of budgetary considerations as much as anything.

Ted laughed at that.

'I honestly don't think she has one. She certainly has some serious questions to answer, and I'm convinced she's not simply going to agree to come in to do so. Hence me requesting Firearms.'

'All right. I suppose in the long term it makes more economical sense to bring her in without inconvenient deaths, not to mention the resulting paperwork and awkward questions. How do these people get, and keep, their firearms certificates, I wonder? What are they shooting at?'

Ted wasn't sure whether or not it was a rhetorical question but he answered it anyway.

'Foxes and other wild animals, I believe, to protect their

livestock. And sometimes out of control dogs worrying sheep. The point is they have them, legally, and in Janice Burrows' case, my professional judgement is that if she felt cornered, she would open fire. She's already been spoken to about firing in the air above possible intruders.'

'Fair enough. So is that all on your shopping list? You have a bit of an Oliver Twist look about you. Like you're about to ask for more.'

'I am, I'm afraid. I want to find out what happened to Fred Burrows. The father. And I want another look taken at the circumstances surrounding the mother's death. It wasn't treated as suspicious at the time so it wasn't a Home Office pathologist ...'

'Please tell me you're not about to request an exhumation to add to the budget?'

'Aah ...'

Sammy gave a theatrical glance to the heavens.

'Anything else, while we're at it? And what possible relevance to the current situation is what happened to the parents? I take it we're not talking recent death and disappearance?'

'About five years ago now. Miss Burrows came back to the farm from where she was working in Birmingham when apparently, her mother phoned her to say her father had disappeared. At least that was her story. She waited a couple of days or so before reporting him missing, which is fair enough. But it seems she was probably at the farm when he disappeared, so her story doesn't add up. I've got DC Burgess on looking at when she handed in her notice at work. That could prove to be very significant.'

'Are we talking a money motive here? Presumably she inherits the farm after presumption of death. Is it worth much? I know nothing about agricultural land prices, I have to confess.'

'More than I thought, but a lot of hard work required in the interim. Another thing DC Burgess is looking into is the family history. There were allegations of physical and sexual abuse of both the wife and the daughter by Fred Burrows, which don't seem to have been taken seriously enough at the time. If they're true, that might be a much more likely motive. A revenge killing for what he'd done to her as a child, perhaps?'

'But then why kill her mother? Especially if she'd been going through the same sort of thing?'

'It wouldn't be the first case where someone has blamed a parent for not protecting them from an abuser and gone on to take revenge because of it.'

'All right. That's plausible. So if Fred hasn't been found in five years, how are you proposing to solve that little mystery?'

'I thought we could start with an aerial survey of the farm and surrounding areas. I know it's a long shot, but it has been done successfully on other cases, to look for historical signs of ground disturbance which might possibly indicate a burial site. There's a place nearby which warrants a closer look. There's something strange about it.'

Sammy Sampson was now looking at him as if she didn't recognise him at all.

'Ted, are you telling me you want me to sign off on an expensive operation because you have a hunch this woman might be a serial killer? I'm supposed to authorise a high cost aerial overview because you think a place has "something strange" about it?'

Once more she mimed quotes in the air to emphasise her point.

'I know it sounds far-fetched. But we have the start of a case against her because of her DNA found on Brendan Doyle's body. And imagine if she has killed before. Possibly twice. That's got to be a nice tick on the books, if we can pull it off and prove that.'

'Well, for goodness sake don't let anyone shoot her before we know if she's guilty or not. The press and media would slaughter us if she was innocent. And speaking of which, remind me to send you on a course, soon, for Best Practice in

Managing the Image of the Police Service in the Public Eye. Or some such thing.'

* * *

Ted went in person to see Janice Burrows brought in for questioning. It was far from standard procedure, but it would be his responsibility, for which he would be held to account, if things went wrong and shots were fired. Especially if anyone was hit, so he preferred to be there to try to keep a lid on the situation.

Inspector Bridger had sent him a unit of four AFOs led by an experienced sergeant, Mark Booth, whom Ted knew from his own Firearms days. It made Ted at least optimistic of a positive outcome, despite the sceptical looks Sergeant Booth was giving him when he explained the situation.

'I know I don't have to remind you not to let the fact that it's a woman we're here to arrest on suspicion alter your judgement. Sergeant Thomas here can tell you that Miss Burrows is seldom seen without either her shotgun or the .22 close to hand, and there's every reason to believe her instinct would be to shoot if she felt herself backed into a corner.

'That's why we want to tackle her in the open, rather than risk her coming to the door if we knock and opening fire the minute she sees who it is. She'll know by now about Jamie Robinson being taken away. It might hopefully lull her into a false sense of security. Assuming of course she is our killer. But let's not be under any illusions. She's as potentially dangerous as anyone pointing a firearm at us. Let's hope she'll listen to reason.'

Cai Thomas's local knowledge was invaluable to them. He knew pretty much every inch of every farm on his patch. He was hoping they'd find Janice Burrows out in one of the fields where they might stand a chance of getting AFOs on all sides of her. He was also praying she had the shotgun with her, not the rifle. He knew she'd not be left standing after firing the first shot, whatever weapon she had.

Much as he found her an unpleasant person to deal with, he wasn't particularly looking forward to seeing her shot dead in front of him, if it came to that.

Ted had told the AFO Sergeant he'd prefer to take her alive, but he knew that the safety of the officers present was the utmost priority.

They found Miss Burrows' quad bike parked in a gateway. Yet more of those big stone gateposts, Ted noticed. They must have been a job lot from somewhere. At least he now knew they'd stop a bullet.

'This is good news for us,' Cai Thomas told Booth. 'If we can't see her from here, she's down in the hollow over there. That means you can easily get your shooters to surround her, or at least cover her from both sides, if you go round and keep behind the wall. The tricky bit will be for whoever approaches her from the front where there's no cover. Oh, and watch out for her dogs. They're not the nicest, although if I'm near enough, I can shout at them in Welsh and they'll usually lie down, at least.'

The Firearms sergeant shook his head firmly.

'No one approaches without cover. Not even you, sir,' he looked pointedly at Ted as he said it. 'You should know better than most than to even try that. We all approach from the sides and we all stay behind the wall.'

He gave a steely-eyed look as he said, 'And sir, you may be the ranking officer here, but you know as well as I do I have the final say on Firearms deployment. Despite your background. So we do it my way.'

Ted had known he would say that. Knew, too, that he was right. In a sense, he would welcome a shot from Miss Burrows, as long as it didn't find a target. It would give him the excuse to arrest her on the spot, rather than simply trying to take her in for questioning. The AFOs would return fire the moment they considered there was any danger to life, but Ted wanted more than anything to take her alive so he might finally get some answers to his many questions.

Sergeant Booth got Cai Thomas to scratch out a rough map of the terrain for him in the soil of the track up to the gateway. Only when he was sure he'd placed his officers where they'd be the most effective, and in a place of safety, did he give the go ahead.

Ted left it to Sergeant Thomas to open negotiations. He'd gone with the other two AFOs so was on the opposite side to Ted. From where they were now, any of them could get a glimpse of Janice Burrows, right down the bottom of the sloping field, doing something with the drystone wall, while her two dogs fixed a few sheep with hypnotic eyes, holding them in place.

There was no immediate sign of either firearm within reach.

'Miss Burrows?' Thomas called out, from the sanctuary of the drystone walls. 'Cai Thomas, Miss Burrows. I wonder if I can have a word, please?'

The shotgun appeared in an instant from the grass up against the wall, both barrels swinging towards where the voice was coming from as she whirled to face the perceived threat.

From her stance, it was clear that in that moment the time for negotiation had passed.

The next voice was Booth's, barking at her from behind the wall.

'Armed police! Drop the weapon!'

She hesitated, the shotgun still raised to a position from which she could easily fire.

Another voice, this time from behind her on the far side of the field.

'Armed police! Put the gun down. Now!'

Cai Thomas risked a familiarity. He wasn't appealing to a

better nature he didn't think she had. He was simply trying to defuse the situation to avoid bloodshed on his patch.

'Janice, please. Put the gun down. There are Authorised Firearms Officers all around you. Your life is at risk if you don't put the gun down and step well away from it. We just need to talk to you.'

There was a collective holding of breath as the woman stood her ground, gun still levelled, trying to get a sight of the men behind the voices.

Nobody spoke.

What happened next depended entirely on the actions of one woman with a shotgun and a short fuse of her own.

Finally, so slowly she seemed barely to be moving, she lowered the weapon, bent her knees then laid it carefully down in the grass, raising her now empty hands above her head.

'Step back away from the gun!' Sergeant Booth barked. 'Keep your hands raised, palms open, facing towards me. Don't make any sudden movements.'

He waited first for the two officers behind the woman to climb over the wall, one at a time, and cover her with their weapons, closely followed by Cai Thomas.

'Keep stepping back. Further away from the weapon. Any movement towards it may result in you being shot.'

The sergeant and the other AFO went over the wall next, again moving individually. Only then was Ted told to follow them.

As soon as they appeared, Janice Burrows barked a command at her dogs which saw them flying over the grass towards the three men. Cai Thomas shouted something to them from the far side of the field. They took no notice, gaining ground, looking menacing.

'Shall I shoot, skip?' the AFO asked his sergeant.

To his own surprise, Ted straightened himself up and shouted, with as much authority as he could muster, the Welsh command Thomas had used, at the same time fixing the dogs with what he hoped was a stern stare which brooked no argument.

'*Lawr*!'

To his surprise, they dropped to the ground, tongues lolling, on full alert for the first sign of movement.

'Nice one, sir,' Sergeant Booth told him. 'I didn't know you were a dog whisperer. Right, shall we go and secure your suspect for you? I can see why you thought Firearms were needed. What a nice friendly lady.'

* * *

'So, Jezza, I'd like you to be the one to start the initial interview with Janice Burrows, once her solicitor gets here and she's had time to talk to them,' Ted told DC Vine.

For an instant, her eyes flashed with something like anger. Ted was puzzled. He'd thought she would jump at the responsibility.

'So because we were both raped by our fathers, you thought we might be able to bond a bit?'

Ted looked at her in surprise.

'Jezza, I thought you knew me better than that. That thought never crossed my mind. I'm sorry if I upset you. I'll get someone else, of course.'

'No, no, don't do that. I'm sorry. I wasn't being professional and I do know you better than that. Sorry. Of course I'll do it.'

'Is anything wrong, Jezza? I hope you know you can always talk to me if there's a problem.'

She stifled a yawn as she replied, 'I don't suppose you want to adopt a small boy, boss? Goes by the name of Tommy? Autistic. Prone to having meltdowns and being an absolute pain in the arse, pardon my French. He's got a new class teacher at school and it's apparently the end of the world. He doesn't cope well with change. I don't think I slept a wink last night.

'But that's my problem. I shouldn't bring it into work.

Sorry, boss. And yes, perhaps locking horns with someone stroppy who is determined not to give anything away is just what my sleep-deprived brain needs.

'So, brief away. Tell me what you want me to attempt to find out from her and I'll do my very best.'

Chapter Twenty-five

Cai Thomas stayed behind while Janice Burrows was taken to the station to be questioned. Once more, he would need to sort out care and feeding for the livestock, including the dogs. Neighbours had always been willing to rally round and help out when it was Jamie Robinson, but nobody cared much for the truculent woman and her menacing ways. She'd never gone out of her way to win friends and influence people. It might need to be a call to the RSPCA in this case.

Tom Taylor was her nearest neighbour. The sergeant suspected he wouldn't want Miss Burrows' dogs anywhere near his place because of the children, but they would be safe enough shut in a shed with plenty of food and water for now. That would be a novelty for them as they always looked in need of a good meal. The sergeant knew, too, that the woman could be rough with her animals. He'd seen her lose her temper with them on more than one occasion.

He could well imagine the reaction of someone like Brendan Doyle if he'd ever seen such evidence of neglect and ill-treatment.

He'd need to check with Tom to see if he could at least keep an eye on the livestock for the time being, until something could be sorted. He'd no idea whether or not Janice Burrows would be remanded in custody. He thought it very likely in the circumstances.

'What's all this about, Cai?' Tom Taylor asked him when he called round. 'I mean, I'm not surprised about Jamie. He's been on a knife-edge for a while now, poor sod. But what's Janice been up to? Have you dug up her dad's body finally?'

Unsurprisingly, he seemed to know already what had gone on. The sergeant imagined he'd been watching the whole show from a distant vantage point.

Cai Thomas was sipping the welcome mug of tea Tom's wife had put in front of him, together with a slice of fruit loaf like a door step. There were two such slices on Tom's plate and he was already halfway through the first.

'What makes you say that?' he asked, never knowing with Tom Taylor if anything he said was worth listening to. Sod's Law decreed that the day he took no notice would be the day the man had something of value to say.

'Well, I always wondered if she'd done away with him, after that last blazing row I heard them having, and then him never being seen since. Remember, Maggie love, I came in the house and said there was going to be murder done. I could hear them shouting from up on my fields where I was working at the time.'

'I remember,' his wife said. 'She'd barely been back home a week, if that, and they were going at it like cat and dog. And it's true, I never saw Fred again after that day, but good riddance to him, I say. Horrible man. I never liked him. He made me uneasy, the way he leered at me whenever I drove past.'

'Did you never say anything about this, Tom? When officers came round asking about him? Only it's the first I've heard of this.'

'I did!' Tom sounded indignant. 'I told old Lardy-arse, what's his name, when he came round. You know, the lazy one. Always came cadging tea and cake and happy to sit on his bum to chat, but never seemed to do any work. Keith, was it?'

'That's the one, Keith Lewis. He retired not long after that, I seem to remember. Right, tell me everything you told him, and anything you remember about what you heard. But, Tom, I need the facts on this. Only the facts. Nothing added, nothing left out. It could be important.'

* * *

'Now, Tom's not the most reliable witness in the world,' PS Thomas stressed, as he fed back to the team at the end of the day. 'But he's adamant Janice Burrows was back at the farm a good few days, maybe a week, before her father was reported missing. And he swears he heard a blazing row between the two of them, with threats from both sides, shortly before Fred disappeared.'

DC Alan Burgess was clearly bursting to add something, watching with barely concealed impatience for the sergeant to stop speaking. He jumped in as soon as he did, addressing Ted.

'Sir, yes, that's exactly what I've found out talking to the people where Miss Burrows used to work in Birmingham. She left there under a bit of a cloud, but they let her resign rather than sacking her. She was spot on with figures, they couldn't fault her. The problem was what they called her interpersonal skills.

'Prickly doesn't begin to cover it. There was some trouble with an older man. Apparently he called her "ducky", she took it the wrong way and it all kicked off. The management looked into it, because it wasn't the first time something like that had happened with her. But they decided there was nothing to it and she didn't like that. In the end they suggested, quite forcefully, that she'd do better to find another position, so she handed in her notice and left the same day. That was the week before her father disappeared.'

'Good work, DC Burgess,' Ted told him.

Burgess was grinning and looking pleased with himself as he said, 'Oh, that's not the best bit yet, sir. I thought I'd try tracking down the older man to see if he had anything of use to tell me. Brian Barnes, his name is. Retired now, gone back to

Lincolnshire, where he's from. He called me "duck", but I think it's a thing there, a figure of speech, like mate or something, even between men sometimes, not a chat-up line at all.

'Anyway he felt really bad about Janice Burrows leaving. He never wanted to make a fuss, but he said it seemed like the management were just looking for an excuse to get rid of her. Her work with figures was faultless but she seemed to rub everyone up the wrong way, or take offence at the slightest thing. It didn't make for a good atmosphere in the workplace.

'Now we get to the good bit. Even after her accusations against him, Brian tried to make peace with Janice, for the sake of the working relationship. She was having none of it. She told him she was having self-defence lessons to deal with workplace pests like him. And she told him in great detail what she'd do to him if he didn't leave her alone.'

'So it looks as if Tom might not have been spinning a yarn, for once, when he says he heard a blazing row between Janice and her dad just before he disappeared,' Cai Thomas responded to that. 'And it seems she could have been better prepared to defend herself against him than he might have thought.'

'What's happening now with Miss Burrows, boss?' Jo Rodriguez asked him. 'When's she being interviewed? Because all of what Alan's found out will be very useful to introduce during interview. Even though her solicitor will dismiss it as hearsay.'

'She's with her solicitor now, then Jezza will start the interview process. I'm going to suggest we keep her overnight at least and oppose bail. Considering we needed Firearms to bring her in for questioning in the first place, that would seem to be a reasonable precaution,' Ted told him.

'We can at least assure her and her solicitor that her livestock are being taken care of. I would certainly want all her firearms seizing and her licence pulling, in view of what happened earlier, before we could even think of allowing her to go back, even on bail.

'DC Burgess, very good work. What you need to do now is go over to Lincolnshire and get a full detailed statement from this man, Brian Barnes. I doubt the solicitor will allow Miss Burrows to answer any questions about it, even after disclosure. And even if we find where she was having these lessons, I can't imagine any instructor admitting to having taught her a lethal technique. But it's a very good start.

'Next stage, once the Super's signed off on it, is to get some aerial shots of the area, looking for any sign of comparatively recent earth disturbance which might possibly suggest a burial. It can apparently show up some years afterwards, so let's hope we get lucky with an indication, at least.

'Well done, everyone. We're getting somewhere, finally.'

* * *

Another morning call to Stockport for Ted, where he found Mike Hallam looking pleased, and no sign of Steve Ellis.

'He sorted us out in no time at all, boss,' Mike said in response to Ted's questioning look. 'It was a piece of cake for him, so now we're all over bar the shouting on this case. Especially with the specialist help we had from Sal, too. We did try to hold Steve hostage, but he said he had to get back to Central Park.

'He's changed a lot. Much more self-assured than he used to be. I don't think he blushed once while he was here. So when can we have him back on the team?'

'Like I said, Mike, it's not my decision to make. I'd have him back like a shot. I have to talk to the Super again now so I'll raise it once more, but I doubt her answer has changed from last time.'

It hadn't.

'Give it time, Ted. Working magic with a computer from the safety of the office is a long way from doing his job in full. I've been hearing amazing things about him, though. Arresting his own father. That takes some bottle.

'It's worrying how much domestic abuse there is amongst coppers. Even more worrying the number of officers who think it's acceptable to cover up for colleagues. Young DC Ellis has shown incredible courage. That should be recognised, but not at the expense of his welfare. Once we're sure he's fully fit, it would make sense for him to return to a supportive team he knows well. Like yours.

'So, what's next with the farm frolics? Who are you proposing to arrest today and what back-up do you need? A platoon of Marines? The SAS?'

It was clearly going to be a long time before she let Ted forget this case. She was enjoying pulling his leg too much, for one thing.

The aerial survey Ted had requested was taking place that day, so pending what, if anything, that revealed, they may have another angle to go on. He had plenty of loose ends to tie up in the meantime, starting with a phone call.

'Am I interrupting you, or have you a moment to answer a couple of questions, please?'

'Edwin!' Professor Nelson always sounded pleased to hear Ted's voice. 'I have no students or other audience and I'm quite able to chop and chat, so ask away.'

Ted outlined for her the scenario he was interested in, the apparently accidental death of Janice Burrows' mother in a fall down the stairs brought on by a TIA, and the possibility that she was in fact pushed to her death by her own daughter, or had had her neck broken and was then pushed.

'Absolutely impossible, I'm afraid,' she told him cheerfully. 'Even if we dug up the poor old dear, I couldn't give you anything of much use. Your only chance would have been possible DNA traces from soft tissue, as on your hippy fellow. But no chance at all after all this time.

'I take it you're suspecting murder most foul? A quick push and a convenient fall to mask an injury? The best I can offer you, I'm afraid, is to take a look at some of her recent medical notes, and have a glance at the death certificate, but don't expect any miracles. Sadly circumstances like these happen all the time and are so seldom queried I'm sure a good few people do get away with murder.'

Ted made a brief stop at the Ashton station to see how the interview of Miss Burrows was going. He found Jo watching over the monitor and joined him briefly.

'Pretty much as you'd expect, boss,' Jo told him in reply to his question. 'Flat "No comment" to everything. Are you going to go for a remand in custody?'

'I think we have to. At least until the whole of the property has been searched for signs of Brendan Doyle's presence there, and that could take some time. We can certainly make a case on the basis of a real risk of her interfering with evidence, if we released her.

'What's her solicitor like? How much of a fight will we have over it?'

'He looks bored rigid and I'm surprised he's not fallen asleep yet, the amount of yawning he's been doing.'

'All the better. I'll leave that to you to sort out, then. Liaise with Jo for the remand. I want another trip out to Hippy Valley with Cai Thomas. There's still a few loose threads there I want to get my head round.

'Oh, and once we've finally wrapped this one up, I want to put someone onto looking again at that planning application from Greg Whittaker. Something's not right with that whole thing. Corruption, extortion, I don't know what. But I'd like to find out.'

* * *

'It's a shame about Jamie Robinson, if he loses his farm on top of everything, when it looks more and more likely he had nothing to do with the murder,' Cai Thomas began as he drove them out towards Hippy Valley.

'We can't take no action though, not after what he put PC Nield through. And remember, if one of us had tried to go through that front door, rather than Army personnel who knew what they were doing, we wouldn't be here to tell the tale.

'But I agree, he needs proper help, urgently, and whatever the outcome of any legal action, he's clearly not fit to go back to running the farm on his own. Probably not for a long while, if ever.'

'I've been in touch with a charity which helps ex-servicemen like him. It's an unusual one for them, but they're going to see if there's anything they can do to help. More than anything he needs to be back with his dog. She helps him more than any pills can do.'

Ted leaned forward in the passenger seat, looking up at a light aircraft in the sky above them.

'With any luck, that might be our aerial survey. It's a long shot, and a costly one if I'm wrong, but it might just produce some sort of a clue as to where Fred Burrows might be lying, if he didn't simply leave the farm of his own accord and choose to disappear.'

'She might have chucked him in the slurry pit. Certainly there were no efforts like draining it even considered when he disappeared. If it was a missing child, that would have been done, for sure. But with him being an adult, and not a vulnerable one, there wasn't much of a search at all, to be honest with you.'

Ted shook his head at that.

'Janice Burrows doesn't strike me as a stupid woman and that would surely be too obvious. Would it not normally be one of the first places to be searched on a farm? Assuming there was any suspicion of foul play or anything else. It could have been an accident, for one thing. Or even a fairly grisly way to commit suicide.'

'That's true enough. And after all, no one would take much

notice of a tractor with a back actor digging somewhere on a farm. It would be easy enough to dig a hole and plant a body that way.

'And what is it you're hoping to find out from Hippy Valley this time?'

'We now know that Brendan Doyle owned the land up at The Stones and that his ashes are to be scattered up there. That's fair enough. It's the time frame I'm curious about. He made that will just over three and a half years ago, leaving everything to Ruby. But why then? Why at that particular time? I could understand it when she was first born, especially if she is his daughter, or he thinks she might be. But why wait the few months before making the will?

'One thing we've not yet asked John Alexander, although I highly doubt he's going to give us an answer, is was there a previous will and if so, what were the terms?'

'He's not going to divulge that, I bet you anything. He takes the confidentiality thing seriously, even now his client is deceased. Even if there was an earlier will, there's no guarantee that all traces of it haven't been destroyed.'

They'd reached their destination now, parked the car, and were walking down to Hippy Valley. The first thing they encountered was little Ruby, running happily and laughing at the top of her voice in front of the house where she lived with her mother.

A small hand reached out to touch something neither of the men could see.

'Tick, Gracie, tick. You're it. You chase me now, Gracie. Catch me if you can.'

Chapter Twenty-six

For once there was no sign of the solicitor, John Alexander, sitting on a log by the campfire, although its embers were still aglow. Apart from the little girl, still engrossed in her game of tag with her invisible playmate, there was no one about, although the door to the house was open and smoke was rising from the chimney.

'Where is everyone?' Ted asked the sergeant.

'Most of them work,' he told him. 'It's easy to assume folks like these are all benefits scroungers, but apart from John the solicitor, there's a graphic designer, a cabinet maker and a Russian translator amongst them, to mention just a few. Those who can earn support those who don't or can't.'

'As I've said before, I don't make assumptions, sergeant,' Ted told him, softening the words with a smile.

'Sorry, sir. Noted. That was me making assumptions, then. We'd better go and have a look round to see where John is.'

'Before we do, tell me a bit more about Ruby. How old is she exactly, do you know?'

'About four now, she must be, I think. I don't know for sure. Ali wouldn't let anyone near her when she was tiny. You know how bad she is now with her, but when Ruby was first born, she was like a she-wolf. Kept her shut inside the house if any outsiders came anywhere near. I know Ruby was just about sitting up the first time I saw her.'

They walked as they talked and found John Alexander in Brendan Doyle's bus, sorting through paperwork.

'All right, John?' the sergeant greeted him. 'The DCI wanted another word, if that's all right with you?'

'It's fine with me. I won't insist you make an appointment. But I'll step outside to talk, if you don't mind. Letting you take a toothbrush to identify him by was one thing, but I know Spike would never have allowed police standing talking about him in his living space. And I'll remind you once more. I will still respect the confidentiality of my client, even though he is no longer here, unless and until I am compelled by a court to say something.'

Once he was outside the living space, he asked, 'So, are you any nearer finding who killed him?'

'We're currently interviewing a person of interest,' was all Ted would tell him.

'Admirable discretion, chief inspector. So I hope you will accept that any questions you intend to ask me about my late client will be treated in the same way. So what was it you wanted to know?'

'First off, Mr Doyle's campaign about animals. I understand he was inclined to make a bit of a nuisance of himself around the local farms. Do you know of any in particular he might have targeted?'

'Now my client is no longer here to speak for himself, I don't feel I can answer that on his behalf. In the spirit of cooperation, however, I will say that he would always take a stand against any perceived cruelty to, or neglect of, any animal, from farm animals to pets. He hated to see any animal ill-treated, or underfed.

'He was passionately against animals being reared for food. Not only on purely ethical grounds to do with killing and eating them, but also because he believed that it was a primary cause of climate change. And those views also held for the larger-scale organic, free-range farmers, as much as for the intensive ones.'

'Thank you. Next question. The place you refer to as The

Stones. Brendan Doyle was the owner of that land, I understand, so it will now pass to Ruby, in time. Is that correct?'

'Perfectly correct.'

'He bought the land around the same time he made the will, I believe. How old was little Ruby when he made that will?'

John Alexander's eyes narrowed so briefly that Ted wasn't sure if he'd seen the motion or simply imagined it.

'About six months, I think, from memory. Is that significant in some way?'

'Possibly. You would know better than me but if, for instance, Ruby was Mr Doyle's daughter, or he believed her to be, wouldn't it be more normal to make a will in her favour shortly after she was born, rather than to wait a few months? Isn't that what most people tend to do?'

'I can't speak for most people, chief inspector, only my client. And that's how he chose to do it. It wasn't my place to question his wishes, simply to carry them out.'

'Fair enough. Tell me a bit more about The Stones. What's the special significance of that place to you all? If there is a vibe of some sort about it, it passed me by when I was there, I'm afraid. And the stones themselves looked like relatively modern discarded gateposts to me.'

'Ah, chief inspector, not everyone can feel the beating heart of a place like that. It's a special place for all of us, particularly for Spike, so when it was available to buy, he bought it, and bequeathed it to Ruby, with the rest of his worldly goods. As simple as that.'

'Thank you,' Ted told him, and made to turn away.

Then he stopped and looked back.

'Just one more thing, before I forget. The sergeant tells me that you and Mr Doyle have both been living here for about ten years. So I wondered, was the current will the only one you'd made for Mr Doyle or had there been a previous one? Perhaps one from before he bought The Stones? Had he perhaps changed his will when little Ruby came on the scene, for instance?'

This time there was no mistaking the fleeting change in the solicitor's expression at the question before he regained control and his face became impassive once more.

'Any previous wills are surely now irrelevant, since the current one would automatically replace any and all of them, as set out in the terms.'

'Yes, of course. Purely idle curiosity on my part. Thank you, Mr Alexander. You've been very helpful. We'll leave you in peace now.'

Cai Thomas chuckled quietly as the two of them started walking back towards the car.

'That was straight out of a Columbo episode that, sir. But you certainly hit a nail on the head there about an earlier will.'

'I may well have hit a nail, sergeant. The problem is I've no idea if I'm hammering it into a piece of wood or a mains cable.'

* * *

Their next port of call was Janice Burrows' farm, where Crime Scene Investigators had begun the work of trying to find any sign of Brendan Doyle's presence on the property. Ted thought it unlikely that Doyle would ever have got inside the house, not with Janice Burrows and her guns and dogs around, but they couldn't afford to overlook anything, so the forensic examination was beginning there.

'The livestock will need moving before they can get into the outbuildings,' Cai Thomas told him as they drove into the farmyard. 'And I'll need to let whoever's crime scene manager know that no one should go near the dogs, for any reason. I've got the RSPCA coming later today. It may be safer all round if they take the dogs into their care for the time being. At least that way they'd be well looked after, for a change.'

'With Miss Burrows still saying nothing at all, we desperately need some trace of Mr Doyle's presence. We can show she was the last person to have physical contact with him but she'll doubtless claim that happened when she was lawfully evicting him from her property or even preventing him from entering it. I could see a jury giving her the benefit of the doubt on that, if it was all we managed to produce.'

'Surely they'd see right through her, sir? Unless the defence send her on a crash course at charm school.'

'The solicitor she has so far is useless. Bored and useless. But if we can get enough to take it to trial and if she gets a decent barrister, they'd see that she was properly prepared to present the right image in court.'

He heard an aircraft again, flying low over the farm, and looked up towards it.

'What we need is our friends up there to come up with some likely burial sites for us, preferably on Miss Burrows' land. Then we might have a sporting chance of getting her remanded in custody while we come and dig up her fields for her.

'In fact, we need two miracles. The first is to find Fred Burrows. The second is to discover that he died from a similar injury to Brendan Doyle.'

* * *

Ted didn't hear anything about the aerial survey until late afternoon, when he'd almost given up hope of any news.

'Chief inspector Darling?' It was a woman's voice calling him. 'I'm sorry it's late in the day. Jennifer Channing. I've been in charge of the aerial search you requested. I wanted to have a quick look at what we'd got before I spoke to you. I didn't want to raise false hopes.'

'Does that mean you've found something?' Ted asked.

'I'm afraid it's not quite as simple as that,' she told him with a small laugh. 'Ours is only the preliminary role, and it's not an infallible one. All we can do is report on sites which show possible signs of disturbance within the time frame we're given, which is luckily a comparatively short one, in your case. Certainly in archaeological terms.

'Together with the probable dates, we also consider the geographical parameters set by your enquiries. All in all, this has been a lot simpler than some cases we get called in to advise on.'

Ted was trying to curb his mounting impatience.

'But has it revealed anything of any use?'

'That's rather for you to determine. We've got the data, we've been processing it since we got back. What I would suggest as the next step is for you to come here, perhaps first thing tomorrow, if you're available, and we'll go over together what we found. With your local knowledge and my input, we should, between us, be able to narrow down your best places to search.'

'But you think there might be some potential search sites?' Ted pressed.

'Oh, yes, undoubtedly, I would say. And one of them is certainly at a site which you highlighted as being of interest. I'll see you in the morning, then.'

She gave him the address and rang off.

Ted dared to let himself feel a small glimmer of hope as he went to find Jo Rodriguez.

'We'll need to push briefing back in the morning to when I've got the result of the aerial survey, Jo. I'm hoping this might possibly be the breakthrough we've been waiting for. Another body could be just what we're looking for, especially if it turns out to be Fred Burrows. Although I suppose we need to prepare for the fact that if they are burial sites, they might be for dead farm animals, or even pet dogs or something. Ms Channing did say one was very small.

'How's Jezza been getting on with Miss Burrows?'

'Not that I intend to, but I would never commit a crime anywhere that Jezza might be the one to question me. She's ruthless. By the book, but relentless. She should have put in for promotion. She'd be the boss of all of us by now, no doubt.'

Ted shook his head.

'Not interested, she tells me. Happy to stay a DC for the rest of her days. All the better for us. That way we can probably keep her for as long as she wants to stay.

'Right, so that I'm as sharp as I can be tomorrow morning, I'm going to go and spend an hour or so kicking people. And I might hopefully hear some more from my *sensei* or the other members of the club about rogue instructors teaching lethal techniques. Now we can pretty much pin it down to Birmingham, we might be able to get somewhere. One of them will have contacts in the West Midlands, for sure. Martial arts is a fairly small world and pretty much a closed circle.'

* * *

'It's not often we get asked for such a short and specific time frame with these searches, chief inspector,' Jennifer Channing told Ted when he went to her office the following morning. 'It makes a pleasant change. I have to warn you, though, that it's not an entirely exact science. A lot of it depends on intuition, plus good intelligence, which we have in your case.'

'Ted is fine, Ms Channing,' he told her.

'In which case, so is Jenny. So, to business. Here's the map of the area we covered for you, and here are the highlighted spots which may be of interest. The farm, first of all. It's not, of course, unusual to see evidence of earthworks on farms, for all sorts of reasons. Drainage issues are quite common, for one thing.

'There's evidence of some much earlier work at the farm in question, which a rapid bit of research quickly showed us was connected to the installation of mains water to the buildings there and the surrounding properties. That happened much earlier than your five-year window, though, so we can probably dismiss that for now.

'That leaves us with these three locations which show signs of much more recent disturbance. Here, here, and here. And this one, going a little more on intuition than science, appears to be at least within the right sort of dates.'

Ted put his glasses on to study the map carefully. A spot not far from the farm's slurry tank, in a field where young cattle grazed. He'd noticed when he'd been to the farm that the land had a tendency to be wet and poached at that spot. That would have masked any signs of disturbed earth to the naked eye.

'You had me intrigued with your talk of this so-called spiritual place. The Stones. Henges are a bit of a hobby of mine and I know of no evidence at all for any such thing in that area. We overflew that a few times and analysed all that data, but using much wider parameters. I also researched it thoroughly. No known reference anywhere to early settlements, stone circles, anything remotely of a spiritual nature.

'That's not to say there isn't anything, of course,' she went on hurriedly. 'Strange as it may sound, new discoveries are being made all the time, even on a small and relatively crowded island like ours. I have friends who specialise in such things so I've emailed all of them. Some replies have come back already and all are negative. No one knows of any established historic pagan or other site at that location.'

She saw the disappointment on Ted's face and went on with a smile, 'However, all is not lost. But once again, don't get your hopes up too high. There is evidence of some earthwork having gone on comparatively recently - that is to say within the right parameters - roughly in the centre of the site.

'The puzzle is, it's very small. We can't of course, accurately tell how deep, but it appears to be much smaller than the normal surface area required to bury a human body, for instance. So it could conceivably be somebody's dog, as an example.'

'Probably not that in this case. The land belonged to one of the residents of what they call Hippy Valley and they don't keep domestic pets. It goes against their beliefs in the freedom of choice for animals, as I understand it.'

'Another distinct possibility, then, which would appear to fit with their ethos, is a vertical burial. It's apparently becoming quite a thing, because clearly it takes up a lot less surface area than horizontal burials and therefore saves precious space. Also I think some religions and cults may stipulate such burials.'

She paused for a drink from the cup on a nearby desk. Ted had declined her offer of one for himself. He was anxious not to linger but to get back to the team as soon as possible with an update on whatever she told him.

'So now we come to the third option. It could, quite conceivably, mark the burial place of a small child.'

Chapter Twenty-seven

'You do know people can legally be buried pretty much anywhere these days, don't you?' Superintendent Sammy Sampson asked Ted when he paid her a quick visit on his way back to Ashton to brief the team on the latest developments.

'I like telling my family I want to be buried in the back garden, so I can carry on annoying them long after I'm gone. You can't be planted near a watercourse, for one thing, but there aren't many other restrictions. If you want me to authorise a search of these stones based on nothing more than a hunch and a speculative aerial photo, you'll have to agree to it being your head on the block, not mine, if it's all a costly waste of time. What if it's someone's pet parrot or something?'

'Yes, humans can be buried anywhere, more or less. Except, for it to be lawful, the death needs to be properly registered, with the burial location recorded. And there must be a valid death certificate with a cause of death which doesn't raise red flags,' Ted countered. 'So we need to find out first if there's anything on record for this site, and if it's all in order. Nothing's shown up so far.'

'But you don't even have a missing child, within the right time frame, do you? Search the farm, yes, by all means. That needs to be done as a priority. You have a murder suspect with a missing father. Not to investigate the sites highlighted on the farm would be negligent. Let's get that done, as soon as possible, then take it from there. I'm more than happy to sign off on that for a start. But The Stones site? I'd first like to see some evidence of a missing child from anywhere, not just our patch, within the right time frame.'

'I'll get DC Burgess on to that, after I've reminded him again about the need for confidentiality. He's getting to be good at the Mispers stuff, and at least it keeps him out of mischief. I'll also get someone to check further with the authorities in case there has ever been an application for a woodland burial up there. But if we start with the farm search and we get lucky with finding Fred Burrows quite quickly, would it be that much of a strain on the budget to use the same equipment up at The Stones straight afterwards, just to make sure? It's not a big site and the aerial footage has pinpointed a very small surface area of note. It wouldn't take long and they'll already be not far away.'

Sammy was studying him as he spoke.

'You can be very persuasive, Ted, d'you know that? I'm still not keen on using up budget for a body which may not exist. Find Fred Burrows first, then let's see what's left in the pot.'

'There is a possible shortcut, which would save us wasting money. I worked with Victim Recovery Dogs out in Spain, on the case of little Storm Moonchild. A good one can detect a cadaver that's been buried for some years and they can do an initial survey without any major earthworks. The dog handlers put probes down on a site under investigation and the dogs will only react to the scent of a human body.

'What if I bring one in, before the excavation team leaves the Burrows farm? Then if the dog should give a positive indication at The Stones, it's surely going to be more economical simply to divert them to the second site, rather than standing them down and having to call them back out?'

'You're appealing to my surprisingly soft, cuddly granny side, Ted, damn you. I could never live with myself if I turned out to be the senior officer who had the chance to bring home a missing child and failed to act. You and I both know about one child in particular who was never brought back to his family from the Moors to be properly laid to rest.

'Let's do it. The dog first, at least. And if it turns out to be a budgie in the grave, you can explain to the ACC, and no doubt to the Chief too, why the quarterly budget got gobbled up.

'Now, do we need to inform the land owner?'

'Technically, that's still Brendan Doyle, until the will has gone through probate. Arguably, we should inform John Alexander, as the executor. I'd really prefer not to, though, if we could possibly get away without doing so. From a PR point of view, the last thing we need is a stand-off with the hippies at The Stones if they get wind of the search. The press and media would have a field-day with that, and I wouldn't mind betting someone from the Valley would make very sure they knew about it, before we even cut the first turf.'

Sammy gave an exaggerated sigh.

'All right, all right. Let's do it. Let's see what we can find and then worry about the fall-out afterwards.'

* * *

All the team members were quiet for a moment after Ted told them of the findings of the aerial survey, and the possible implications. Especially of a smaller potential burial site.

'As the Super pointed out, it could turn out to be nothing more sinister than a pet. But we need to investigate, in case it's more than that.

'With that in mind, DC Burgess, you've been doing well on Mispers so I want you, please, to look for any missing children, from anywhere, nationwide, within the last five or so years. Perhaps start at four years ago than widen the search out up to ten years. And no, I've no idea what age or gender we're talking about. Nor even if there is a child buried up there. Let's just start by seeing how many there are listed as missing. Don't give up if there's nothing listed in the UK, either. Widen the search to other countries, just in case.'

Ted's eyes caught Rob O'Connell, yawning expansively at his desk. Rob jumped visibly when the boss spoke to him.

'Rob, I was going to put you in charge of overseeing the search of the Burrows' farm, if you're up to it?'

'Yes, boss, sorry. Just a bit sleep deprived.'

'Problems with the fostering?' Ted asked him.

'Faye's been to stay with us before but now she knows it's long-term, it seems to have rattled her a bit. It's a big step for her.'

Maurice's eyes lit up at the news.

'Mate! You're a new foster dad? That's wonderful. We should all go for a pint to celebrate.'

'I don't want to be the pourer of cold water,' Ted spoke above the buzz which went round the team at Rob's news, 'but can we hold off any public celebrations until after the outcome of these two searches, please?'

He was thinking of Sammy's words about image projection. Imagining what a field day the press and media could have with pictures of officers out in public for celebratory drinks with ongoing searches still in progress. Especially if any word should get out that one of them was for a possible dead child.

'Once we've found Fred Burrows and discovered who, if anyone, is buried up at The Stones, we'll all go for a drink and I'll get the first round in. But a bit of discretion before then, please.

'We're going to need to apply for a further remand in custody for Miss Burrows, on the grounds of her possibly trying to interfere with the search of her property. Jezza, has she said anything of any use yet?'

'Nothing, boss. Nothing at all. If she did kill and bury her father she seems pretty confident we won't find him, but then she doesn't yet know about the aerial survey. Do you want me to mention that to her when I interview her again today?'

'No, let's keep that to ourselves for now, until we've finished searching. She and the solicitor have had the warrants in disclosure now, have they?'

'They have, boss. Miss Burrows was not amused. At least her solicitor appeared to stay awake long enough to glance at them. He's as much use to her as a chocolate teapot, but that's all to the good for us. I'm doing it all carefully by the book, but even so I'm posing questions most solicitors would object to.'

'Don't stray off limits, though. We don't want any case against her to come unstuck because you pushed boundaries too far.

'And thinking of possible suspects, how did it go with your visit to the woman who reported the body? Anything there to make you think she was anything other than the unlucky person who came across a corpse while out with her camera?'

'Nothing at all, boss. Quite the reverse, in fact. She doesn't own a vehicle, for a start. I checked, rather than just take her word, and there's nothing registered to her. Never has been. Plus she doesn't have a driving licence. She takes a bus out into the wilds, walks and shoots with the camera, then gets another bus back from wherever she ends up. Not the ideal way to transport a body.

'I let her show me all the photos she'd taken that day on her way to the waterfall, and there were a lot of them, all date-stamped. She doesn't appear to me to be techie enough to know how to have faked all of that. She takes nice photos and posts them to Facebook, but that appears to be the extent of her knowledge.

'If you want that side of it checking, you'd need to send someone with local knowledge to find out how long it would take to walk from one place to another, then factor in the delay of doing it with a dead hippy slung over her shoulder.'

'All right, let's bump her down the list of possible suspects, as none of that seems to make her a probable,' Ted told her.

'Rob, I'll be around most of tomorrow, if anything comes to light, but there's somewhere I have to be on Sunday morning and into the early afternoon. Jo, if the search does turn up Fred

Burrows, the Super has agreed that we should at least have a quick look up at The Stones before the team stands down. That is unless we turn up any official record of a burial up there. I'll sort the paperwork for that. We can't afford to get anything wrong with that.

'We're also going to try to get a Victim Recovery Dog in at some point over the weekend, although they're sometimes hard to source as demand can be high. That should at least tell us if there is any point digging around up there. But Fred Burrows remains the priority for now.'

'Do you really think there could be a kiddy buried there, sir?' Cai Thomas asked him.

'You said yourself they don't keep pets at Hippy Valley so I'm in a sense hoping that's not all it is. Of course little Ruby could have been feeding a wild animal, a rabbit, perhaps, or maybe a fox, and if it died of natural causes, they might have let her bury it there with full ceremony, I suppose. In which case I am going to look very stupid indeed.'

* * *

It was late on Saturday afternoon when Ted got the phone call. He was using Jo Rodriguez's office to try to keep on top of paperwork. He'd let Jo take the day off as he'd be working the following day. Ted hadn't dared hope for an early result from the farm search until he heard Rob tell him, 'Boss, we found a body.

'It was in that very boggy patch down below the slurry tank, and from the look of things there's been a leak from that for some time which has never been properly fixed. The body's clearly been there a good while so there's not much to give us any clue as to identity or anything. What remains of the clothing, and the Welly boots, look like a man's but it's hard to tell.

'The coroner's been informed and the professor is coming out in person, so obviously I'll stay until she gets here.

'The VRD has been delayed on another shout but the handler has been in touch and is promising to try to get here first thing in the morning. The thing is, she didn't sound all that hopeful. She said if there is a body and if it's in a properly sealed coffin it will be harder for the dog to pick up on any scent. So it might not show much interest, although she did at least say her dog isn't known for giving false positives. I think basically she was asking if it's worth delaying the search team waiting for her and the dog to get there and then not getting a firm indication either way.

'Now that we know there's no burial officially recorded up there, I spoke to the team about shifting their kit to the site. They're coming to the end of their hours for today so the officer in charge said it made more sense to leave the equipment where it is for now, pending what happens about the dog. Makes sense to me. No sense lugging the kit to a site with tricky access if it doesn't need to be there. But it does potentially leave that team and the equipment sitting around idly waiting, and they might, of course, get another more urgent shout in the meantime.'

Ted reflected for the briefest of moments before he said, 'Stand the dog down and tell the search team to go ahead without its input. I'll take full responsibility if it's a wild goose chase. When you write up your notes, make sure you record our conversation. It's on me if I've got it badly wrong.

'Jo's in charge tomorrow. I'm strictly do not disturb from late morning, hopefully until mid-afternoon, with a bit of luck. But make sure everyone knows they can always text me if my input is needed and I'll respond as soon as I can. Thanks, Rob.'

* * *

It was rare for Ted to find himself in a church. As far as he could remember, this was his first time in a Catholic one.

The baptism of little Aspen Jade had brought out the

Cheshire Set in abundance. The first child of top models Willow and Ebony was always going to attract media attention and the paparazzi were laying siege to the church long before the ceremony finished. There were plenty of other celebrities amongst the congregation, some of them showing clearly that the setting was a novelty to them, too. Even Ted recognised quite a few of them from television or the press and he took little interest in such things.

Trev was in his element, perfectly at home amongst the Beautiful People and looking as stunning as any of them.

The paps were to be granted a photo opportunity outside the church immediately after the baptism ceremony, then the guests were invited to a lunch at a nearby exclusive hotel. In theory, no press were allowed there, but no doubt some of the more determined photographers would attempt to gatecrash for the best photo opportunity.

Once they'd finished in the church and everyone moved outside, the photographers went into a frenzy of activity. Ted had to fight an irresistible urge to lamp one of them, he found their behaviour so obnoxious and intrusive. One in particular was very vocal and seemed to hold some sort of seniority over the others.

'One with just you and Ebony and the godparents now, Willow, love. Don't hold the baby up too high. The readers want to see you've got your figure back.

'Who's the gorgeous bloke with the black hair, at the end? One of the godparents? Shit, he's hot, the readers will wet themselves. Move in, move in. What's his name, Willow?'

He spoke about Trev as if he wasn't there. Willow gave Trev a conspiratorial smile and he put on his poshest accent as he answered for himself.

'I'm Trevor Patrick Costello Armstrong, godfather to Aspen Jade.'

'Give him the babe to hold, Willow, and let's have a shot of just you two together. Fuck, the readers will cream themselves.

Sorry, Ebony, but I have to get this shot.'

The cameras clicked endlessly, with much shuffling about of people in the frame. It all got a bit much for little Aspen whose tiny face wrinkled and went pink as she started to cry.

'Oh god, lose the sprog while it's gurning like that,' the same obnoxious photographer ordered.

Trev was still holding the baby at the time and brought her across to where Ted was standing.

'Here you are, Mr Grumpy, you look after my god-daughter for a moment. I know you're hating all of this but I'm having a fabulous time, and we won't be long now. And before you say you don't know anything about babies, just cuddle her like you do little Adam and sing her that nice Welsh lullaby your mam taught you.'

Then he was gone, back in front of the clicking cameras leaving a bewildered Ted not really knowing what he was meant to do.

'Don't cry, little Aspen,' he told her hopefully. 'I'm not enjoying myself either. Shall I sing to you? It might make it worse. My Welsh is rubbish these days, but I don't know what else to try.

He started softly, hesitantly. The haunting Suo Gân.

'Huna blentyn ar fy mynwes

Clyd a chynnes ydyw hon.'

He surprised himself with how many of the words came back to him as he sang, although no doubt he was massacring the pronunciation and the grammar with the unfamiliarity of it.

He could only remember the first verse but by the time he'd stumbled through it twice, not only had the baby stopped crying, she was slowly nodding off in his arms.

Then his phone pinged with an incoming text from Jo Rodriguez.

'Boss phone when you can please. We've found a body.'

Chapter Twenty-eight

Trev always maintained there was some special psychic bond between him and Ted. Ted was never sure whether he believed in such things or not, but it was true that sometimes, if he looked at him hard enough, even when Trev wasn't looking in his direction, he would suddenly turn and make eye contact.

Ted tried it now. The last thing he wanted was to make a fuss on Willow's special day, or to make other guests start asking questions. Nor was he anxious to waken the baby. Once he had Trev's attention, he jerked his head for him to come across to where he was standing, still cradling the now peacefully sleeping Aspen.

Trev didn't look pleased and as soon as he reached where Ted was standing, at a distance from everyone, he started to speak.

'Ted, if this is you saying you have to go ...'

Ted's expression was serious as he cut in.

'Take the baby, please, and I'll explain, but don't wake her up.'

He transferred Aspen to her godfather's arms then reached up to pull Trev's head lower so he could speak quietly into his ear.

'I'm sorry, it's not planned, but I have to go. Please make my apologies but clearly don't tell anyone the reason. I've heard from Jo. He's been out with a team looking for another body. They've found one, but I don't yet know whose. There's a good chance that this one could be a child, so clearly, I need to go.'

Trev looked stricken as he said, 'God, Ted, I am so sorry. Of course you must, and I hope the news is better than you fear.'

Ted got his wallet out, found a large note and folded it into Trev's pocket.

'You'll need a taxi home because clearly I'll need to take the car. And I have no idea when I'll be back, but I'll try to let you know. Please make my excuses to Willow and I'll see you when I see you.'

He called Jo as soon as he set off.

'Jo, tell me what you know. I'm on my way.'

'Really sorry to spoil your day but I thought you'd want to be involved from the start. The team found a coffin buried, more or less where the aerial survey indicated. A very small one.

'I took an executive decision, rather than bother you if I didn't need to, so I hope I haven't ballsed up. I didn't want to call up the cavalry if it really was a dog or something, although the coffin looked too smart for that. So I had it opened. It's a child, Ted. A very young one. A baby.

'And, get this. There's a name engraved on the lid of the coffin. Gracie.

'I've informed CSI. I was going to let the search team go now, unless you think there might be any more for them to find? They did dig down below where the coffin was located, in case there was anything else in the same grave, but they found nothing.'

'No, let them go. I'm hoping there's no one else there. One small child is enough. I'll be there as soon as I can. There shouldn't be too much traffic on a Sunday, with any luck. With the search team going, make sure you have enough other officers to secure the site. Have you informed the coroner's office?'

He knew he was teaching his granny to suck eggs. Jo was a capable DI. He'd have thought of everything, but Ted wanted every I dotted and every T crossed for this one. It was going to be a delicate situation. They couldn't afford any slip-ups.

'We'll need a female officer with appropriate training if we have to go and talk to distraught parents. Who's there with you?'

'I've got PC Heather Wright. She'll be ideal.'

'Good. I'll hopefully not be too long getting there. And, Jo, if you can have a word with one of your saints who handles such things, can you please ask them to make this nothing more than an unregistered burial?'

* * *

The search team were still finishing loading up their vehicles at the bottom of the track when Ted arrived so he had a word with the officer in charge before they left.

Ted had a change of clothes and footwear in the boot of his car, as ever, which he quickly donned before walking up to The Stones. He was glad he didn't have to do it in his best suit and shoes.

Jo was quieter than usual, the gold tooth revealing smile much less evident. He looked rattled.

'I hope we've not got this wrong, boss. What if it's another bureaucratic cock-up and the burial here was official? For any parent to lose a baby is dreadful, but then if a load of flat-foot coppers come along and dig them up because someone in an office misplaced a document ... well, that doesn't bear thinking about.'

'I know,' Ted told him. 'But imagine if it's more sinister than that? The child could be the victim of a crime. We've done the only thing we could do, in the circumstances.'

Jo was shaking his head.

'I just can't see it, boss. That little coffin is beautifully made. Really professional. If we're talking child killer here, would they really do that for a victim? And the little engraved name plaque on the lid? That doesn't ring true somehow. Do you want to take a look?'

'I think probably the less we do with it for the moment the better. But you did absolutely the right thing in opening it. As you said, until we knew if the remains were human or not, we didn't have anything to go on.

'With regard to the coffin, it wouldn't be the first time a kidnapper had taken a child, lavished care and attention, and gifts, on them before killing them. It could conceivably be an extension of that type of behaviour.

'Any idea of the approximate age of the child?'

'I have six to judge against, so I would say under six months. But it's not much more a skeleton now so it's not that easy to estimate.'

'And with the name Gracie on the coffin, not to mention Brendan Doyle owning the land, there must be a connection with Hippy Valley, so that's a good place to start asking questions. I'll take that myself, for now, and take Heather Wright with me ...'

An angry roar interrupted him. Both men turned in the direction of the sound and saw a red-faced John Alexander striding towards them, out of breath from the climb up to the site and clearly furious.

'What the bloody hell have you done, you total cretins? You had no right. No authority to desecrate a grave.'

'Mr Alexander, we have a warrant, of course. We became aware of a possible burial site here which is not registered. Clearly we had to investigate.

'Who is Gracie, Mr Alexander? And why is she buried here, with no record?'

The solicitor was still breathing hard, as much from his anger as from exertion, but making a visible effort to compose himself.

Ted looked round the site. The Rural Crime Team's 4x4 had been driven up the track carrying equipment and was parked some distance away from the grave.

'Look, why don't we go and sit in the vehicle while you tell me everything. We've had to notify the coroner of our findings here. I had no choice in the matter. You know that as well as I do. Any unregistered burial is always going to be treated as a suspicious death, especially that of a child. So let's go and sit down and you can tell me everything you know. Then if there's any way I can put the brakes on what's happening here, you have my word that I will do.'

They went across and got into the vehicle. Sat in silence for several moments. Then Ted asked again, 'Who is Gracie, Mr Alexander?'

The man let out a long and not very steady sigh.

'She is - was - Ali's other daughter. Ruby's twin.'

'And how did she die?'

'Nothing sinister. A cot death. They call it something different now, I think. Sudden Infant Death? Something like that.

'Gracie and Ruby were inseparable from the moment they were born. Identical twins. They slept practically glued to one another in the same cot. They hated to be apart, even for a moment.

'They were such good babies, too.' There was a fond smile on his lips as he said that. 'They slept really well, as long as they were together.

'Then one night Ruby was crying so loudly it woke Ali immediately she started. She went to the cot and she found Gracie there, cold and still. No visible signs of anything. She could almost have been asleep. Except she wasn't. She was dead.

'Ruby was distraught. She simply wouldn't settle. They just a few months old but it was as if she knew what had happened to her sister.'

The man paused so Ted asked, 'And was the death properly certified and recorded? There'll be a death certificate if we search for one, will there? If all of that is in order and you can prove it to me, then we can simply lay Gracie to rest once more, straight away, and I'll apologise in person to her mother.'

The solicitor sighed as he said, 'No, chief inspector, there was no death certificate, and there is nothing anywhere on record about the death or burial. You may have noticed that Ali doesn't like to have any contact with any sort of officialdom.'

'But there's a birth certificate? For Ruby, at least? Because you would know the difficulties she would have in claiming her inheritance without such proof.'

The man gave him a grudging smile.

'You're sharp, I have to grant you that. Yes, there is a birth certificate.'

'For both of the twins?' Ted pressed.

This time Alexander gave a dry chuckle.

'Yes, for both of the twins and, in anticipation of your next question, yes, there was an earlier will leaving everything half and half to the two of them.

'Brendan Doyle was their father. I imagine you will be able to confirm that from DNA, should you need to. As soon as they were born, Spike got me to draw up the will jointly in their favour. When Gracie died, rather than add to Ali's grief with a will which mentions a dead child by name - one for whom no documentation exists after her birth certificate - Spike had me make a new will naming Ruby as sole beneficiary.

'All of this is going to destroy Ali. She's been through so much already.'

'I can't simply turn a blind eye, Mr Alexander. You know that. I have a dead child - a baby - with no death certificate and unlawfully buried. There will have to be a post-mortem examination, and an inquest, because of the circumstances.

'As long as the PM doesn't throw up anything of concern and the proper paperwork is completed, I see no reason why little Gracie shouldn't be laid to rest again here, after due process.

'I should warn you, though, that this whole case is going to bring unwanted attention to your community. Questions may be raised, for instance, about Ruby's welfare. Living alone as she does, with no contact with other children. Some may find it worrying that her sole playmate seems to be her dead twin sister, in whichever way she perceives her.'

Another sigh.

'Ali has always been frank and honest with Ruby about Gracie and what happened to her. Ruby's seen photos of the two of them together as babies and she knows Gracie is no longer around, in mortal form. Some cultures would find it normal and healthy that she still acknowledges her existence.'

'Speaking of such things, how did you know we were here?'

The solicitor turned to look at Ted. This time his smile reached his eyes.

'You admitted to me that you didn't feel the vibe of this place. You perhaps dismiss such things as woo. But to us, and not just because of Gracie, this place is special. It speaks to us. I felt it calling me, so I came to see what was wrong.'

Ted studied him hard for a moment, trying to decide whether his leg was being pulled or not.

'So what happens next?' Alexander asked him.

'The next steps are up to the coroner. He's been informed. I don't imagine he'll ask for a pathologist to attend the scene in this instance. Even if there was a crime involved, this is unlikely to be the crime scene, in the circumstances. But he will almost certainly request a PM by the Home Office pathologist. That's standard with any unexpected death with even the possibility of a crime.'

The man made to speak again but Ted cut across him.

'Yes, I know you say a cot death, but we can't simply accept your word for that. The first thing I'm going to need to do is to speak to the mother, Ali. I'll be as tactful and discreet as I can, and I'll have a female officer with me, but I have to do that, as I suspect you know.'

Alexander made to leave the vehicle.

'At least let me go and prepare the way first. This is all going to come as a dreadful shock to her. I'm not sure what the consequences will be. I really wish you'd spoken to me first. After all, as executor of the will, the land is currently under my custodianship.'

'Would you have answered my questions if I had?' Ted asked him.

The solicitor responded with a rueful smile.

'Probably not. My first loyalty is always to my clients.

'Whether I go first or at the same time as you do, my advice to Ali will not change, and that will be to say nothing at all at this stage. To let you make all the running. So now will you let me go to her first? I promise I'm not about to whisk her away. I simply have very real concerns for her state of mind when all of this comes out.'

Ted hesitated. Procedure said he shouldn't allow it. Human decency told him it might be better to let someone the woman knew and apparently trusted give her the news first.

Finally, he nodded.

'All right, but I won't be far behind you. As things stand, we might be able to emerge from all of this with not much more than some document irregularity to be sorted out. Anything else and it would become much more serious.'

'I doubt Ali can imagine anything more serious than her baby daughter being exhumed against her will, chief inspector,' the solicitor said dryly as he got out of the car, straightened his hat and headed off to walk back down towards Hippy Valley.

The encounter which followed was one of the hardest Ted could remember in his career. Ali, the mother of what they now knew to have been twins, was hysterically aggressive from the start, despite the efforts of Ted and PC Wright to keep the situation as calm as circumstances allowed. At one point John Alexander had to physically restrain her.

The little girl Ruby seemed happily unaware of what was going on in the house. Through the open door they could see and hear occasional evidence of her happy games with Gracie. There was something unsettling about it, now they knew the truth.

Ted had instructed the PC to ensure her body cam was running the whole time for the record as he explained patiently that the decision was not his. There would have to be a post-mortem because of the absence of a death certificate, or any form of registration.

When they got back into the car, Heather Wright let out a long, shaky breath.

'Well, that was a first for me, sir, and I hope it's the last one like that,' she told Ted. 'I can't begin to imagine what that poor woman was going through. But why didn't the solicitor make sure she did it all properly? He could have prevented all this. Will she be prosecuted?'

'I honestly don't know. I sincerely hope not. I can't see how it would be in the public interest, after all she's been through. But we will have to wait for the PM results, in case all was not as it seems. As long as that doesn't throw up anything suspicious, I think it can all be dealt with as a paperwork lapse. Then everything, including little Gracie, can go back to how it was.'

It was late by the time Ted finally got home. He'd spent time notifying everyone who needed to be kept in the picture, starting with the Super, then writing up everything to go on file.

The lights in the living room told him Trev was still up but he found him asleep on the sofa, buried under cats, the television on low in the background. Adam had padded out to the hall as soon as he'd heard Ted's key in the door, and stood watching him while he took off his walking boots and hung up his coat.

He picked the little cat up then went to sit on the few scant inches of spare space next to his sleeping partner, who stirred, feeling his presence.

'Hey, you,' Trev greeted him, stretching sleepily. 'Was it a child? A murder?'

'A little baby. Possibly natural causes. I hope so. The uncomfortable thing is that when you and I were trying to find the vibe, up at The Stones, you remember?

'We actually walked over her grave.'

Chapter Twenty-nine

Ted received a call from pathologist Bizzie Nelson before he had even left the house the following morning. She was always an early bird, especially on Mondays when she had her students visiting her post-mortem suite and she always liked to find unusual cases for them.

'I would have loved to have made baby Gracie the subject of one of my working lectures for the eager young things. I can't sort it in time for this morning and I'm sure you need information as soon as possible. Which is your priority, the baby or Welly Man?'

'Am I off your Christmas card list if I say both of them?' Ted asked her, ironically, since neither of them marked Christmas particularly and certainly didn't send cards to one another.

'Welly Man, as you call him, is the more likely of the two to involve a crime, I think, so an early ID and cause of death on him would really move things forward for us,' he went on. 'If it's who I suspect it is, his DNA is already on file.'

'As you were kept waiting a ludicrously long time for DNA results for your previous victim, I will make it my personal mission to see that these come through in world record-breaking time. I pre-empted a bit on that, trying to get ahead, and samples have already been sent for him, and for the baby.

'Regarding full examination of the bodies, if James and I rearrange our schedule, we could do both PMs tomorrow morning, first thing, if that would help you?'

Ted knew that Bizzie's idea of first thing meant before the birds were even awake, let alone tuning up for the dawn chorus. That would suit him ideally. The sooner they got some results in both cases, the sooner they could move forward.

'Perfect, thank you.'

'An early caveat for the baby though,' Bizzie warned him. 'Given the length of time since the death, the most I will probably be able to tell you tomorrow is whether or not there are any signs of physical trauma which could explain the death. Things like skull fractures, for example. I should be able to rule out anything like that, but I would have to wait for analysis of bones and tissue to discover traces of toxins or pathogens. Always assuming any were administered and may still show lingering traces in the skeleton. That's not common, I should warn you from the start.'

'I've been told it was a cot death.'

'Bugger,' Bizzie told him cheerfully. 'Hard enough to diagnose accurately with a recent death. Next to nigh on impossible to do so after such a time lapse. What was on the death certificate?'

'There wasn't one,' Ted told her.

'I see. Well, I've always said my epitaph should read "I liked a challenge" so I will do my very best for you, as always. And I'll have the whole procedure recorded in minute detail so I will at least be able to share it that way with my students.

'I'll see you in the morning, then, bright-eyed and bushy-tailed.'

Ted arrived at Ashton before the appointed hour for morning briefing following the early morning call. No one was late. If the officers hadn't realised by now what a stickler for time-keeping the DCI was, there was no hope for them.

He let Jo Rodriguez start off with details of both the suspicious deaths they were now investigating. A murmur rippled round the room at the news of little Gracie, which not all of them had yet heard. Big soft Maurice reached for his handkerchief to wipe his eyes and blow his nose noisily.

Once Jo had finished, Ted took over.

'Professor Nelson is doing both PMs tomorrow. Jo, you and I should be there for that. Best possible outcome for us, but probably the stuff of crime fiction only, is if the body from the farm is found to have the same fatal neck injury as Mr Doyle.

'Speaking of which, DC Burgess, where's your report on what you discovered from Janice Burrows' former colleague? Brian Barnes, was it? I've not yet seen that.'

Ted knew the name perfectly well. He had the ability to retain information from the countless reports he had to plough through. Barnes' evidence could be strong in any case against Janice Burrows.

Burgess shifted in his seat as he said, 'Nearly there, sir, just a few more details to check.'

'Nearly there is not on the file, where it should be, DC Burgess,' Ted told him.

The last thing he needed now was Burgess slipping back into his old ways of skiving and not completing tasks unless someone was riding shotgun on him the whole time.

'Same goes for all of you, please. Detailed reports, filed promptly. It's my job to filter out anything not needed. I can't do that if I don't have anything to start from.

'Jezza, where are you up to with Miss Burrows?'

'I was working yesterday, boss, so I went to interview her again at the remand centre, with her solicitor present, and only nodding off part of the time.'

'Did you get anything more out of her?'

'Oh, she was very talkative this time, but only to complain about the standard of the food she's being served inside. She says the meat is only fit for dogs and she's used to better.

'I did tell her we'd found a body on her land, at which point she clammed up quickly.'

'Did she seem surprised by the news?'

'I'd say surprised that we'd found it rather than surprised there was one, boss. But that's only supposition, nothing at all of any use in a court of law.'

'We desperately need something a bit more substantial than her DNA on Brendan Doyle's body to hold her much longer,' Ted reminded them. 'We've been lucky up to now that her solicitor is so passive, but the press will have a field day if they get wind of it. Jezza, is she likely to admit to anything, do you think?'

'Nothing at all, boss,' Jezza told him cheerfully. 'She barely admits to being called Janice Burrows so she's not going to cough for anything else. Not without thumbscrews.'

Ted frowned at the misplaced humour. He wasn't in the mood for jokes, but said nothing, simply pressed on.

'Jo, we need to show intent to kill rather than pure self-defence, for both of the deaths, if we can make a case against her for either or both. Get someone down to Birmingham to talk to people at the place where she worked and find out if she said anything to anyone else, other than Mr Barnes, about what she would do to them if they invaded her personal space.

'I've also now got a couple of names from that area, through my martial arts clubs, of instructors down there who've been known to teach the dodgy stuff. See if you can get anything out of anyone about having taught Janice Burrows anything at all. Let them know I'm not interested in pursuing them as accessories, as long as they agree to stop teaching such lethal force. If not, tell them I'll be down to see them myself.

'Let's find anyone who's ever had any contact with the woman and get their statements. The more we have, the more likely we are to find something we can use.

'In the meantime, everyone keep your fingers crossed for some sort of result from the PM tomorrow. If anyone can find anything, the professor will, and she's promised to prioritise results this time.

'Anything else, anyone? Even straws to clutch? We need

anything we can get at the moment.'

'Sir, there's a possible glimmer of good news about Jamie Robinson's farm,' Sergeant Cai Thomas told them.

'As you know, I've been talking to the RSPCA and to an ex-serviceman's charity about what to do with his livestock. The charity people have another former soldier on their books, from a farming background, who's been working on a community farm, is doing very well, and now needs to move on, but is homeless when he leaves there. They're looking at the possibility of him at least care-taking Jamie's place while he's away.

'Will he face charges, sir? Jamie? Only going to prison would probably kill him, and it's not his fault he's as broken as he is.'

'He could have killed someone,' Ted pointed out. 'Not just PC Nield, but anyone going in the house to try to get him out. Not my decision, thankfully, it's up to CPS. He needs specialist psychiatric help rather than simply a custodial sentence, but we all know how often people like him are let down by the system.'

'So are we saying he's not a suspect for the killing of Brendan Doyle?' Jo asked.

'I think Janice Burrows is far more likely,' Ted replied. 'Jamie would almost certainly have the capabilities to break his neck, but when he started the hostage situation, he didn't seem capable of much rational thought. So would he have gone to the trouble of taking Brendan Doyle's body to the waterfall and dumping it there, if he was the one who killed him? I'd have said he was far more likely to leave a victim lying where it was, rather than go through such an elaborate charade.

'Plus it's Janice Burrows' DNA on the body, not Jamie's, don't forget. That's hard to get round.'

'That's my feeling too, sir,' the sergeant told him. 'I don't think Jamie would have seen anything wrong with killing an intruder, especially during one of his episodes, so I also think it's far more likely he would have left him where he fell rather than try to cover it up.'

'So at the moment, Janice Burrows remains our prime suspect for the murder of Brendan Doyle. Let's build a case against her and see if CPS think it's got legs.'

* * *

Jo Rodriguez was having a crafty swift smoke as he hurried across the hospital car park to where the boss was waiting for him, two minutes before the appointed hour. He knew the DCI had his menthol lozenges to get him through post-mortems but he preferred a nicotine hit in preparation for the ordeal ahead.

'Your wife still hasn't twigged that you've not given up smoking after all?' Ted asked him.

He was never sure whether the picture Jo painted of his wife being the dominant one in the partnership was true or not.

Jo chuckled as he said, 'As long as no one drops me in it, I'll keep getting away with it. Besides, I've hinted you're the smoker, when she claims my clothes smell of tobacco.

'By the way, before I forget, boss, is it this weekend you go off on your holidays?'

'Well, depending on how the case is going ...' Ted began, but got no further.

'Oh no you don't. Your Trev would never, ever forgive me, let alone you, if you let him down on this one. Where is it you're going? Corsica, did you say?'

'That's the idea. Horse riding in the mountains. Just Trev's cup of tea.'

'Right, well, that's settled. You're going, if I have to drive you to the airport myself and load you, handcuffed, onto the plane.

'So, shall we go and do this?' he asked as he pinched out his cigarillo between finger and thumb, then followed the boss down into the basement of the hospital, where the professor had her autopsy suite.

Bizzie Nelson began without preamble as soon as the coroner arrived, slightly later than anyone else.

'As I promised you, chief inspector, after the debacle of the last DNA results, I personally pushed these through as fast as possible, on both bodies, and received the results in the promised record time.

'The person I have been irreverently referring to as Welly Man, because of the remains of his footwear, is a positive match for the DNA of a Fred Burrows, who is listed as a Missing Person.

'The little baby, Gracie's, DNA tells us that she is the daughter of our earlier guest, Brendan Doyle. So we now at least have identities sorted for both of them. Let's see what we can find out about how they died.'

As usual, she kept up a steady running commentary as she worked, every word and every movement recorded audiovisually. Her assistant, James, worked alongside her, anticipating each request with the familiarity of long hours spent together on similar cases.

When they'd finally finished, the professor summed up for those present.

'Whether or not there is a link to the earlier death of Brendan Doyle is for the chief inspector and his team to determine. With a body that's been in the ground for as long as this one has, especially with the effects of slurry contamination, there's not a great deal of information it can tell us. Nothing in the form of contact DNA, for instance.

'What I can say with some certainty is that the neck fractures which killed the two men are almost identical. As you know I'm a woman of science, not a guesser nor yet a gambler. But I would go so far as to say that the odds of two different people each having a broken neck with significant similarities, especially on two bodies found within such a narrow area of one another, with no connection between the two deaths, would probably be infinitesimal. Particularly a technique which is so specific. If that helps at all.

'I will, of course, send you the photographic evidence of the similarity between the two injuries. I would be intrigued by whoever a defence team would produce to try to argue that the similarity was purely coincidental. I have to confess that I would relish being called by the prosecution to play duelling pathologists on that subject.'

'It does indeed help, thanks. And I agree. It's the sort of statistical coincidence which is so improbable it's likely to show a connection. Thank you.'

'I warned you that with baby Gracie I might not be able to tell you anything at this stage about what may have killed her. Until the results come back, I can't rule anything out. What I can tell you, however, is that whatever did kill her, there are no signs at all of physical injuries. No damage anywhere to any of the bones, particularly not to the skull or the neck, the most common sites for fatal injuries.

'So pending any surprises from the test results, all the indications so far are that this was indeed a tragic case of Sudden Infant Death Syndrome.'

Ted waited to catch a word with the coroner before he left. Their relationship was only ever formally polite, at best, but he was the one in authority when it came to when the body of baby Gracie could be released back to her mother for reburial.

'I'd like to see it happen as soon as possible, sir,' Ted told him.

'I'm sure we all would, chief inspector. For what it's worth, I think your actions throughout were beyond any criticism, so I hope you're not experiencing any feelings of guilt about authorising the disinterment. Had the mother gone through the proper channels right from the beginning, none of this would have been necessary and the poor child could have been buried with the right certification to rest in peace for all eternity.

'Alternative lifestyles are all very well, but the implications need to be carefully considered. I'll order the release of the body as soon as I can. You have nothing for which to reproach yourself.'

Ted watched in surprise as the man walked off in the direction of his car. It was as close to a ringing endorsement as he had ever heard from him.

* * *

Ted called a briefing for the end of the day to update the team what information they had to date from the post-mortems, particularly the confirmation of the identity of Fred Burrows, and to hear anything new anyone had to report.

'Boss, Rob is on his way back from Birmingham but currently stuck in traffic because of an accident,' Jo told him. 'He hopes to be here within half an hour, if not he'll phone through what he has. He did say he has something pretty damning on Janice Burrows, though.'

'I'd say the PM results are fairly damning against her, too. The professor pointed out how long the odds are on two such similar causes of death having two separate perpetrators. Plus we have the fact that Fred Burrows was her father, buried on his own farm, and her DNA was found on Brendan Doyle's body.

'Jezza, I'll let you have the details as soon as I can so you can disclose to Miss Burrows and her solicitor. I'll also talk to CPS about how close we are to being able to charge her.'

'No doubt she'll claim self-defence, boss,' Jezza replied.

'She might even have got away with it where her father was concerned. There's detail on file about alleged physical and sexual abuse by him which was never acted on. She could say he'd assaulted her again, she killed him in self-defence then panicked and hid the body.

'Once is just about plausible. But a second time? To do it then stage the body to make it look accidental? I doubt any jury would buy that, although you never know.'

Rob O'Connell must have had his foot down flat and the blue lights on the minute he had a clear bit of road because he arrived earlier than he'd feared, out of breath and full of apology.

'Boss, sorry to be delayed but I've got something which might help. Janice Burrows' first guinea pig, you could say. Another bloke from where she used to work. She tried the technique on him because she said he was getting over familiar, which he denies. He said she attacked him, tried to twist his neck but he knows a bit of self-defence himself and managed to break the hold, although it did give him a nasty sprain and he was in a collar for a while. He never said anything to anyone, although he had to take a bit of time off work and couldn't drive safely, because he was too embarrassed by the whole thing.

'So we have a living witness to Janice Burrows trying a neck-breaking technique.'

Chapter Thirty

'I also tracked down the two instructors you were given contact details for, boss,' Rob went on. 'I found the first one on a building site where he's working. He was quite happy to talk to me, and quite open. He does know the technique and he admitted having shown it to a couple of people where he was convinced it was safe to do so. One was an older lady who writes crime fiction. She was doing book research, she told him.'

'Did you believe him? That wasn't simply Janice Burrows giving herself a cover story?' Ted asked him.

'Definitely not her, boss,' Rob told him. 'Description didn't tally at all, and the lady is visually impaired, with a guide dog. I checked up on her and she is who she says she is.'

'And the other one?'

'A young bloke, charity aid worker. Goes abroad to some pretty dodgy parts of the world with rebel forces you wouldn't want to get on the wrong side of. And again, I checked it out and it seems genuine.'

'Did you tell him his fortune? Remind him of the dangers of teaching such stuff?'

'I did, boss, and I think he got the message. I also asked him who else might teach such a technique. Without hesitation he gave me the other name you'd already been given, and he didn't have a good word to say about him, either. That could just be professional rivalry, of course, but I got the feeling it was more than that. So I went round to see him. Eric Bolton, he's called.

'He was at home and he came to the door. As soon as I said who I was and what I wanted, he started to slam the door in my face. I tried to block it but he's incredibly strong. In the end, I decided it would be safer to wimp out and not try to talk to him on my own. Sorry, boss.'

Ted shook his head.

'No need, it was exactly the right decision in the circumstances. The potential risk was too high.'

'I spoke to the local nick before I came back. He's known to them but has no record yet. They're going to try to lift him, hopefully tomorrow, for me. If they succeed, they'll let me know when they have, then I can go down and do a formal interview. If he realises he's implicated up to his own neck, excuse the pun, I'd say there's a good chance he would talk, to save himself.'

'Good work, Rob. If you can get him to talk, that's another very powerful nail in the coffin of our Miss Burrows.'

* * *

The domino effect. They'd all seen it happen so many times before. Once the first tile fell, the others quickly came clattering down.

They were suddenly starting to build a more convincing case against Janice Burrows for both murders, getting close enough to charging her with at least one of them.

'We're going to need something really solid though, Ted. We both know she's going to go for the self-defence card, and with previous reports on record about the father's abuse towards her, especially as it appears they were never acted upon, that's a strong argument for the defence, straight away. Plus the number of times she's reported intruders on her farm.'

Ted was in conference with one of the newer Crown Prosecutors. Young, dynamic and with an impressive record of successful trial outcomes.

'I mean, could she come up with some story that he died in some sort of an accident she didn't know about? Perhaps the cows attacked him, trampled him into the mud and she simply thought he'd disappeared?'

'I think the defence would have a hard time making that one stick, Laura,' Ted told her. 'The body was buried some way down. It looked as if the hole had been dug with a back actor.'

'Back actor?' Laura queried. 'Is that some sort of smutty euphemism I don't know about?'

Ted had to chuckle at that.

'No, it's a digger attachment on the back of a tractor. Most farms would have one, for all sorts of routine maintenance and jobs. And the cows certainly couldn't operate one, so she'd have some explaining to do for burying him rather than reporting it, if it really was an accident.'

'I'm a townie, I know little about what goes on in farming. So the next thing we would argue from the prosecution side is that the father was in his seventies, so would he really have posed the same level of threat to her as in her childhood? And therefore was it really necessary to kill him, even in self-defence, rather than just stop him from attacking her?'

'To which the defence would no doubt counter that he was fit and strong enough to be still running the farm on his own, so he might well have been strong enough to present a perceived threat.'

'You're rather good at this, aren't you?' Laura asked him with a chuckle of her own. 'So now you're going to want to know if you have enough to charge her. Based on what you've told me so far, and subject to seeing the full file, I would say yes, just. By the skin of your teeth. But I would want a witness statement from the person who taught her the technique, which could show pre-meditation. With, of course, a positive identification of it having been her.

'If you could find me the evidence that she had been asking around for a lethal force technique rather than simple self-defence that would show pre-meditation to kill.

'Or on the other hand, it might just be another gift to the defence by showing she was so much in fear of her life at her father's hands that she'd made plans of how best to defend herself with whatever force it took.

'What we need is an expert witness on all this self-defence stuff. About fine lines between self-preservation and intent to kill. I don't suppose you happen to know of anyone, do you, or can you find someone?'

'As it happens, I can. Several of them. Martial arts are my way of unwinding, and I teach self-defence to children in my spare time. My karate *sensei* might well agree to do it, or he'd know who would. I've already mentioned it to him, and it was through him we found the rogue instructor down in Birmingham.

'I also happen to know the country's top expert on such things, unquestionably, but I'm not sure we'd get him to testify. He lives on one of the remote Scottish isles and isn't the most approachable person there is. He guards his anonymity fiercely, too.'

'He sounds ideal, though. Could he at least testify via video link?'

Ted was trying to think how he could get Mr Green to agree to any such thing. Apart from anything else, the man was beyond paranoid about staying off the radar for security reasons.

'I can try to ask him,' he said doubtfully.

'Excellent. Even a written statement from Witness A, if he prefers that method, would be better than nothing,' Laura went on.

'Now, what about the hippy chap, Brendan Doyle? They'll no doubt use the same defence and say she was bravely protecting her livestock, and then herself, if he turned nasty. What was he likely to have been doing trespassing on her property, anyway? Assuming that's where the incident happened, and if

CSI can find any traces at all for us to prove that.'

'From what we know of him, Brendan Doyle would take direct action against anyone mistreating animals, as he saw it, whether they were farm animals, working dogs or pets,' Ted told her. 'Her dogs certainly look in need of a few square meals, and Sergeant Thomas tells me she can be very rough with the livestock. Mr Doyle might well have gone round there intending to do something about that. Have it out with her, at the very least.'

'So if she came on him up to no good on her property, why didn't she simply shoot him? She's in lawful possession of firearms and could play the frightened lone female card, acting in fear of her life. Surely it would be more risky for her to creep up on an unknown intruder to get close enough to break his neck?'

'Several reasons spring to mind,' Ted replied. 'The most obvious, apart from the chance of someone hearing the shot, being that if she shot him and reported it, there was always a chance her version wouldn't have been believed. Especially if she approached him from behind and shot him in the back. Hard to make a self-defence case out of that.'

'And would the fatal neck injury have been inflicted from the front or from the back?' Laura asked him.

'I asked the pathologist about that and she said almost certainly from in front. She asked me to demonstrate the move to her students, and it's certainly easier to get strong leverage under the chin that way. And it's likely, though not guaranteed, that his guard was down, seeing an unarmed woman approaching him.'

'You know how to do it?' Laura asked him, a note of astonishment in her voice. 'I'm talking to a police officer who knows how to snap someone's neck like a stick of celery? I hope you won't be offended if I always insist on conference calls.'

Then she was businesslike again as she went on, 'We still need to place Doyle at the scene, unequivocally. I imagine there's a good chance that if this happened in some livestock shed she might not have thought to don her rubber gloves and give the place a thorough clean afterwards.'

'Whatever we find, I imagine the defence will concede that Mr Doyle was on the premises but continue to claim that Miss Burrows was acting in self-defence,' Ted replied. 'I suppose a lot of it will come down to what the jury think of her performance. Assuming she pleads not guilty to murder, which is looking likely at this stage.'

'Right, send me what you have straight away and I'll let you know by end of play whether or not you can go ahead and charge her with one or both of the deaths. This surviving witness she practised on is an absolute godsend, as long as he would be reliable in court, I have to say. With the instructor, that now gives us two witnesses to testify that she knew full well the technique she had been taught was potentially lethal, so that should give us premeditation to kill.

'And this neighbouring farmer who heard the big row between her and her father. That might help. If she was staying to argue, could she really have been all that afraid of him and what he might do to her?' Laura speculated.

'I imagine the chap who walked away with nothing worse than a stiff neck is going to be more than a little bit rattled when he discovers what could have happened to him. That might make him much more eager to testify.

'Oh, and get me this dodgy instructor, Ted. I want a full statement from him on what exactly the Burrows woman asked him for. The specifics of it. And I want him put on notice that he's likely to be called as a witness for the prosecution.'

* * *

Sammy Sampson phoned Ted mid-morning for an update on the double murder case.

'I'm just putting the finishing touches to the file, but CPS think we've pretty much met the threshold to charge. Once I get the go-ahead from them, I'm planning to have Miss Burrows brought to the station tomorrow morning for a formal interview under caution. Depending on what she has to say for herself, I'll then charge her.

'DC Vine has been interviewing her so far and doing her usual good job of it, but I'd rather like to take the lead for the final stage. It's an intriguing case.'

'And what about the little baby? Where are you up to on that?'

'The coroner will release the body for reburial as soon as possible, but we need to wait for all the test results to come back. Cot death is a strong likelihood, unless those results throw up anything sinister.

'I was going to go up to Hippy Valley myself, perhaps tomorrow, to update them ...'

'No, don't do that,' the Super told him, her tone almost sharp. 'It's commendable that you want to but it could be a PR disaster. We can't afford for anyone to do or say anything which implies the police actions were somehow at fault. And they weren't. You did everything by the book, as always. You going there could be misinterpreted, not to mention being the proverbial red rag to a bull, and I don't want us to have to start searching for your body if you don't come back from there. Besides, aren't you going on leave this weekend?'

'I'm meant to be, as long as everything here is wrapped up ...'

'You are going, full stop, Ted,' she told him firmly. 'You have good teams in place and they all know where to find me. Go, and enjoy yourself.'

It was late afternoon when Ted got the go-ahead to formally charge Janice Burrows with the murders of her father, Fred Burrows, and of Brendan Doyle, known as Spike.

Prosecutors were still deciding on the most appropriate way of dealing with Jamie Robinson over the siege. Ted was relieved the final decision wasn't down to him. It was another PR nightmare in the making.

Janice Burrows said nothing other than 'No comment' throughout her interview with Ted and Jezza the following morning when she was brought from the remand centre. She had plenty to say when she was formally charged with two counts of murder, mostly obscenities and threats of violence. She had to be restrained to be taken back to the remand centre.

Ted called the team together at the end of the day to address them.

'Firstly, well done, everyone. A good job, professionally done. The rest is down to the courts.

'Now, I did say that as soon as the time was right, I'd get the first round in, not only to celebrate Rob's new status as a foster dad but also the way you've all handled these cases. So as soon as we've finished up here, everyone round to the pub for a swift one.

'And as soon as all the paperwork for this is finished, next priority, Jo, please, is let's have a really good dig into Greg Whittaker. Liaise with Sergeant Thomas about some of the things he's suspected of. Let's see if you can't turn up something - anything - which would give us a lead on which to obtain warrants to delve deeper into his business affairs.

'I'm particularly interested in any money trails anywhere which might hint that he's been bribing someone with influence on planning matters into trying to get his application through, despite all the obvious reasons why it should be rejected out of hand.'

'And for that, boss, we're going to need a computer expert,' Jo told him with a broad smile. 'Someone from Central Park who knows how to make computers give up their innermost secrets in a way that none of us possibly could.'

'Someone like DC Steve Ellis, you mean?' Ted asked him with a smile of his own. 'It's just possible that I was thinking along the same lines, if he's available to us. Make the necessary enquiries, Jo, please. I didn't take to Mr Whittaker much. If everything he's doing is on the level, fair enough. But I'd probably bet my pension that it's not.

'And just a reminder everyone, I'm away all next week. Abroad. Out of touch. Do not disturb, and so on. Jo's in charge, Superintendent Sampson is there as back-up, and you've all proved yourselves capable of managing without me. I'll see you all when I get back.'

* * *

Trev was like a child on take-off, almost bouncing in his seat, Tigger fashion, watching the tarmac runway slip away beneath them as the plane began its ascent.

Ted disliked everything about flying but the take-off most of all. The knowledge that he had no control over his own destiny. His life was literally in the hands of people he didn't know and he hated that feeling.

Once they'd reached cruising altitude, bumping slightly with some turbulence on the way, Trev turned to face Ted, his eyes sparkling, face split by a beaming smile.

'I can't believe this. It's wonderful, and so exciting. I'm actually on a plane, with my husband, flying off on a fabulous holiday he's treating me to, like any normal couple. Where you're going to be a person, not a policeman, and where you're not going to be called at any hour of the day or night to rush off to look at bodies or other policemanly things.

'We are going to have so much fun!'

The End

Printed in Great Britain
by Amazon

81931182R10171